BLACKBIRD

REDEEMED

BLACKBIRD REDEEMED

JENNIFER OSUFSEN

LITTLE TYRANT press

BLACKBIRD REDEEMED by Jennifer Osufsen

Little Tyrant Press
Aurora, Minnesota 55705
www.littletyrantpress.com

ISBN-13: 978-0692767849

ISBN-10: 0692767843

10 9 8 7 6 5 4 3 2 1

Visit **www.jenniferosufsen.com** for more information about the author and her upcoming projects.

To my best friend, Dawn Breen, who was quick to say, "Sure!" when asked if she wanted to read the unconventional chapter of my first novel, and has stuck with me ever since.

There is no way I could do this without you, nor would I want to.

Also by Jennifer Osufsen

Mercy Springs

A Reckoning of Fire

To Those Who Make It Possible

This third installment was hard. Bleeding words onto the page hard. The enemy attacked, guns blazing, in the writing of *Blackbird Redeemed*. I know from experience what this means. It means that God has big things in store for this novel. I do not claim to know what that entails, however. It could be one soul saved, or a dozen people finding hope where once none existed. I ask God to write for me, and He never fails.

My dear readers, you mean the world to me. Without you (or *y'all*, if we're speaking Texan) I would have a pretty small cheerleading squad spurring me forward. But all of you who send encouraging words and kind compliments are a balm to my soul. From the bottom of my wordy heart: Thank you.

To Dawn: I have no idea how you waited patiently for so long between chapters, but I am grateful. You stood in the gap as I battled spiritually, most of the time never knowing you held a shield against the onslaught of fear and uncertainty over the last year.

To Erin Siber and Nikole Anderson: No typo too big, no inconsistency too small. I appreciate you taking the time to beta read for me. My eyes and brain are eternally grateful for your attention to detail. Thank you for loving on me.

To Wendy Sweney: For the fine-toothed comb you applied to the proof copy, thank you. Your continued encouragement and friendship, despite my flaws, means the world to me.

Last, but never least, to my beloved husband, Jesse. You fortify my heart with your very existence. I love you.

The Collapse

In 2040, a catastrophic economic disintegration, known as The Collapse, rocked the United States. For a decade, the country floundered, eventually imploding. A few members of Congress remained; and taking advantage of a weakened society, seized control and redesigned the country as Unified Socialist America. Two years after the Reformation of the U.S.A., Texas seceded. The Second War of Secession followed, lasting a year and a half. In the end, the Republic of Texas was once again an independent nation.

After The Collapse, leery citizens reverted to a more primitive way of life. The economy shifted to a precious metals (gold, silver, copper, etc.) and barter system. While technology advanced, it was generally reserved for the wealthy and those in government, both in Socialist America and in Texas. Primitive modes of transportation and barter systems remained in place as a semblance of security for the people, should turmoil once again wreak havoc on the nations.

Unified Socialist America outlawed any one faith during the Reformation. The government decided that faith in one God violated the rights of all the people, persecuting those believing in other faiths. Hence, the people could worship all gods or none at all in designated centers of worship. The Republic of Texas, however, clung to the fundamental religious beliefs upon which the original United States of America was founded.

"So you are no longer a slave, but God's child; and since you are His child, God has also made you an heir."

Galatians 4:7 (NIV)

Prologue

Liza ran, blinded by the ink of a moonless night, her stride eating the rock-strewn desert floor in stretchy gulps. In the distance, the lights of El Paso glared, a tenuous hope. A mile, maybe two. She was strong; not tall, but fit and shapely. Her arms pumped at her sides, but her pace remained steady, measured. Controlled. She pulled the dusty spring air into her lungs, exhaled through her nose as her legs churned, each step one closer to freedom.

She took a chance and glanced behind her. The camp remained dark, lit only by scattered fires; the heavy canvas of the tents was military-grade, designed to blend in with the darkness by night, and the desert sand by day. At the northern edge of the sprawl, she caught a glimpse of two armed guards patrolling the perimeter. The sight spurred her forward with renewed vigor and stealth; she kicked up the pace, arms pumping harder, elongating the length of her stride.

Gravel grated under the soft-soled slippers she wore. She gasped deeply as a prickly pear cactus seemed to appear out of nowhere, and she was barely able to avoid running headlong into the plant's spiny daggers. The sudden course-correction wrecked her balance. Her right ankle rolled on the slippery gravel. Liza threw her arms out in front of her to break her fall.

Pain exploded as she fell headlong across the rocky, sandy floor. Her chin connected with the sharp edge of a rock, jarring her head back. She tasted copper as flecks of light danced around her eyes. Fire spread from her shredded hands and down her body as she slid to a stop. She groaned and pulled her skinned knees to her chest, placing both hands protectively over her abdomen. No time, no time to cry. Have to go, have to run. Tears tracked across dust-covered cheeks, but she pushed herself harder, rising to stand on shaking legs. She cried silently. First one step, then the next, and she shoved the searing ache into the dark recesses of her mind.

It was one of the first things she had learned, after being taken. How to shove the hurt, the agony, the loneliness and confusion into the dark corner of her brain. There the bad stuff burned, a torch in the gloom; and once the fire blazed, she imagined a great wind, snuffing fear and pain into oblivion. Weakness vanished long ago, fueling conflagrations with an innocence lost to the bosses. Each ruthless beating and every night forced to entertain another john propelled her pounding feet toward El Paso.

With the stars overhead loaning their weak light to Liza's eyes, she could see the outline of Tent City. The name was a misnomer. Clay brick huts, lean-tos constructed of woven brush, and tents ranging from miniscule to enormous crowded one another in a mad warren of desperate humanity. Even from this distance the stench of unwashed bodies, refuse, and sewage assaulted her nose. Tent City housed the lost, the hopeless, the unwanted. The two times she had worked in the forsaken barrio had left her soul bruised. But tonight, Tent City was hope.

Liza was closing in, less than a hundred yards from the outskirts when the alarm sounded across the desert behind her. Floodlights lit the sky and perimeter of the camp behind her. Her heart skipped, stuttered. They knew. She expected it, the alarm. But she was delayed because of the earlier fall. Gulping panicked breaths, she sprinted.

There! Mother said to look for a stake with a white ribbon tied at its tip. The signal hung limply in the still night air, bright against the blackness. Behind it crouched a simple tent, and a shadow hunkered within shadow in the narrow triangle of an open flap. Liza halted, bent over with hands on knees, drinking in precious air. A gnarly hand latched onto her wrist, dragging her inside. The tiny amount of light from a shuttered lantern seemed as bright as the sun.

"You're late." Mother never minced words. The white ribbon dangled from one arthritic fist. With the other hand the old woman pointed at a stack of folded cloth on the ground. "For you. Strip."

Liza obeyed the garbled instructions with a question on her face, but it remained unasked. Mother turned her back, allowed her to undress in privacy. Such a simple courtesy, but one she had not witnessed in over a decade. Grateful tears welled in her eyes. Mother saw her as a person worthy of respect, and if for no other reason, Liza would be forever in her debt.

"Nonsense," the old woman whispered as she peeked through a small crack in the flap.

"How do you do that?"

"Do what?" The old woman chuckled lowly, letting the tent flap fall closed.

"Know what I'm thinking."

"You wear your emotions for everyone to see."

Liza shook her head and put on the new clothes Mother provided. "You're not even looking at me to see my emotions."

Mother looked over her shoulder then and gave her a crooked smile. "Hmm. That's true."

Dogs brayed in the distance, and Liza's eyes grew wide. "No! It's too soon. They shouldn't have released the dogs for another minute or two."

"Quick, hand me your old clothes." Mother snatched them from Liza's hands just as a small boy ducked inside the canvas tent. He was filthy, no more than six years old, maybe younger. Bony wrists peeked from the ends of his tattered shirt. Mother handed the youngster her old clothes, shredded to rags. He grinned, stretching his mouth from one ear to the other. In the dim light, Liza saw him wink.

"Don't worry, miss. We'll give them a good run."

And in a blink he was gone.

"Is it just him?" Liza wasn't sure how one boy could throw off a scent trail by himself.

Mother snorted. "No. All the boys in his pack will run with a piece of your garments. The dogs will come here first, of course. After that, your scent will be scattered in the wind."

Liza enveloped Mother in a hug, breathed in her earthy scent, felt her wind-dried skin alongside her cheek. "I am so grateful. I can never repay you, Mother. Never."

"I do not seek payment, child. Now, go! Run! You remember who to meet across the river, and where?" Liza nodded, wiped a tear from her eye. "Good. Run, girl. And don't look back."

Mother cast the flap aside and they both ducked out into the cool spring night. The old woman flashed Liza a smile, extinguished the meager flame, and vanished into the night. The wind carried Mother's departing words. "May God bless you and keep you, child."

The pack snarled and yipped, their desperate braying growing closer. Too close.

Once more, Liza ran, weaving in and out along beaten footpaths. Hers would be one more scent trail for the pack to follow, and if Mother was right, there would be dozens to confuse the dogs. But she still had to move quickly, because she knew how capable the handlers were. She had seen them work, watched them track down their prey and bring them in. They were one with the dog; and while the dogs worked on scent, their human counterparts added visual tracking and intuition to the hunt. The scent fan would work, but not for long.

Roads in Tent City were non-existent. There were main thoroughfares, of course, but nothing more than three horse-widths across. Liza kept away from the wide swaths for the most part, stayed in the darkest shadows between the more permanent clay brick buildings and the lean-to structures. Sort of like the alleys she had seen in the bigger cities. At this time of night, the city was quiet but not silent. Her footfalls startled man and rat alike, but both paid her the same amount of attention. In and out, weave and duck, but forward. Always forward.

On the far edge of Tent City rose the gutted remains of a small theme park. A Ferris wheel stood bleak, the circular skeleton barely distinguishable against the black sky. It reminded Liza of her life before. She had vague memories of her parents looking up at her as she rose into the air, her hands gripped tightly around a safety bar. Tonight, though, she

5

ducked beneath the abandoned structure, and ran, faster. Her chest heaved as she left the last edges of Tent City behind her.

The Rio Grande River twinkled darkly ahead, a glittering onyx ribbon dividing the two countries. Texas waited on the other side. Hope swelled in her chest, and she picked up the pace. A snarl behind her was followed by a vicious barking and a howl. One of the trackers had found her.

An all-out sprint now, each frantic step bringing her closer to the river. The team was fifty, maybe sixty yards behind her, but gaining. Deep breaths coursed through her lungs and out her mouth. So close! More tracking teams would be just behind this one. It was only a matter of time. Minutes, possibly seconds.

Head down, she flew across the desert floor, praying to any and all gods to not let her fall, to get her to the river. She had to get to the culvert, the one Mother told her to find. The grate across it had been rigged to appear intact, but would open for her. She found the outcropping the old woman described, honed in on it, and let it draw her like a lifeline.

The snarls and growls edged closer, the scent of their prey pushing them forward, nearer. She could hear the trackers now, yelling at one another over their communicators. She didn't dare look back, not for a second.

Every breath was agony, like shards of glass slicing her lungs, but still she sprinted on leaden legs. There! Her feet splashed once, twice, and then she dove. The river was deep here, dug out intentionally during the second Civil War, like a moat dividing Texas from America. Her arms sliced the water, and she kicked, heard the splashes behind her that meant the dogs were in the water. She swam for her life, for freedom. At the last second she sucked air into her straining lungs and submerged herself completely under the water. She knew she was close to the culvert. There was no turning back; she was fully committed.

Like an arrow shot from a bow, she swam directly to the grate-covered culvert. Desperate for air, her lungs burning, Liza yanked on the metal grille, her movements exaggerated and slow beneath the water. Once, twice she pulled, beginning to panic. With one last heave she pulled on the grate, and with a screech, it opened. Her head began to feel fuzzy, like it was packed with cotton. She needed oxygen, felt the lack of it in her eyes, in the desire to suck in air, water, whatever. Liza pulled the metal grate shut behind her, and pushed off the culvert floor, angling for the gap of air the old woman promised would be there. Mother said the drainage tube was buried at an angle, slanting from the higher Texas ground to the lower level of the river.

Her face broke the surface of the water and she gulped sweet, stagnant air, filled her lungs to bursting with oxygen. Water sloshed and echoed in the hollow tube, and darkness deeper than any she'd known surrounded her, enveloped her in a watery cocoon. Faint barking echoes skimmed across the surface of the water, filling her ears with trepidation. One minute, then two passed as she rested her weary body, but she still had to reach the opening of the culvert unseen by border guards.

Liza lost track of time as she pushed against the flow of water, uphill until the stream was only a trickle and her toes gained traction on the corrugated floor. She crept up the incline until she reached the opening, and then laid prone, watching. Her eyes adjusted to the night sky once more, and minutes passed without a guard in sight.

She closed her eyes, counting the seconds, and gathered her resolve to emerge from the tunnel depths. Liza eased her head out into the open air, searched the area and saw no one. Good. Mother said arrangements had been made on the other side to make sure the guards would be away from this post. Once more, she whispered thanks to the stars above, to whomever may be listening. Maybe there was a God, just as Mother had said. If so, maybe He helped her escape.

It was something to consider.

Chapter 1

Friday, September 13, 2097

The roasted earth scent of fresh coffee beans infiltrated his exhausted brain in welcome waves as he pushed through the heavy glass door of Capitol Grind. Dozens of patrons perched on industrial backless stools, pulled up to waist-high round tables. Conversation buzzed, rising and falling in a symphony directed by expressive hands and waggling eyebrows. The combination coffee house and bakery was popular with the govvies after hours; well, those that weren't four doors down at Three Sheets, ordering a different kind of brew. Since all the tables were full, he sidled up to the long, stainless steel bar in front of the barista's station. He opened his mouth to get her attention just as she switched on the grinder. It grated and brayed, pulverizing beans and sending out another pungent wave. The barista caught him in the reflection of the mirror behind the machines and smiled, holding a finger in the air. He nodded, content to wait. Or fall asleep. That was another viable option.

"Early morning?"

"And a long day."

The embossed tag on her chest provided a name to the cute, sun-kissed face. "Elise, you have what I want."

She raised a manicured brow. "Really? Well, this sounds interesting."

He laughed. "Coffee. Dark, in great quantities, with two shots of espresso. Preferably in IV form."

"Oooh, a long day indeed. Tell me something, Mister Lawman."

"If you're holding my drink hostage for information, I'll say anything."

"What tiny town did you ride in from?"

He assessed the petite woman in front of him. Observant, feisty. Chocolate brown eyes a few shades lighter than her cropped, raven-black hair. Somewhat nosy, too.

"How do you know I'm not from Austin?"

She rolled her eyes, and snagged a tall ceramic mug from beneath the countertop. "Oh, come on, cowboy. I can smell the country on you from here." Elise turned to the machine and started yanking on handles. Gulps and hisses blended as she worked her magic. "Your accent, for one," she said over her shoulder. "Somewhere east, I'd say. And your eyes aren't jaded enough to be Capitol police."

"Who says I'm law enforcement?"

Elise plunked the mug in front of him, and lifted her chin slightly. "That slight bulge under your sport jacket, behind your left shoulder. And the one at your right ankle."

Observant. "I'm impressed, Elise."

"It pays to be attentive. But you have me at a disadvantage."

"How so?"

"You're not wearing a nametag."

"Jimmy," he said, extending a hand. "Deputy James Wilson, at your service, ma'am."

"Ah, a country gentleman," she laughed. "Elise Gomez. Pleased to make your acquaintance, officer."

Jimmy sipped the hot beverage and felt his eyebrows climb. "Wow," he said around a swallow. "That has a kick."

"You did say make it strong."

"I didn't say strong enough to fell a horse," Jimmy retorted, holding the warm mug in mock salute. "Gracias."

"De nada."

A shout at the end of the bar interrupted their banter, and Elise excused herself with an apologetic shrug. "Be right back," she whispered.

"I may need resuscitation when you get here," he mumbled.

Was he flirting? With a complete, but adorable, stranger? Man, he really must be exhausted. His inhibitions were compromised by sleep deprivation.

Several hasty, mouth-singeing gulps later, he felt as though he could fly. Tired? Who was tired? No, he was ready to dance, to skip through Capitol Square, maybe show the locals a thing or two about two-stepping. He admired the way Elise glided around the shop, ducking behind the pastry showcase, serving steaming, frothy cups of who-knows-what kind of coffee concoction. It was as though she danced, a barista ballerina. When he imagined a tutu around her waist, he laughed out loud, spewing a bit of java onto the counter in front of him and turning a few heads in the process.

"Something tickle your fancy, officer?"

He spun on the swivel seat to find Elise grinning behind him. Jimmy felt the flush in his cheeks, tried to cover it with a gulp of hot joe. He shook his head with a closed-mouth smile as the steaming liquid scorched the roof of his mouth and his esophagus. His eyes watered, but he swallowed.

"No, nothing," he answered when he had breath. "Just thinking, ruminating over the day."

"Ah, well, I wouldn't want to interfere with ruminations." The serious expression did nothing to hide the laughing twinkle in her eyes. She reached behind her, untied the strings fastening the apron around her waist. Neatly, she folded the apron until it was a small rectangle in her hands, then she cocked her head to the side as if considering a question he hadn't asked.

"You're leaving, then?" Jimmy asked, surprised.

"End of my shift. Like you, I've had a long day and am ready to get home."

With unexpected panic, Jimmy raked a hand through his short hair, thinking furiously. She couldn't leave. Not now, not when the conversation was so interesting. Captivating.

"Uh, well, I guess –" he stuttered.

"I'll see you around?"

Think, Wilson, think. "Yep."

Great. A one-word response. Brilliant banter, genius.

With a grin, she turned and pushed through the door with a tiny wave. No, no, no. He thudded his fist onto the bar top. Throwing judgment out of the proverbial window, he hopped off the stool, threw two coins on the counter, and prayed like the dickens that it was enough to cover the bill. He rushed after her, bumping into milling govvies leaving work in the nearby Capitol building.

Why couldn't she have been taller, he wondered, standing on tip-toe to see over the crowd.

There! Near the fountain.

Jimmy quickened his step, apologizing and grunting as he wormed his way through opposing foot traffic. He reached the fountain only to find she had vanished once more. Hastily, he jumped onto the raised stone rim surrounding the water feature. When he spotted her, reason departed and he yelled into the crowd.

"Elise Gomez! Wait!"

She jump-turned, startled, and a hundred other spectators followed suit. Blood rushed to his cheeks once more, but relief outweighed embarrassment. He grinned, maneuvering around the stone rim until he stood in front of and above her. Elise waited patiently as a river of humanity swelled around her, like she was an island in the middle of a rushing creek after a rainstorm.

And yet, she smiled. It was all the encouragement he needed.

The black soles of his dress shoes slapped cement still wet from an earlier rain shower. Jimmy ducked his head and grinned sheepishly at the curious bystanders, making his way through the milling crowd until he drew to Elise's side.

"You have a flair for the dramatic, Deputy Wilson," she stated, grinning. "Are you sure you're not a stage actor on the side?"

"Look, I'm not usually like this. Honest," he said, wringing his hands. "But, I, uh, just had this gut feeling and I needed to ask you something. And please, call me Jimmy."

"Okay?" Her voice was tenuous, curious. She checked her wristcom. "Can we walk and talk? I have to be home by six."

"Oh. Yeah, sure." Suddenly unsure, he stuttered, "Now I feel weird. You're probably headed home, and your husband is waiting for you."

She held up her left hand. "No ring, no husband. But I'm pretty sure you noticed that earlier. So," she said, motioning for him to keep up, "what's so pressing that you had to chase me down?"

For a tiny little lady, she had a long stride. Her hair glinted in the dying light of the day, like streaks of black fire in the dark of night.

"I, um, was wondering if you'd like to go to dinner with me." Well, here goes nothing. "Tonight."

Elise halted midstride, stumbling to a stop. She searched his face, surprise painted all over hers. "Wow, you country boys don't waste any time, do you?"

Around them, Austin pulsed. Folks leaving work, and others showing up early for Friday night dates and entertainment. It was as though a giant foot kicked an anthill, and the ants scrambled, fervent in their attempt to put it to rights again. But her eyes held his in their chocolate depths, and he barely noticed the shoulder bumps and hip nudges as people parted around them.

Hesitation and a tinge of regret clawed his throat. He was an idiot. "Um, too soon. Okay. Now I seem like a creepy weirdo, don't I?"

Her slight grin drew the left side of her mouth toward her ear. "Oddly, no. Any other man who stalked me and jumped on top of a fountain to gain my attention would usually send alarm bells clanging in my head. But you? Nope. And that's weird. Nice," she clarified. "But weird."

She glanced at her wrist once more, and looked up at Jimmy.

He took the hint. "Lead the way."

Their reflections skipped from shop window to shop window west along Tenth Street. The President's Mansion loomed ahead. They walked in silence until they stopped at the corner of Lavaca and Tenth. Elise came to a standstill at the city transit shelter.

With hands on her slim hips, she clicked her tongue and said, "All right, Jimmy. Tell me about dinner. I'm intrigued. You have two minutes until the bus arrives."

Two minutes to explain why he asked a complete stranger to dinner, in a city he didn't live in, and quite honestly hated to visit.

"Jimmy?"

He cleared his throat. "Right. Okay, here's the deal. I'm in town for two reasons. The first was yearly law enforcement training."

"Oooh, fun."

With a snort, he rolled his eyes to the sky. "Yeah, it's a high point every September."

"And the other?"

"I'm here for a wedding."

Her widened eyes showed glints of gold in the dark brown irises. "Not your own, I assume?"

"No!" he said too quickly. "Gosh, no. I'm an usher in a friend's wedding. Tomorrow."

"And that would make dinner tonight the *rehearsal* dinner?" Elise's voice rose an octave.

Squirming, he nodded. "Yep."

The bus turned the corner and glided toward the stop. Elise twisted her mouth. His heart pounded in anticipation, hoping her silence meant consideration, and not a plot to escape.

Finally, she asked, "What time?"

"Eight."

The bus rolled to a stop beside them, the air brakes hissing as it lowered to boarding height. Jimmy fished a business card out of his wallet. Beside them, passengers lined up to exchange seats with those exiting the vehicle.

Elise flicked the card between her fingers, making a popping noise barely audible over the rush hour din. She chewed her lip, glancing at the line of people boarding the bus. With a grin, she gave a quick nod, and joined the end of the queue.

"I think I can arrange it, but I'll call to let you know for sure. Give me an hour?"

Jimmy smiled, at ease for the first time since he stumbled out of Capitol Grind.

"I'll be waiting on pins and needles."

She laughed and stepped onto the bottom step. "Don't do that. You'll hurt yourself."

Then the doors whisked shut, the bus returned to cruising height, and it pulled away from the curb. Elise waved from the window, her bright smile shining amidst her tanned face.

He watched his heart roll north on Lavaca Street, and wondered if he would see it again.

Chapter 2

"Miss? Miss?"

Elise turned from the fingerprint-smudged window to find an older gentleman looking at her with expectant eyes.

"Hmm?"

"I asked if the seat next to you was taken," he said.

"No, sorry. You caught me daydreaming. Please, sit."

A grand daydream it was, too. The cityscape rolled by outside, but her mind took her to a cozy candlelit restaurant and a glossy wood dance floor. The possibility of an evening out with a handsome country boy she would never see again appealed on so many levels. How long had it been since she even looked at a man with interest, much less flirted with one?

Years. Not since the one fling she indulged in which ended in complete disaster. But she had been young, finally free, and comfortable in her new surroundings. Joaquin, her personal mariachi singer. A voice like warm honey, dexterous fingers gracefully dancing across guitar strings, moonlit nights on the Riverwalk in San Antonio. He wooed her, serenaded her, and abandoned her, all within the span of a month. Elise should have known a man like him would never agree to tote the baggage she came with.

Her stop approached, and she glanced at her wristcom again. If she picked up the pace, she would be home right at six. This was the best part of her day, the light in her darkness, the hope she clung to when nightmares raged in sleep.

Minutes later, Elise's sides heaved from the three-block jog from the bus stop to her first floor apartment in Stoneridge Manor. She jabbed the key into the lock, and as always, it stuck. Somewhere along the way, it had gotten bent. From the other side of the door, she heard muffled laughter and outrage. It painted happiness across on her face. Ten to one, Matthew and Trudy were engaged in an epic battle.

The lock snicked open, and she entered the modest two-bedroom residence. Cool air bathed her face, and Matthew's voice soothed her. Home.

"You're going down this time, Aunt Trudy!"

"Not on your life, sucker!"

Elise was right. She watched, amused, as Matthew and Trudy waged war in her living room. They faced each other, holovisors covering their faces and sim-gauntlets surrounding their forearms.

Matthew, his charcoal hair tousled beyond combing, dodged to his left, barely missing the lamp on the end table. Elise hissed, but neither her son or Trudy noticed. He had changed from his school uniform into a comic book character tee and shorts. With a beleaguered sigh, Elise noted the inches the hem of the shorts had shrunk above his knobbed knees. The boy had grown at least two inches in the last few months.

Trudy, however, remained ageless, as though she had found the fountain of youth twelve years ago, and hogged it all for herself. Her curvy best friend jabbed the air between her and Matthew with a quick flash of her fist. The strap holding the holovisor in place compressed the writhing mass of corkscrew curls pulled back into a long ponytail. Trudy pursed her lips, her head on a swivel, and Elise imagined those concealed slanted hazel eyes of hers sought out a hidden foe. They must have been fighting for a while, as a sheen of sweat glistened on Trudy's mocha skin.

Elise glanced at the viewscreen, and her face registered surprise. Level seven? It was a new high for him. The pair ducked and punched, flicked and twisted, squatted and jumped. The screen only held the stats. Elise quietly edged around them and snagged another holovisor from the game stand. Making sure to leave room for the opponents, she settled in on the plush sofa, and slid the visor over her head. After a slight adjustment, she tapped the on-switch.

Her apartment vanished, replaced by a lifelike image of a decimated cityscape. Buildings crumbled in obliterated ruins; vehicles were scattered and crushed along streets and in alleys. Some cars hung suspended precariously from windows several stories above the ground. Matthew and Trudy fought in the middle of a square strewn with twisted metal, bits of scuttling paper, and broken glass. They battled hand-to-hand, throwing each other around the apocalyptic square. Plasma cannons spewed deadly streaks across her vision as the two ducked and covered behind various obstacles. Elise smiled, watching Trudy go to ground and edge her way around an overturned transit bus. Matthew stood in the open, his head swiveling to locate his enemy. Elise clenched her jaw to keep from laughing and ruining Trudy's ambush. Then Trudy popped out of a second story window and fired a well-placed shot from her plasma cannon, punching Matthew in the chest and laying him out on the littered concrete.

His character blinked out of existence, and a frustrated growl escaped from his real-life lips in her living room. Elise removed her visor and laughed as Trudy launched into a victory dance. Matthew tossed his visor onto the slipper chair with a grunt.

"Don't hurt yourself," he advised Trudy with a pout. "I let you have that one."

Trudy threw her head back and laughed, then walked over to ruffle Matthew's messy black hair. "Sure you did, kid."

"Nice job," Elise said from the couch. She chuckled when they both hopped in surprise.

"Dang it, Mom!" Matthew exhaled. "You scared me to death!"

"Come here and give your tired mama a hug, silly boy."

Matthew rolled his eyes, but plopped beside her anyway, enveloping her in a hug. He was long and lanky, and in desperate need of a haircut. She hugged him back.

"I missed you." To Trudy she said, "Sorry I'm a little late."

"Phaw," she dismissed with a flung hand. "You're never late. And I didn't have anything going on tonight anyway."

"About that. Can I talk to you in the kitchen?"

"I'll be in my room," Matthew said, heading down the short hallway.

"No screen!" Elise yelled. She thought she heard a muffled, "Yeah, yeah," in response.

Trudy eyed Elise, scrutinized her with squinted lids. She tapped her chin with a manicured fingernail and hummed. Then her friend's eyes flew open, and her long lashes framed surprised eyes. She pointed a finger at Elise.

"You met a man!"

Rolling her own eyes, Elise opened a cupboard and withdrew a clear drinking glass. She filled it at the tap, and sipped, careful to avoid Trudy's pinning glare until the last moment.

Finally, she gave in. "Yes, I did."

Trudy let out a hoot and jumped up and down. "I *knew* it! Who? What's his name? Is he cute? What does he do? Is he rich?"

Elise laughed. "Slow down, hot shot. His name is Jimmy, and I met him at work."

"He works at the coffee shop? Definitely not rich, then."

Slapping her friend lightly on the arm, Elise said, "Customer. Not employee."

"Hmm. You don't date customers. I think I may have heard that mantra a thousand billion times."

"I know. Which is why this is weird."

Trudy stood on tip-toe, backing up to sit on the counter. She leaned over in anticipation. "And?"

"And what?"

"You are not allowed to clam up now. Why is this guy an exception to the stone-chiseled rule?"

Elise pictured his crooked smile, and golden-brown irises. The kind set to his face. The way his cheeks pinked, and the heat in his eyes when he stared at her. She cleared her throat. "Honestly, I don't know. Maybe because he's not a local?"

"Really? This is getting more interesting."

"He chews his nails."

Trudy twisted her mouth in disgust. "Eww. That's a good thing?"

"No. Yes. Maybe. I noticed them wrapped around his mug, when I was looking for a wedding ring. And he blushes when he's embarrassed."

"Go on."

"He's a deputy somewhere out east," Elise continued. "Come to think of it, he didn't say where."

Elise held a finger in the air, and dashed over to the couch. Rifling through her purse, she found the business card he handed her before she boarded the bus.

"Angelina County."

"Nothing but briars and pine trees out there. And hicks. Lots of sticks and hicks."

"Shut up," Elise laughed playfully. She bit her lower lip. "He asked me to dinner tonight."

"Ah, there it is. You want me to sit with Matthew, still, right?"

Elise shuffled her feet. "I understand if you can't," she began.

"He's twelve years old, honey. Too old for a babysitter."

"You're not just the babysitter, Trudy, and you know it."

"I do," her friend said, rubbing her shoulders. "You have to learn to let go. You're safe here. How long has it been since the last scare?"

"Two years."

"There you go. They've given up, Elise."

She had heard the lecture a dozen times. "Soon. Not yet. Plus, Matthew loves spending time with you."

"And I love him," Trudy reassured her. She pulled Elise in for a squeeze. When she let go, she asked, "Where is Deputy Handsome taking you tonight?"

"To dinner."

"Do you know where?"

"It's, um, a rehearsal dinner," Elise mumbled.

Trudy's brows climbed into her hairline. "He asked you to a rehearsal dinner? As in, a *wedding* rehearsal dinner? On the first date?"

Nodding, Elise slipped off one work shoe, then the other, tossing them in the entryway. "He's an usher in a wedding tomorrow."

"Huh. Popular day for weddings."

"What do you mean?"

"It's been all over the newscasts. The President-Elect's son, remember? He's getting hitched tomorrow, too. What is his name? Carter? Kevin?"

"Cullen," Elise provided. "But there are probably dozens of couples getting married tomorrow. Besides, I doubt a country lawman would be rubbing elbows with pseudo-royalty."

Trudy consulted her wrist. "What time does this shindig go down?"

"He said eight. I still need to confirm it with him."

"Does he know about Matthew?"

Elise shook her head.

"Well, he's here and gone soon. What he doesn't know can't send him running for the hill country, right?"

"Exactly."

"Okay, I'll head up and get a shower. Grab something to eat. I'll be back at 7:30."

Trudy bounced out the door, her curls bounding behind her. A few seconds later, she heard her best friend's footsteps sound across the ceiling. Having her best friend and babysitter living directly above her was a wonderful perk.

She flicked the small rectangular piece of cardstock between her fingers, then ran a light fingertip over the raised embossing of his name. She took a deep breath and keyed in Jimmy's number.

He answered on the third ring, breathless. "Hello?" Water trickled loudly in the background, and she realized he had been in the shower.

Her mind wandered into embarrassing territory, and she was grateful he couldn't see her burning cheeks. "Jimmy? It's Elise. We met earlier?"

"Hey, girl." His country twang tickled her ear, made her stomach jump rope. "You coming out with me tonight?"

"Yes," she blurted a little too loudly. "Yes, I'd love to go to dinner with you."

She thought she heard him exhale on the other end of the call.

"I can't wait. Pick you up at 7:30?"

Matthew. He couldn't see her son. He would run away with his tail between his legs, and leave a dust cloud in his wake.

"How about I meet you there?"

After a brief hesitation, he said, "Fantastic. Eight o'clock at The Driskill Hotel."

With an anxious gulp, she said, "The Driskill?"

"Yep. I'll see you there."

Only the wealthiest people scheduled events at The Driskill. Echoes of Trudy's statement echoed in her mind. *The President-elect's son? He's getting married tomorrow.*

Elise flopped onto the comfortable secondhand sofa and stared at the wall. It couldn't be.

What had she gotten herself into?

Chapter 3

Twinkling white lights swarmed the stunted decorative trees along the sidewalk flanking The Driskill, like fireflies blinking along a country road at twilight. The mid-September air kissed the nape of her neck, cool and flirty. Elise clutched the diminutive black beaded purse between her side and elbow, enjoying the clear night sky above and the breeze fluttering her cocktail dress against her calves. The beaded bodice reflected miniature copies of the light from streetlamps. Foot traffic was heavy on Sixth Street, normal for a Friday night. An open-air restaurant down the block hosted an up and coming local band, The Wicked Minors. Their haunting minor-key echoed and traveled along the street, lending an otherworldly feel to the evening.

Overhead, the half-moon hung expectantly, unencumbered by clouds. Elise angled her head, admiring the clear evening, wishing Jimmy would hurry up and join her. Granted, she had arrived early. But her toes wiggled impatiently in completely insensible high heels, and her ankles screamed in protest. Other than a night out now and then with Trudy, she found little excuse to dress up. Though her feet objected, she couldn't help feeling giddy.

Crowds flowed in waves. Groups of giggling college students, and enraptured couples, oblivious to the world around them, wove around her. A sleek, black sedan whisked to the curb, its solar motor nearly silent. The driver exited with a confident stride around the front of the vehicle, and an elegant woman unfolded herself from the backseat with a nod to the chauffeur. A graying gentleman, smart in his tailored pewter gray suit, followed his companion. A twinkle of silver shone briefly as he tipped the driver. He took the arm of his leggy blonde and escorted her to the entry of The Driskill, where a doorman in black and red livery awaited with the wide oak door opened in anticipation.

Elise glided her clammy hands over silk-draped hips, staring at her toes. She was out of her league. The hotel demanded elegance and found her lacking, despite the borrowed cocktail dress. What had she been thinking, agreeing to go to a wedding rehearsal dinner with a complete stranger, in a place like The Driskill? Her right thumb rubbed circles on her left palm, a nervous habit never quite snuffed. Was it too late to join the laughing throng on the sidewalk, to meld herself with the masses and disappear?

"Elise?" a deep, honeyed voice behind her asked.

She spun around and found Jimmy grinning at her. Too late to escape now. She forced a smile and dropped her hands to her sides.

"Hey there."

"You look," he paused, his eyes devouring every inch of her, "stunning."

She blushed and returned the compliment. "You clean up nice yourself."

His dress jeans could have stood up on their own legs with the amount of starch encasing the denim fibers. A sharp crease extended the length of the front of each pant leg. His pressed white long-sleeved shirt glowed in the evening light, and the pearl snaps shimmered pink, blue, and cool yellow. She expected a giant belt buckle to go along with his shined, brown leather boots. Instead, an elegant, silver buckle with carved filigrees swirling around a pecan tree fastened the belt in style.

Jimmy held an elbow crooked in invitation. "Shall we?"

With a nod, she took his arm. Could he feel her shaking?

Just as he had with the sophisticated couple before them, the doorman guided them into The Driskill with a quick bow of the head.

Jimmy leaned down to whisper into her ear as they walked through the hotel. "Relax. You are beautiful."

Were her doubts painted on her face, or was he simply good at reading people? Probably a little of both, she decided, considering his line of work.

The Driskill lobby snatched her breath away. Her heels clicked atop mosaic marbled floors done in warm tans, taupes, and gold; gilded leaves atop maroon caps topped the creamy white columns marching off into the distance. Overhead, intricate paneled wood ceilings commanded attention. When she and Jimmy stopped in the center of the spacious entry, Elise gazed upward. A stained glass tiled mosaic glowed a rich yellow with accents of red, blue, and green. Tiles of colored glass formed a square, and in the center an inverted dome dropped from the main piece. The dome boasted golden diamonds interwoven so that it resembled a blazing sun.

Pieced stars encircled the circumference of the feature, with blue glass above which brought a starry night to mind.

Jimmy brought her out of her reverie. "Am I the only one who feels out of my element, here?"

Elise laughed, a quiet chuckling. She squeezed his arm. "No, you are not. I feel like Cinderella in Prince Charming's palace."

"Does that make me Prince Charming?"

He had the cutest grin. A tiny dimple winked under his left cheek, and his amber eyes sparkled in the warm ambience.

She smiled. "Only if I'm an overworked, underpaid servant. So, yes," Elise chuckled. "I suppose you are."

Jimmy shook a finger in mock sternness. "No pumpkin act, all right? Austin is a big city, and I'd hate to have to scour the streets trying to find the match to your black stilts. Plus, I have to be at work on Monday," he added with a wink.

"You got it, Charming."

Foot traffic eased in the hallway outside the room marked with a placard naming the room The Citadel. Well-dressed guests glided along carpeted runners, their footsteps muffled. Conversation floated from the dining room. From her vantage point, she could only see bits and parts of the wedding party within; a silk-draped arm here, a wingtip shoe there.

Jimmy took her by the elbows and pulled her close, gazing down at her. Elise's heart thumped, beating out a warning. Her skin tingled where he touched her; her breath hitched in her chest. But when he smiled, her nervousness faded to a slow, warm glow.

"Listen," he began with a side-cocked smile. "It was crazy for me to invite you to this shindig. Honestly, I don't know why I did. Instinct, maybe?"

She exhaled softly and laid a calloused hand on his upper arm. "It will be fun. I'm looking forward to it. And Jimmy?"

"Hmm?"

"I'm glad you asked me."

He started to run a hand through his hair, but pulled away at the last second. "I don't usually get all gussied up like this."

"Okay, why are you acting nervous all of a sudden? You know the couple. You're in their wedding party."

Jimmy arched his neck and gazed at the ceiling, letting out a slow breath that smelled of peppermint. "Yep. I know the happy couple. But it will be my first time meeting the groom's father. And I hear he's formidable."

Alarm bells clanged, and she licked her top lip ever so slightly. "Formidable?"

Laughter spilled from the private room, and glasses clinked. It seemed to break the spell, and Jimmy rolled his head and shoulders. "Shall we, Cinderella?"

With a decisive nod, she squared her shoulders. Then she flinched as Jimmy took her hand in his. Sparks fired between their palms, and Elise felt the jolt deep in her core. As though he felt it too, he brought her hand to his lips. The innocent pressure of his lips on her hand flared like a firebrand. His eyes simmered with the same fire. They stood that way, his breath hot on her upraised hand, until a guest behind them cleared his throat. Elise jolted from his stare, her cheeks rosy. Boy, oh boy, this man took her breath away.

After a brief apology to the guest behind them, Jimmy and Elise took one step forward. They came to an abrupt halt when a procession of dark suits with solemn faces flooded the hallway. Elise shot a questioning glance at Jimmy, but he simply shrugged; nonchalant, like this type of interruption happened all the time.

"Ma'am, sir?" Black Suit asked. "Please step into the dining room. Now."

Again, Jimmy shrugged, and guided her into the room. Couples mingled and small talk buzzed, enveloping Elise in a surreal cocoon. Pearls and diamonds flashed around necks and on earlobes. Here and there, an emerald flashed, a ruby blazed. Elegant dresses flirted with sophisticated tailored suits.

When her eyes swept across the giant on the far side of the room, Elise did a double-take. He was undoubtedly the largest human she had ever laid eyes upon. A fiery redhead in a stunning green dress stood at his side, a slender arm laced through his immense one. The striking couple kept to themselves, standing next to the fireplace; he dwarfed the massive carved mantle at his back.

Elise dubbed the guy Mount Everest, and tried not to stare. The mountain of a man grinned and raised a hand in greeting, and Jimmy returned the gesture.

"The best man," he whispered to her.

"Are you sure he's a man?" she whispered back.

"Aw, Ben's an old softy. Trust me. Cora is the one to reckon with."

"The lady on his arm?"

Jimmy nodded. "His wife, and a talented midwife physician."

"I look forward to meeting them."

A few feet away, another Black Suit mouthed a silent sentence, then nodded. The giant and the redhead were momentarily forgotten.

The President's son is getting married tomorrow.

The mental version of Trudy's voice gloated, full of mischief and self-validating amusement. Elise's suspicions were confirmed when Sterling Miles, President-Elect of the Republic of Texas, strode into the room. His soon to be First Lady, Betsy Miles, beamed above a diamond choker from her husband's side. Black Suits followed in their wake, their eyes sweeping the room. The one who had ushered her and Jimmy into the room nodded to a colleague standing beside a potted palm with wide, kelly-green fronds in the far corner of the room. President-Elect Miles flashed whitened teeth, and shook a few outstretched hands; others he clapped into a boisterous embrace with slaps on the back. Mrs. Miles leaned in to kiss the cheek of a younger woman. The junior of the two grinned and raised a surprised eyebrow.

Elise yearned to scratch the sudden itch between her shoulder blades. The memory was close, niggling at the raised hair on her neck, something to do with the younger of the two women. She averted her eyes, and found Jimmy smiling down at her once more.

He leaned down to whisper in her ear. "Do you forgive me?"

"For not warning me that we would be attending the rehearsal dinner for the wedding of the decade?"

"Something like that."

Elise laughed quietly. "Yeah, you're forgiven. As long as you buy me dessert."

"Dessert, huh?" Jimmy's eyes sparkled with mirth in the low light of the dining room. He cocked his head to the side. "I didn't peg you as the sweet tooth type."

"There's a lot you don't know about me, mister."

"Ooh, a woman with a secret. Intriguing."

If he knew, he would speed away in the opposite direction without a backward glance.

Rather than meet his probing stare, Elise swiveled a look around the increasingly crowded space.

"Are you here for the bride or groom?"

"Both, really. I met Cullen and his soon-to-be wife, Jo Camden, last year when they visited my other friends, Ben and Cora. We've gotten to be pretty good friends over the months. Cullen's a good guy, and the polar opposite of his father. Jo is ... impressive."

Hoots and hollers accompanied handclapping as what could only be the honored couple entered the room. Whistles echoed off the paneled walls. The woman who grabbed her attention earlier – what was it about her? Mystery Woman inserted two fingers in the corners of her mouth, and emitted the shrillest whistle yet; the President-Elect grabbed her in a side hug and squeezed her close to his side.

While the rest of the room cheered Cullen and Jo, Elise studied the lady in the President's familiar embrace. Short, but taller than Elise, with long, wavy hair the color of toasted almonds. Confident, perfect posture. She had President Miles' nose, and Betsy Miles' ears. A daughter?

No, *the* daughter. The attorney. Elise had not recognized her out of her stiff business suit and slicked-back bun. But it was her, all right.

Elise felt her stomach bottom out, and her shoulders stiffened. Jimmy must have noticed.

"Everything okay?"

She managed a nod, though her smile was more a grim slash across her face than anything resembling happiness.

Friends and family edged toward seats assigned with embossed note cards. The tented cardstock nested at her place setting simply read *Guest* in a filigreed gilded font. Jimmy pulled her chair toward his chest, and gestured with a gallant hand for her to sit. Again, her smile never reached her eyes. Her stomach somersaulted. Elise kept her eyes cast downward, avoiding the eyes of the attorney.

Over the next few minutes, while conversation ebbed and flowed, Jimmy tried his best to introduce her to the people at their sides and in front of them. Forks and spoons clinked against the fine china service, and hearty laughter seasoned the first course. The sounds melded together into a buzzing cacophony. Elise was suffocating in an ocean of mirth and festivity, drowning in polite tête-à-tête. Yet she nodded and smiled, gave one and two-word answers to well-meaning questions.

Her concentration remained on not making eye contact with the President's daughter. Katherine Miles, Federal Prosecutor for the Central Texas District. Elise felt foolish for not connecting the dots sooner. The one woman she had evaded for the last twelve years sat five chairs away.

"Elise?"

"Hmm?"

Quizzically, Jimmy pointed to the uneaten salad in front of her. "I was asking if the food was to your liking."

"Oh. Yes," she lied. She barely remembered the soup, and had no recollection of the wait staff sliding the chilled plate in front of her.

"You seem distracted," he pointed out. "We can go for a walk, if you want."

She was ruining his evening. He didn't deserve this, her mess of a life. "You stay. I think I'll run to the ladies' room. It is a little overwhelming, you know?" She angled her chin to the sophisticated collection of souls surrounding her. "Can you manage on your own for a bit?"

He placed his hand atop hers and squeezed. "Take your time. I feel awful for not preparing you."

"Don't. I'm having a lovely evening, Jimmy. I just need some air."

She excused herself, clutching her beaded bag to her side. Elise hoped the eyes she felt on her back were those of the man she was leaving behind, and not those of the petite lawyer she never wanted to see again.

***

Jimmy peeked at his watch for the third time in as many minutes. Elise must have been more upset than he thought for her to need more than fifteen minutes alone. For the thousandth time, he scolded himself for not telling her who Cullen was. He was a coward and a jerk.

Resolved, he pushed away from the table and laid his napkin on his seat. Cullen watched him rise with a questioning expression, to which Jimmy could only shrug and nod toward the door. The groom-to-be nodded and whispered to Jo, who excused herself with a strained smile.

In the hallway, Jo exhaled with gusto. "Thank you."

Jimmy chuckled. "For what?" He glanced around the hallway in search of Elise, but she was nowhere in sight.

"Needing me to go into the ladies' room to find your date. And to catch my breath as well. All these highfalutin bigwigs are stressing me the heck out."

"Those bigwigs are soon to be your in-laws."

"Don't remind me," she said, shuddering.

"You don't strike me as the cold feet kind of girl."

"Hang out with Betsy Miles for ten minutes, and then reevaluate," she sneered. "Here we are. I'll retrieve your lady in no time."

Jo returned with empty hands and a puzzled look. Jimmy opened his mouth to ask the obvious; but just as he did, a light tap fell on his shoulder.

"Excuse me, sir?" The smartly dressed concierge greeted them with a slight frown and an envelope. "Are you Jimmy?"

"Yes." His face mirrored that of the annoyed employee.

"A guest left this for you, and asked that we deliver it."

Jimmy took the envelope, and the concierge turned on his heel, disappearing down the hallway. The lip of the envelope was tucked, not sealed. He withdrew the note, and his forehead wrinkled in response to the missive inside.

Jimmy,

Please forgive my hasty departure. I will forever be grateful for the chance you took in asking me to dinner tonight. But unfortunately, circumstances demanded I leave early.

Regretfully,
Elise

The note dropped to his side, where Jo snatched it from his idle hand. It was short, and she read quickly.

"The nerve of that woman!"

"Hey, it's really okay," Jimmy said. "Something was off. I could tell. After your future in-laws arrived, Elise tensed up. She probably felt intimidated. I knew I should have prepared her."

"Well, still. I hate that you will go stag for the rest of the evening."

"I'll survive," he laughed, but he felt no amusement.

For the duration of the evening, his thoughts were on an exotic raven-haired barista, her sharp wit, and easy sultry laugh. He attempted to remain upbeat for his friends' sake, and failed. Jo met his eyes with sympathy, and Cullen dragged him to meet every single lady in the room.

His Cinderella had left him high and dry, without even a stilted black pump to go on.

Chapter 4

A sonorous chime rang sedately, increasing in volume and permeating the hotel room from all sides. Jimmy paused in the act of zipping his too-full suitcase.

"Room 213, go ahead," he acknowledged to the expectant air.

"Deputy Wilson," a pleasant voice responded. "Your vehicle has been brought around and is waiting in the loading bay. We have allotted twenty minutes for your departure."

"Thank you. I'll be right down."

"Very good, sir."

He leaned onto the swollen leather travel case with one hand, letting his weight push the lid toward the base, while coaxing the zipper one interlocking tooth at time. With jaw clenched and mental pleading, he managed to shut the thing without breaking the zipper. Successful and out of breath, Jimmy shot a guilty glance at it, knowing the only reason he had difficulty shutting it was because of the impeccable silvery gray tuxedo haphazardly folded inside.

He dropped the case by the door, and prowled around the room, flicking the duvet to the foot of the bed, pulling out smooth mahogany dresser and nightstand drawers, verifying he left nothing behind. The bathroom was devoid of his belongings as well.

Another annual training weekend in the big city on the books, but his lungs craved the sweet country air of Cotton Springs. In Austin, there were too many people breathing the same oxygen, too much busyness and shoulder-bumping passersby. The Capitol was good for a visit, but definitely not his choice for the long haul.

Two bright spots scorched his memory.

The dark, raven hair of a woman turned ghost; one he would never see again, but who had ripped a chunk of hope from his soul and absconded with it. Jimmy could still hear her husky laugh, picture her chocolate eyes.

Did soul regrow? Was it healed by patience and time, or would they only serve to be reminders of that brief spark when his heart leapt into his throat and danced there?

In contrast, he would carry bright memories of a beautiful and hilarious wedding. Jo, in her gorgeous hand-beaded ivory gown, with wildflowers woven into a crown and her blonde hair piled high in loose curls around it. The way Cullen practically skipped down the aisle of emerald green grass, and those gathered chuckling under their breath. In the distance, the setting sun sparkling like cut diamonds on the snaking Colorado River behind the President's mansion. He wondered ...

Before exiting the room, he tapped the clear glass media wall. It appeared to be a simple, if oversized, section of plate glass adhered to the wall. But with a couple quick taps and swipes of a finger, it displayed any number of things: weather forecasts, traffic information, television broadcasts, SatNet, and more. His finger dragged a window open, and he navigated to the national news. As he expected, the headlines featured the President Elect's new daughter-in-law hooking a well-aimed uppercut to the chin of an intruding member of the paparazzi. A laugh bubbled up, and he shook his head as the scene replayed.

Truthfully, the guy had it coming. Security had been at understandably elevated levels. As an usher, Jimmy had been required to memorize the modest guest list, and verify the identity of every person he guided to the seating area. President Miles also had his personal security detail undercover in the guise of ushers. The voracious interloper had masqueraded as a violinist, part of the limited string orchestra situated under the gazebo. After the minister pronounced Cullen and Jo to be man and wife, they turned, greeting the applauding crowd with mile-wide grins. They had stepped off to begin the exit down the aisle, Cullen with his eyes glued on his bride, Jo laughing with her wildflower bouquet dangling at her side, when the paparazzo lunged at them. The idiot flew up the aisle, snapping photos with his sleek high-speed camera, a lapelcam secured to his tuxedo jacket. Cullen and Jo were brought up short, and exchanged startled glances.

Then Jo handed her bouquet of flowers to her groom, wordlessly met the enthusiastic cameraman at the aisle's midway point, and assessed him with a tilt of the head and narrowed eyes.

"Mrs. Miles! Do you have anything to say to the audience?"

The man's eyes danced, a wide smile splitting his face.

"Nope," she replied.

The guy never saw the wicked punch coming.

The stunning bride then wiggled her fingers, shook out her hand, nodded once, and took the bouquet from her husband. Cullen had looked to the heavens for guidance, then barked a laugh in response. The couple split, their hands clutched in the middle, skirting the unconscious man on the ground, and glided the rest of the way into the house amidst shouts and applause. The blacksmith bride dropped a curtsy before waving one last time, entering the mansion with Cullen in tow.

Jimmy, still smiling at the footage replaying on the news, closed out the news screen and tapped the media wall to shut it down. Leave it to Jo to authorize the official photographer to release video of the knocked-out paparazzo. That woman was a firecracker!

With a last scoping glance around the room, he extinguished the lights. The elevator descent was uneventful, and he checked out of his room with a palm placed on the clerk's scanner. In four hours, he would ease back into the slow pace of Angelina County. A sigh escaped at the thought.

His unmarked government vehicle waited in the loading zone. The President's daughter leaned against the front of it, jutting out like a carved beauty on the front of a Viking longship. The ghost of a smile played on her smirked lips.

"Deputy Wilson," said Katherine Miles.

"Madam Prosecutor."

"Oh, please," she laughed. "We're practically family now, right?"

Her amusement sounded like gravel sliding down a rocky ridge. Throaty, coarse. Appealing. She had the reputation of a wildcat in the courtroom.

"If you say so, ma'am." He swept eyes over his cruiser, and returned her stare with a quirked eyebrow. "Something I can do for you, Miss Miles?"

When her pout yielded no results, she huffed and stood, brushing off her hips and backside.

"Please, call me Katherine. I had a couple questions for you."

"Okay, then, *Katherine*. Shoot."

He moved to the passenger door, dropped his suitcase in the seat. She angled to stand beside him, and folded her arms across her midsection.

"The woman you brought to the rehearsal dinner. What do you know about her?"

Surprised, his thick eyebrows climbed his forehead. "Not much, really. Her name is Elise Gomez, and she works at Capitol Grind. Other than that, I don't know her at all." An ache lodged itself in his throat, and he swallowed around it. Jet black hair, a wicked smile, an ease he had never felt around anyone else. The zing when his lips touched her skin. "Why do you ask?"

"You're sure?"

"Yes," he gritted through clenched teeth. "So I picked up a barista at a coffee shop? Am I under arrest for uncouth etiquette?" His laugh sounded forced, even to him.

She blinked, shrugged. Then he realized she wasn't really interested in *his* relationship to her, but in Elise herself.

"Who is she?"

"A ghost," she said with a shrug. "One who, I suspect from her hasty departure the other night, is long gone."

The attorney clapped him on the shoulder, gave it a squeeze.

"It's probably for the best she's gone, Jimmy."

"You know I'm going to look into this," he pointed out.

Katherine brushed her long, unbound hair over her shoulder. "You can try. Like I said, Deputy. She's a ghost."

So they were back to deputy?

Her high heels clacked on the paved road a few paces before she turned around. "Oh, Jimmy?"

"Yeah," he answered, wary.

"If you find anything in your search, you are legally obligated to inform me. The warrant is waiting for you in Cotton Springs."

For the second time in three days, a woman left him with more questions than answers.

Chapter 5

"You waiting for the form to submit itself?"

Betty's honeyed drawl yanked him from the internal argument he was losing with himself. How long had his receptionist been standing over his shoulder? He tapped the lower left corner of the screen, snoozing it, then lazily spun around in his chair and steepled his fingers beneath his chin.

"You gonna stop nagging me any time soon?"

The long-time secretary rolled her wire-framed eyes, shaking a finger in his direction. "We both know you want to."

Jimmy sighed, mainly because she was right; and because she had done nothing but nip at him about it every single day for the last month.

"Has less to do with me wanting to be Sheriff than it does dreading the politics. I'm not sure I'm up for it, to be honest."

"Pah! Shake some hands, kiss some babies, cut some opening day ribbons. Everyone in Angelina County knows you're the man for the job."

"It feels like a betrayal," he admitted quietly.

Unshed tears glistened in her eyes. "Jimmy, honey. Tom Bronson served our county well, and I liked him. Called him my friend. But," she said, sniffing and dabbing at her nose, "he's gone. And the void he left needs a good, strong man to step up and do the job he loved."

Sheriff Bronson had been in office for the last ten years. His tenure was a legacy of honesty, sound judgment, and fairness. The massive heart attack had claimed a husband, a father, and a reputable lawman in one tragic blow; and it left a vacant office in its wake. Instead of holding a special election, the commissioners court had decided to appoint a new sheriff. After a month of no one in the position, Judge Waters was getting antsy.

Jimmy rubbed a calloused palm across his stubbly chin. How long since he had shaved? Two days, three? The deadline for candidate submission had consumed his thoughts, not only during the working day, but in the wee hours of darkness. Sleepless nights, the precarious stacks of dishes in and next to his sink, the piles of soiled laundry ... all because of this application. It gnawed at him. He should go ahead and put his name in the proverbial hat, if for no other reason than to reclaim his once orderly life.

He growled and swiped the screen awake. Betty's thin eyebrows rose in surprise as he held his palm against the screen's security scanner. Once more, the submission form appeared. He inhaled once, held his breath, and signed the bottom of the page with a stylus. His index finger hovered over the Submit icon.

"Oh, for Pete's sake, just tap that thing already."

Jimmy closed his eyes and submitted his tender for Angelina County Sheriff.

***

"What can I get you, *Sheriff* Wilson?" Dixie's quirky smile lit up the diner.

Jimmy rolled his eyes heavenward. "How?"

He glanced at his wristcom. Thirteen minutes since he made it official. "You need to ask?"

He hung his head, shook it slowly. Betty excelled at her profession, but her mouth was legendary.

Silverware clinked against plates, conversation buzzed low and steadily. A handful of regular bottoms warmed their red-covered stools; half a dozen booths were filled with an animated lunch crowd. Dixie slid a beaded glass of sweet tea in front of him, and he nodded his thanks.

"Want the usual?"

"Yeah, but onion rings today."

"Sure thing. Sheriff." The wink flashed alongside her grin.

Jimmy chuckled, rolling his eyes. "We'll see what happens, Dix. Feels surreal, like a dream. But you and I both know dreams can go any which way."

"At least it's not a nightmare."

"Not yet," he chuckled.

While the café owner flittered around her domain, Jimmy passed the time sipping and half-paying attention to the news report playing onscreen above the kitchen pass-through. President Miles continued his international trade negotiations with Mexico. Lines etched around the leader of the Republic's smile hinted at the strain involved, despite the amicable handshaking. According to Jo, steel prices had improved, but only by a hair, and just enough to encourage the trade talks.

Behind him, the brass bell tinkled entrances and exits. Forks tinked against plates, conversation buzzed low, and meat sizzled on the grill in the kitchen. The news channel showed clips of angry, fiery protests in eastern America, but the diner noise drowned out the words.

"Hey, Dix? Turn that up for me, will ya?" Jimmy pointed at the viewscreen.

She tapped the screen and slid the volume bar.

"*Demonstrations have bled into a second day around America's capitol city, baffling city officials and stressing the resources of federal police. Multiple injuries have been reported, but so far, no fatalities. Federal police are seeking information into the leadership of the so-called 'Dissenters'. Citizens are instructed to report to their district precinct with any pertinent information.*"

Porcelain scraped across the bar top, and his lunch skidded to a stop between his triangled arms. "Didn't your mama ever teach you not to sit with your elbows on the table?"

He peeled his eyes from the mob scene on the news, grinning at Dixie. "Yeah, but I betcha don't know the origins of it."

Intrigued, she cocked her head to the side and tipped her chin, urging him with a raised eyebrow. "Do tell, oh fountain of knowledge."

Jimmy flicked his napkin at her. "Smartaleck. Anyway, back in the old days, sailors frequented the bars and pubs near the docks. Experienced sailors knew to anchor their plates onboard the ships by bracketing the plate with their elbows. That habit was hard to get out of, and carried over to when they were ashore. So mothers, fearful that their sons would be pressganged into sea service, began telling their young children it was bad manners to put their elbows on the table."

"You're making that up!"

He drew a finger across his chest. "Cross my heart, God's honest truth."

"Huh. See? You'll make a great sheriff."

The bit of onion ring he had just plopped into his mouth nearly flew right out. He cleared his throat. "Because I know useless trivia?"

"Naw. Because you can still surprise me, after all these years." Dixie beamed at him, her smile wide and pristine.

He flicked his chin at the viewscreen behind her. "What's going on in Washington?"

"Freedom fighters, calling themselves 'The Dissenters' these days. They want to return to the days of a democratic republic, rather than living under the socialist government's regime. Creeps up every few years, it seems. Except it looks like they've moved past covertly published manifestos into public rallies."

"That's more than a rally," he noted, nodding at the report. Police in riot gear held the bulging line against impassioned protestors. A glass bottle flew through the air, shattering near the startled reporter. More than a rally for sure. Interesting.

He bit into the bacon cheeseburger, the grease warm and oozing around his teeth, and he nearly groaned with pleasure. His eyes slid closed as he savored it.

"Should I tell Mack you approve of the burger?"

He grunted, his mouth too full to do anything else.

Dixie laughed and refilled his tea. "I'll just take that as a yes. This one's on me. Sheriff."

Jimmy grunted again, attempting to protest around the mouthful of greasy scrumptiousness. The sweaty tea glass had just tapped his lower lip when Betty's voice sounded in his ear.

"We've got a 10-54 on 58, about a quarter mile north."

"Any idea whose and what?" He wistfully eyed the remaining burger in front of him, and nodded at Dixie. She flicked him a thumbs up, and rummaged under the counter. The paper to-go bag slapped the counter next to his white porcelain plate.

"Weston's sheep, far as I can tell."

"10-4."

Jimmy Wilson, candidate for Angelina County Sheriff.

Sheep wrangler.

Chapter 6

No sooner had he scraped his soiled boot sole across a chiseled rock in the ditch than Betsy's voice rattled his brain once more.

"Jimmy, you copy?"

"Yeah, I'm here." He bent his leg, angled the sole upward to inspect it. He should have known to watch his step around more than fifty mulling sheep. "Whatcha got?"

"Bo got called to escort a prisoner from Lufkin to Nacogdoches, wants you along for the ride."

He glanced at his wristcom. "Call Scott in early."

"I'm sure he'll leave a thank-you card on your desk."

Snorting, he surveyed the area. Weston's collie busied herself nipping at errant sheep heels, as though making up for lost time. A couple of ranch hands milled near the repaired section of fence. Everything looked to be in order.

"I'll be there in two. Tell Bo to be ready."

Thirty minutes later, Jimmy tucked the prisoner's head as he loaded him into the back of his cruiser.

"Y'all got it all wrong, man. I didn't do nothin'. She came at me. I was just defending myself!"

Jimmy eyed the man, then shook his head. "I'm just the runner. Save your explanation for the judge."

The inmate sputtered through the first few miles, progressed to cussing, and then fell silent by the time he and Bo Simmons, his partner from Cotton Springs, drove across the river separating Angelina from Nacogdoches county. Conversation had, for the most part, been shooting the bull.

Bo entered transfer information into the cruiser's on-board computer system. "Hear you finally threw your hat in the ring."

"Yep."

"So, do you have a plan on strengthening law enforcement in Angelina County, Mr. Candidate?"

Rolling his eyes, he smirked. "Yeah, I'd start with fining smart-mouthed junior deputies."

Bo snorted, tapped a final key, and closed the unit. "Good luck with that."

"I'll bring in a fortune."

The March sun broke through the clouds, warming both the vehicle's windows and the greening earth beyond the glass. It seeped through stoic yellow pines to illuminate ferns blanketing the forest floor. Sunlight strobed and winked, and then glared as forest abruptly transitioned to vacant ranchland. Jimmy tapped the top of the windshield. It dimmed, filtering the sun. Abandoned homes sprouted like weeds on the other side of the glass, stubbornly refusing to be reclaimed by the land.

"This drive depresses me," Bo said.

Jimmy turned briefly to find his partner gazing at the scenery, a wistful droop to his face.

"So many families wiped out and scattered. I can't imagine what my grandparents went through, what they had to do to survive."

"Grandad rarely mentioned it," Jimmy admitted. "He always talked about starting up the reclamation foundry, making a go out of hard times. That sort of thing. But The Secession? Only at the end of his life. His regiment fought near Toledo Bend."

His partner winced. "Ah. That's rough."

Silence fell, interrupted only by the ripping snores of the inmate in the back seat. His partner swiveled his head, mumbled something about only the guilty sleeping. Jimmy's thoughts swirled as the miles crept by. Civil unrest in America, his possible appointment as sheriff.

Twenty-five minutes after leaving Lufkin, Jimmy pulled into the Nacogdoches precinct parking lot. He and Bo hauled the spittin' mad inmate to the watch officer at the desk, left thumbprint verification and signatures in the logbook, and waved cheerfully to the protesting inmate who was squirming against his restraints as another officer guided him to the holding pen.

"Well, that was fun," Bo chuckled. "Wanna grab coffee or something in town before we head back?"

"Dinah's?"

A grin split Bo's tanned face. "Read my mind, Sheriff."

"Not Sheriff yet," Jimmy mumbled.

Before they could cross the threshold, the desk sergeant yelled, "Deputies?"

Jimmy turned. "What's up?"

"Run this packet over to city hall, and the coffee's on me."

"You got yourself a deal, Sergeant."

The cruiser grumbled across the cobblestone paved Main Street. The oldest town in Texas was known for its unique paving in the downtown district. Almost a dozen horses twitched tails and bobbed heads at hitching posts in front of a variety of shops; a handful of vehicles, all but one of them trucks, awaited their owners' return. Jimmy angled into an empty slot. The green canvas awning fluttered in the early spring breeze. City Hall, a three-story red brick building with a white-columned overhang, crouched next door to Dinah's. Nine flags flew lazily outside City Hall, signifying the nine countries to rule over the town since its establishment.

He waited outside as Bo acted the courier, then they both angled toward Dinah's.

Jimmy held the door and tipped his brown felt hat to the customer exiting the bakery.

"Ma'am."

The woman, a shapely brunette in a charcoal pants suit grinned. One hand flew to her heart, while the other clutched a paper sack at her side.

"Why, thank you, officer."

A clean, spicy scent drifted in her wake. It reminded him of candlelight dinner in a ritzy restaurant, maybe champagne by the fireside. He watched as she walked along the sidewalk. Hey, he was human, right? When she was nearly thirty feet away, she turned with a smile, a flirty wink, and a tiny wave. He could have sworn laughter floated in the wind.

Bo smacked him on the back. "For real, man. Does this have to happen everywhere we go?"

"What?"

"Pretty ladies practically throwing themselves at your sheep dung-covered boots."

Jimmy snorted. "Heard about that, did you?"

Simmons grunted, shaking his head. "I bet even that pretty little stranger has heard it by now, Sheriff Sheepherder."

"Funny."

The smell of fried pastries and sugar assaulted his nose in a welcome way. At the counter, he ordered an apple fritter and a black coffee with a shot of espresso, then waited as Bo ordered.

The cashier waved him off. "Dutch called in. You're good."

He dropped a five-dollar piece into the tip jar next to the register, and the cashier beamed as it clinked the glass bottom.

"Thanks, deputy. Y'all enjoy, and let me know if you need anything."

At a raised table next to the expansive plate glass window, the two sipped coffee and munched on their glorious baked goodies. Jimmy let his mind wander, daydreaming and planning projects around the house. Maybe he would finally set up the forge Jo Miles had been nagging him about, try to make something. He had space in the barn for it, if he cleaned it out a bit.

He was licking the vanilla glaze off his thumb, staring past the glass, when she rounded the corner. So lost in his imagination, it took a second or two for his mind to register what he saw.

No. It couldn't be her.

She carried a purse, its strap slanted across her chest, and a canvas shopping bag in her left hand. Her stride was clipped, purposeful, but she halted by the window display of the boutique across from the bakery. So engrossed in watching her, Jimmy held his coffee in front of his lips without drinking.

Her jet-black hair was cut short, almost as short as his own. It gave her the appearance of a waif, a pixie, maybe even a faerie. His jaw clenched as he watched her debate going into the shop. He was frozen, afraid to move; terrified that should he move, he would shatter the vision in front of him.

"Boss? Jimmy, you okay?"

Simmons' concern reached his frazzled brain. "Yeah, I uh ... do you see that woman across the street?"

Without taking his eyes off her, he heard Bo's reply. "The sweet little thing eyeing the mannequin?"

"So you see her?"

"You sure you're all right, man?"

The mug clattered against the tabletop, a wave of coffee sloshing over his hand. Hissing in pain, he glanced down at the mess and grabbed a paper towel to mop it up.

When he looked out the window once more, Elise Gomez had vanished.

Chapter 7

Day and night, black and white. East Texas existed on an opposite plane from the Austin area. It had taken Elise a few weeks to accustom herself to the rolling, pine straw-covered hills, and the snail-like pace of Nacogdoches. After a few months, it was home.

She dropped the shopping bag on the floor next to the kitchen island with a thud. Checked her wristcom. Matthew would be home from school in a little over an hour. Enough time to shower and dress for work before Trudy showed up.

Her best friend continued to amaze her. Not one, but two moves at the drop of a hat. The loyal woman had fled San Antonio with her with nary a backward glance more than a decade ago; and now from Austin to the small city nestled less than an hour from the American border. It was as far away from the western Texas border and El Lobo as she could manage, and still find employment to provide for her and Matthew. Trudy had only shrugged when Elise bolted into the apartment the night of the rehearsal dinner and started throwing clothes in suitcases.

"Had to happen eventually," Trudy had said, grabbing her shoes. "I'll meet you downstairs in thirty."

Even now, standing in the cramped two-bedroom flat, her eyes welled. Faithful Trudy. Government-employed Trudy, who could work remotely from anywhere. She had to admit: she would be lost without her best friend. The miracle woman had even managed to secure housing within the hotel where Elise had found a job.

When she had asked Trudy how she swung that one, she cryptically replied, "It's better if you don't ask." Then she had winked.

The hotel maid gig didn't pay much, but it was an income. She valued the job more because in her downtime, the manager of The Fredonia allowed her to shadow and sometimes help in the kitchen, assisting the pastry chef. Though she wished she had *this* day off.

With a wistful twist to her mouth, she closed her eyes, picturing the stylish outfit in the Bluebonnet Boutique's showcase window. The dusky, cobalt top managed to merge wrapped lengths of silky fabric into a fit and flare tailored shape. And the heeled leather boots! Elise sighed. One day.

Hers was a cotton budget, not a silk one.

A sharp rap on the door sounded half a second before Trudy strutted through the door, pulling the key out of the deadbolt lock.

"Hey, sista. What's shakin' bacon?"

Elise raised a manicured brow. "You're early. Way too chipper, and overdressed for babysitting."

Trudy grinned, her smile touching her full, high cheekbones, and tossed her brown satchel on the worn plaid couch. She hitched a hand onto her rounded hip. "You. Me. Going out tonight."

Elise tapped herself on the chest. "Me. Work. Tonight. Why am I talking like a caveman?"

Her best friend grinned. "I already arranged it with Mel. You're off tonight."

What was going on? "O-kay?"

"And Matthew's hanging out with Paul in the kitchen and bussing tables for the night." She held out a hand, forestalling Elise's argument. "Don't. It's your birthday, or did you forget?"

She hadn't forgotten, and nodded at the bag.

"I got myself a little something."

"Oooh. Let me see. Ugh, more books?" Trudy threw exasperated hands in the air. "Woman, you read more than anyone I know." Narrowing her eyes, she continued. "Especially since leaving Austin. It's like you're hiding."

Elise winced, knowing what would come next.

"It's that man! That deputy." Trudy snapped her fingers, then jabbed a red-tipped nail into Elise's chest. "You need to move on."

"I have."

Trudy glared.

"Okay. I will. Soon. Tru, there was something about him. Magnetic. Something, I don't know, *right*."

"It was doomed from the beginning, and you ended up fleeing Austin in a cloud of proverbial dust. Come on, honey. He's gone. You never even knew him. Not really."

Elise knew she was crazy. How could anyone with her sordid past be all there in the head when it came to matters of the heart?

Trudy gripped her by the shoulders, leaned her forehead down to touch Elise's. "I see where you are by the look in your eye. You are *not* that person anymore. She died crossing the Rio Grande, and you were born in her place."

A tear scuttled across the sharp plane of her cheek. "Don't make me cry on my birthday."

Pulling her into a hug, her best friend exhaled. "I can see tonight will be a much needed reprieve. But hang on. I have something that will make it better."

She caught a glimpse of a sly smile before Trudy reached over the back of the sofa, and pulled out a tissue paper-wrapped package. Her friend shoved it into her hands, and bounced on the balls of her feet, clapping her hands.

"Open it!"

There was something soft and pliable beneath the crackly paper. Elise took her time finding the end of the tied red ribbon, pulling extra slowly. Trudy growled. Laughing, she flung the ribbon away and tore into the subtly patterned white paper.

Silk spilled across her hands.

"Oh."

It slithered and snagged over her calloused fingers. Up close she could see that what she thought was a dusky cast to the silk was more of an iridescence, cobalt blue in the shadows, and muted immeasurable colors when the light struck it. Elise couldn't believe she was holding the blouse from the boutique window. It was hers. She nestled it against her cheek.

"How did you know?"

The sly smile returned, but her friend also swiped away a tear. "You pine for it daily."

"I do not."

"Liar."

"I love you, you know."

"I know. Now go try it on and let me see how it looks on you." Trudy shooed her into the miniscule bathroom. "Don't get lost."

Fat chance of that happening.

When she emerged, Elise felt beautiful. A butterfly exploding from a dark cocoon who knew no other life than that of constricted existence.

It was a shirt, for Pete's sake.

But it was love, and friendship, and promise. And silk!

"I – I can't … I don't know what to say," Elise managed. "Thank you."

"Thank me later, hon. Shower, dress, and after Matthew gets home, we'll proceed with the evening's festivities."

"You're not going to tell me, are you?"

There was that smirk again. "Not a peep."

"You have *got* to be kidding me," Elise uttered, stunned. "There is no way you're dragging me in there."

A mound of golden fried shrimp at Clear Springs, window shopping downtown. Trudy had even treated her to another book from The Dusty Bookshelf, her favorite used book store. But this? She eyed the nondescript cinder-block building warily.

"I don't dance."

The parking lot of Jitterbug Revival popped with laughter and loud conversations, shouts and yells. A corral behind the dance hall seethed with the obscured milling silhouettes of horses. Car and truck doors opened and shut closer to Elise and Trudy; her friend slammed shut the driver's side door to her sedan. The smile on her face faltered when she saw Elise's reaction, but she squared her shoulders nonetheless.

"An hour. One hour to listen to music and dance away your funk."

She was twenty-nine years old today. She would not whine.

"I'm a mother. I can't go ..." Elise wiggled her hand in the air. "Shake my butt around strangers."

Rolling her eyes heavenward, Trudy grabbed her hand and tugged her to the nondescript double door. "Stop whining."

Her lips turned down in a frown.

Without turning, Trudy added, "No pouting either."

The bouncer at the door nodded to them as he sucked in his gut and squared his shoulders, all the while appraising Elise as she passed by. "Have fun, little lady."

Oh boy.

Like a kicked anthill, the busy throng shuffled, weaved, and stirred. The air pulsed to the heavy bass drum beat. Strobes flashed, highlighting hands in the air and bodies rocking rhythmically. Waitresses threaded themselves through rowdy groups effortlessly, smiles plastered on their faces. The air reeked of sweat and spilled beer, perfume and musk.

Sunken into the center of the rectangular concrete building, a wood-planked dance floor hosted a couple hundred gyrating bodies. At one end of the club, a stage squatted, vacant. Too bad, because live music might have made this experience more enjoyable. Opposite the stage, on the other end of the oval, was the lengthy, well-populated bar. Tall circle-topped tables dotted the long sides of the oval dance floor. Trudy dragged her to a table midway down the left side. The previous occupants had neglected to trash their bottles in the large bin only five feet away. She grabbed a napkin from the dispenser, and using it to protect her hand from stranger's cooties, gripped the four empties and tossed them into the bin with a shattering crash. Cooties. Now she sounded like her son.

Matthew.

Was he okay? She should have checked in with him before coming into the club. While Trudy surveyed their new environment – probably hatching a plan to get her to dance with a handsome stranger – Elise took the time to send a quick message to Matthew. A minute later she breathed easier. He was home, his assignments complete, watching an episode of an adventure show he loved. He also noted Mel was checking in on him every hour, and he advised her in his sage, pre-teen wisdom to stop worrying about him and just have fun.

That boy. He made her heart smile. Her shoulders relaxed, and she exhaled softly. Maybe she *would* dance with a perfect stranger. What harm could come from it? Trudy beamed at her under the flashing lights, as if she could read her mind. She leaned in and yelled in Elise's ear.

"Shall we?" She jerked her head in the direction of the floor.

Now or never.

A dozen songs later, with sweat trickling down the back of her neck, she pulled Trudy to the women's room. The four stalls were occupied, so they stood in line behind two very tipsy women. At least the bass thump was quieter in here and she could think. Trudy leaned over and laid her head on Elise's shoulder. Her wild mass of curls was damp with sweat.

"You having fun?"

"Yes."

"Truth?"

"I didn't think I would, but yes."

One lady exited, another entered the empty stall, and the line moved ahead to the sound of water splashing in the sink.

"I still don't feel entirely comfortable around this many people," she admitted.

Her friend nodded. "But you're trying. It's not like El Lobo is out there, not in this part of Texas."

Elise swiveled her head, tense, but everyone seemed to be minding their own business.

"Do not say that name again. Ever."

Abashed, Trudy's cheeks flushed. "Sorry, sweetie. But he's far away and you're here in beautiful east Texas, partying for the first time in your life."

Would she ever truly relax? Be able to live life without looking over her shoulder, terrified he would find her? Or worse, the federal attorney she fled just a few short months ago would find her and bring Elise in to testify against him.

"Relax, honey."

"Yeah. You're right. I'll try. I doubt he'd ever show up in a place like this," Elise laughed, trying to lighten the mood. "Unless it was for recruiting purposes."

She couldn't keep the sadness from her voice.

A few minutes later, they washed up and headed back into the bouncing bedlam. She would do her best to forget the past, if only for the next couple of hours, and be someone she never had the chance to become.

A free spirit.

***

The reporter waited until the two women were washing their hands before she exited the stall. She lifted the faucet, deposited soap onto her palms, and smiled at the reflection of the shorter, black-haired pixie next to her. The lady returned the gesture, hesitant, and exited the restroom behind her taller, curvier friend with the wild curls.

El Lobo.

It was a name Tandy knew well. Since last year, when the federal prosecutor announced her involvement with a high-profile human trafficking and slavery case, Tandy Newman had made it a priority to delve deep into the underworld. El Lobo ... he was the top dog.

And the cute woman with the sad eyes knew something about him.

Who knew a night on the town would be the biggest break of her life?

Chapter 8

"What have you done?" Betty demanded from the half-open doorway.

Jimmy jumped, and tapped the screen in front of him, sending the database into the background and bringing up the home page icon. He felt guilt creep up his neck in warm, blushing waves.

"I don't know what you mean."

The woman he thought of as a great-aunt tapped her thick-soled shoe on the oak floor. "Katherine Miles, Federal Prosecutor of the Central Texas District. Mean anything to you?"

Wonderful. "Daughter of the President, my good friend's sister?"

"All of the above, and on the phone for you."

Fantastic. His eyes flicked to the tiny icon on the bottom right of the viewscreen.

He punched the Accept button, and Katherine's smiling face appeared onscreen.

"Katherine! How are you?"

The surprised look on her face let him know his enthusiasm was as clear as glass. "Just fine, Jimmy. You?"

"Oh, you know. Fine." Brilliant reply. He'd love to thump his head against the wall. "What can I do for you today?"

"Encrypt the call, please."

She knew, dagnabbit. Well, it was bound to happen sooner or later.

He secured the call and waited for the hammer to drop. Katherine didn't keep him waiting.

"Where is she?"

"Hmm?"

"Don't play coy with me, James. You've searched for her half a dozen times in the last twenty-four hours. Why?"

Because he couldn't get her out of his head. He closed his eyes and saw her face, smelled her perfume from the night of the rehearsal dinner. Remembered how her hand felt in his, somehow soft and calloused at the same time.

"I was just thinking about her and wanted to check into it. Since I haven't seen her in six months," he lied.

The Federal Prosecutor stared at him through cyberspace. Her chestnut hair was pulled back into some kind of knotty twisty thing, with only the sides evident from his viewpoint. She wore a sharp, slate gray business jacket over a white shirt. Shoulders ramrod straight, she studied him with puckered lips.

"And what have you discovered?"

Two could play this game. "She's a phantom. You know that. I found nothing and no one. Who knows where she is?"

Nacogdoches, on a cobblestoned downtown street.

For whatever reason, he felt the urge to protect Elise. She ran, which means there was something to run from. And judging by the attention given this by the prosecutor on the screen in front of him, he thought he had found the wolf that made his rabbit dart for cover.

"You don't want to get involved, Jimmy," Katherine sighed. "Too much is at stake."

"What aren't you telling me? If you bring me in, I can help."

Katherine sighed, and rolled her neck, relaxed her shoulders. "I wish I could, but my hands are tied. I think you could be an asset."

She rubbed a hand over her eyes, while Jimmy remained silent. He had learned a while back that silence is sometimes the best way to get someone to talk. Silence, and a curious stare.

"I can say if you become involved with Ms. Gomez, you could endanger her. That's it. I shouldn't have said that."

Outside his office door, Betty dropped something on the floor. The echo remained the only sound.

He stared at Katherine Miles.

She watched him, and chewed her bottom lip. "Fine. I'll try to bring you in, if for no other reason than you got close to her once, and could do so again."

The last thing he wanted was to be used as a tool, to maneuver her into whatever position the government wanted her for. But it was still a chance to see her, to be with her.

To protect her.

"Whatever you think is best. Let me know if you find her," he hedged.

The call ended, and he tipped his chair, putting his feet on the top of his desk. He folded hands he didn't realize were shaking across his stomach. There was no way around it.

He needed to find Elise Gomez.

Soon.

Chapter 9

Both the vehicle and the horse lot were full, so he parked his cruiser a couple blocks away and walked into the precinct. Jimmy badged himself through the rear entrance of the Sheriff's Office building, and trudged up the stairs to the conference room. Other brown and khaki-clad deputies were present, either nodding or offering a flick of the head as a greeting. A couple veterans glanced out of the second story window at the gathering below, and shook their heads with wry smiles. The rest milled in groups of threes and fours. Jimmy counted seventeen deputies in attendance; not the full force, but someone had to remain on duty in their areas of operation.

Man, he hated press conferences.

Judge Waters stood at the head of an elongated conference table, pecking at a thin tablet in her hands. Judging by the sour twist to her mouth, she liked dealing with the media as much as he did. Still, if he were selected as sheriff, it would become a normal part of the routine; the stern, but fair, woman in front of him would be in his immediate chain of command.

"If I can have your attention please," the judge announced without looking up from her tablet. "I was surprised at the application turn-out. Or lack thereof."

She turned, pointing unnecessarily at the task screen behind her.

In bold, black letters, the name James Wilson appeared as if typed on a large sheet of solid white paper.

"Gentlemen, the media downstairs wants to meet your new sheriff. The other court officers and I thought we would have several deputy applicants for this important post. Turns out there is clearly one man for the job."

Judge Waters nodded at Jimmy, placing her tablet on the bulky table. "Ladies and gents, let's welcome the new Sheriff."

Hoots, hollers, two-fingered whistles, and genial slaps on the back jarred him, falling just short of hauling him to reality. Was this happening? No other candidates applied?

"All right, all right," the judge admonished. "Sheriff Wilson, you have five minutes before you need to be downstairs for the press conference and swearing in. I'll leave y'all to it."

Congratulatory handshakes pumped his right arm until it ached, but the whole situation continued in surreal slow motion, spotted with bits and flashes in blazing real time color. He plastered happiness on his face that his mind hadn't recognized yet. Sheriff. He was sheriff of Angelina County.

His colleagues formed two lines, shoulder-to-shoulder and facing one another; starched brown cotton shuffled, their rank insignia patches peeking and flashing as they arranged themselves in the gauntlet. He remembered participating in his first gauntlet with a newly elected sheriff;

more recently with Tom Bronson running its length. Jimmy took his place at the head of the line, ducked his head as he thought about what he would say.

He looked up with a sad grin. "Guys, we're here because a good man died. We all loved and respected him." Murmurs and nodding heads, shuffling feet, answered him. "I hope I can do the job as honorably and as well as Tom Bronson did. So before I run this dang thing, let's have a moment of silence."

Jimmy took the opportunity to thank God for His providence, for the position he would shortly accept, and thanks for the life of a God-fearing man who left this forsaken earth.

And for a sassy woman one town over who had captured his heart, and was running from something nasty.

By the time he reached the end of the row, biceps, triceps, and deltoids stung like fire after all the punching. Legend had it a sheriff shouldn't raise his right hand to swear the oath without it hurting. Hence, the gauntlet of his or her peers was born.

They filed down the stairs to the foyer, dozens of boots thumping a staccato rhythm which echoed off the cream colored walls. Conversation ebbed, and finally ceased, as all the deputies gathered in front of Jimmy. Elijah Turner, one of his buddies from school who operated in the Diboll area, took the lead and pushed open the double glass doors. Once more, the gauntlet assembled; this time Jimmy walked through unscathed, his initiation already complete. His friends and fellow officers stood at attention as he strode through them to the podium waiting at the end of the human line.

Jimmy sucked in the crisp March air, faced Judge Waters with his right hand raised, and repeated the oath of office.

So help him, God.

***

As usual, nothing good was on. Matthew slept the deep hibernation that only bears in winter and 13-year old growing young men achieved. The unadorned plate-sized clock on the wall showed a little after eleven o'clock. It was a rare Saturday off work, but she had risen early anyway. Old habits, and whatnot. She had scrubbed the bathroom and kitchen floors; washed, dried, folded, and put away two loads of clothes; and prepped meals for the next week. Now that she could put her feet up guilt-free and watch a little television, she frustratingly flipped through the channels.

More news coverage of the American riots. People selling the latest gadget to make life easier. Pointless talk shows discussing frivolous topics. Elise was just about to power off the wallscreen when a familiar face flashed and disappeared. Hurriedly, she backtracked the channel search until she saw him again.

Jimmy, in dress uniform, with his hand raised in front of a crowd of law enforcement and civilians alike. She unmuted the program and read the ticker caption at the same time: *Newly Appointed Sheriff Takes Oath of Office.* She heard him say the words, "So help me, God." A hairsbreadth before the oath was finished, those assembled erupted in applause, and reporters began shoving their hands in the air, vying for his attention. Nonplussed, Jimmy shook the judge's hand and squared his shoulders.

Elise had crept to the edge of the sofa, perching there and rolling her hands together. Her heart beat wildly, fluttered in her throat; and when he spoke to the media, it felt as though he was speaking to her. Which was absolutely ridiculous, because for all he knew she was still in Austin. She caught her lower lip between her teeth, wedged a fist beneath her chin and listened to the new sheriff promise to uphold the law and keep the needs of the citizens at the forefront.

"The good people of Angelina County, whether native to the area or just arrived, can be assured that your county law enforcement will continue to protect, serve, and defend your rights and keep you safe."

He looked directly at the camera, self-assured, confident. It felt as though he was addressing her. Those sweet burnished eyes, the color of a aged scotch, penetrated her soul. What she wouldn't give to glimpse him in person. Did she dare?

"Whatever the cost, as the sheriff my job is to keep you safe from harm. I take my responsibilities seriously, just as I know and understand the faith you have in me to do just that. I thank the Commissioners Court and Judge Waters for appointing me, and look forward to serving as your sheriff. Thank you."

A young brunette, mid-twenties, appeared superimposed over the lower left corner of the news report as the sound from the press conference faded. Tandy Newman, the caption read below her talking head. Elise paid little heed to the words coming from the reporter's mouth, as she was still fixated on the coverage happening in the background. Jimmy seemed confident, but ... perturbed, maybe? The set to his jaw, creases at the corners of his eyes. Then the press conference coverage faded to black, and the newsperson was alone against a backdrop of what looked like a courthouse, maybe the police station.

"I look forward to my one-on-one interview with Sheriff Wilson in the coming days ahead. This is Tandy Newman, with East Texas News 9."

A dozen thoughts meandered across her mind, vied for attention almost as much as that pert journalist had attempted to do. She had known Angelina County neighbored Nacogdoches, but Texas covered a lot of earth. Maybe a part of her wanted to be near him; the subliminal part that appreciated his full-faced smiles and the fresh smell of his aftershave. More than that, though, she craved a slower life in a smaller town than Austin. Fewer faces in the crowd, not as much stress and looking over her shoulder.

Seeing his face rekindled a fire she thought doused. It awakened a desire to feel for someone deeper than she allowed herself to go.

On a late Saturday morning, with a brisk March breeze howling low outside the window panes of her tiny, rented apartment, Elise Gomez faced herself in the dainty oval mirror over the bathroom sink. The eyes staring back at her were haunted, jaded. Hurt beyond measure, healed despite the pain. And yet, they held a sparkle of hope.

Her past may have chased her here, clear across the Republic of Texas; but her past would no longer dictate her future.

Chapter 10

Sworn in on Friday. By Monday he slumped, buried beneath a stack of forms to be reviewed and signed. He longed for the days of being saddled – literally – to his work. The only animal Jimmy was riding now was of the pine desk breed.

Pete, the deputy manning the assistant post for the week, possessed a particular gait. More of a *thump THUMP* than a *thump-thump*. The swish of his starched jeans rubbing together at the thigh also gave him away. Jimmy thanked Pete without looking up from his tablet.

"Yep," the young man replied. The *thump THUMP* thudded to a standstill at the door. "Um, Sheriff? It's after lunch. You plannin' on eatin' today?"

"Hmm? Maybe." Jimmy waved a half-interested hand in the air. "I'll be fine for an hour. Go get yourself something."

"Yessir."

Read, sign, send. Repeat.

He rolled his neck, and glanced at his inbox. Groaned. A word on the screen caught his attention, reminding him of something he had forgotten to jot down hours ago. Jimmy snatched at the pen on his desk before the idea was lost in the stack of formality, and the pen skittered and bounced off the hardwood floor into the empty leg space beneath the desk.

"Shoot," he mumbled, scooting the chair backward toward the far wall. "Appointment at 3, appointment at 3. Don't forget ... where is that dang pen?"

Clipped footsteps echoed outside his door. Not Pete. He raised his head, and whacked it on the underside of the heavy desk, rattling both the drawer and his brain.

Gripping his head, he subdued a string of vulgar words his mother would pinch his ear for. Instead, he muttered, "Be with you in a sec." He clenched his jaw, and felt a traitorous tear well up.

Across the room, the footsteps halted, and the tear was sucked into a hasty retreat. He sniffed, swiped both hands across his face for good measure, tousling his shaggy hair in the process. All he needed now was one of his deputies seeing him cry, no matter how involuntarily. He cleared his throat, and opened his mouth to tell the deputy to enter.

It wasn't a deputy.

"You're ... you. How? Why?"

Elise grinned at him from the doorway. "It's good to see you, Jimmy."

She was here. Elise was here. Wait!

"You can't be here!"

Her eyes showed her confusion, her doubt. "Oh, I thought maybe we could ... I guess not."

She chewed her bottom lip, fidgeted her fingers at her sides, and then gripped her hands in front of her. Good golly, she was beautiful in well-cut jeans and a fitted white button-down shirt.

Concentrate, man.

"No! No, Elise, honey. That's not what I meant. Not at all. Of course I want you! I mean, here. Want you *here*. It's just the sheriff's station. You'll be seen."

Glancing over her shoulder, she said as calm as a June pond, "No one is here. I'm not careless."

"Cameras are everywhere," he began.

"Two by the front entrance, one at the juncture of the hallway and this row of offices. Don't worry, my head was conveniently tucked to avoid the facial recognition. But you have answered a question for me, at least."

"I know you're an important person to the government." He shrugged. "That's all. The rest?" Shrugging, he pointed to the chair across from him and pulled up the one next to it. He set the glass to privacy, and closed the door. When they were both seated, he couldn't help himself. He grabbed her hand.

Her smile was warm, tentative.

He needed to know. "Why are you here? In Lufkin, I mean. I, um, saw you. In Nacogdoches."

Her brows rose, chocolate eyes open wide.

His turn to be sheepish. "I was at Dinah's the other day, downtown. Saw you window shopping. Then I spilled my coffee, wiped it up, and you disappeared. Want to know something?"

She nodded.

"I was planning to come find you."

Elise blinked rapidly, wiped a hand absently across her cheek. "That's such a relief. I was afraid you wouldn't want to see me after I abandoned you at the rehearsal dinner."

Jimmy decided to be as direct as she had been, waltzing into his office. Well, casing, ducking, and sneaking into his office.

"Katherine Miles came to me the day after the wedding, told me to stay away from you. And that if I came into contact with you," he paused. "I was required by law to report it to her office."

Elise nodded, gripped his hand. "She's the reason I left. And I want to tell you about it, all of it, but your deputy will be back any minute. Jimmy, I have to know. Is there something here?" She touched her chest, at the top of her sternum close to her heart. A tiny gold bird lay nestled in the v-shaped gap of her collar. "I need to know whether I took the chance of a lifetime for nothing."

He swallowed the thick lump of anxiety in his throat, and answered hoarsely. "I have thought about you for six months, Elise. Now that you're here, I don't want to let you out of my sight."

She hiccupped, and a tear rolled down her cheek. "You have no idea how happy that makes me, but ... there is someone else."

The anxious knot he swallowed thudded to the bottom of his stomach. "Someone else?"

His face must have given away his feelings, because she said, "Not that kind of someone. But a very important person in my life."

She reached into a leather purse he hadn't noticed before, and withdrew a palm tablet. With a swipe of her finger, the home screen appeared. An image of a young man appeared, and she swiveled it so Jimmy could see.

He had her eyes and her ears. The same tilt to the head, and the same long fingers, though his were hooked into his jeans' pockets. He looked up to find her searching his face.

"Your son?"

The question was unnecessary, considering the resemblance. She nodded, bit her lip.

"His name is Matthew. He's thirteen now, but this was taken about a year ago."

He savored her faint perfume, sweet with a hint of a dusky evening. Given her age, her son's age, and her life on the run, he knew Matthew was a crucial piece of her puzzling story.

All in good time.

Jimmy stood, pulling Elise up with him. He cupped her face into his hands, his thumbs lightly caressing her cheeks. She had a little fuzz, soft and innocent, on her jawline beneath her ears. He leaned down until their foreheads touched.

"If Matthew is part of you, then I'll need to get to know him. But I want you to know this. I'm not letting you go again. Ever."

Chapter 11

Tandy arrived early; much too early, if truth were known. Another interview had canceled at the last minute, so she caught the earlier train. The fifteen-minute zip between Nacogdoches and Lufkin barely registered in her memory, as she was catching up on yet another assignment while the pines blurred outside the train's tinted windows. The interview with the new Sheriff should be the most interesting of the three reports she was currently juggling. She doubted the fluff piece on the new hair salon in downtown Nac would blow the ratings through the roof; but this one with Sheriff Wilson? If she could draw him out personally, chat him up first, and then wedge in the tough questions, Tandy felt confident the piece could elevate her standings with the more senior reporters on the team.

She stood beneath an emerald green umbrella outside of The Bean and Company, sipping on a chocolatey, frothy concoction which once vaguely resembled coffee. Tandy hated coffee, really, and only drank it to fit in with the guys in the office. Throw a bunch of chocolate and whipped cream into it, and the bitter, scorched earth taste nearly disappeared. Nearly.

The March wind whipped the canvas umbrella above her head, bit into her cheeks. Morty, their weather guy, had mentioned a cold front. Maybe he was right this time? Judging by the number of pedestrians out with scarves and hats, he just might have made an accurate forecast. Another good omen, in her book.

From her vantage, she could see the Sheriff's station, a shoe store, and a deli on the corner. Tandy glanced at her wristcom, slurped around the melting cream, looked up, and nearly spit the stuff all over her business suit.

Sheriff Wilson stepped from the front door onto the concrete downtown sidewalk, swiveled his head and stretched his arms toward the cloudy sky. Was the new head honcho taking a break? She retreated two steps back into the deeper shadow of the umbrella. How embarrassing would it be for him to see her outside the station two hours early, like a dog wagging its pitiful tail at the arrival of its master? Inside, she shuddered, and thanked her lucky stars the man hadn't seen her.

He disappeared into the glassed entryway of the station, but a murky figure joined him. Hmm, not only did the person join him, but he or she hugged him. This was getting interesting.

Two seconds later, a petite woman with large dark sunglasses exited the building, her head scanning her surroundings less nonchalantly than the sheriff had. Her build, that hair. It tickled her memory. When the woman looked over her shoulder and gave a quick wave to the lawman watching from the window, the piece fell into place; but it felt more like a kick to the gut from an ornery mule.

The lady from Jitterbugs, the one who had mentioned El Lobo. Tandy was sure of it. She narrowed her eyes over the steaming cup of froth. There was a story there. It couldn't be a coincidence, running into the same person in a different city. She knew fate when she saw it.

Energized and motivated, she flagged a taxi. A few minutes later, she paid the driver and walked the sidewalk to the Kurth Memorial Library. It may be old school, but the library was her favorite research tool. Not only did it have an extensive bound book collection, but it had public SatNet stations. Not to mention an employee who was sweet on her, and often helped with the shadier side of investigations.

She had just over an hour until her interview with Sheriff Wilson. Tandy rubbed her hands together, excited and determined. The cute library assistant glanced up as she walked the length of the foyer. He grinned and waved, edging from behind the semi-circular desk.

A little sashay, a flirty grin, and a well-placed hand on his forearm, and he was logging into the government database.

Hunting time.

Chapter 12

The interview with the local news reporter ended, and Jimmy rose, shaking Miss Newman's hand. Her grip rated somewhere between limp noodle and awakening comatose patient. So young, incredibly ambitious, but trying too hard and going about it in the wrong way.

"We'll get this edited and on-air tomorrow night, Sheriff Wilson. Oh, before I leave ..."

She left the question hanging with a half-smile, coquettish.

"Yes?"

"Off the record, of course."

He nodded, slowly, his eyebrows drawn. Surely she wasn't interested in him personally?

"Have you ever heard of El Lobo?"

Not personal, then. "Sure. Pretty much any lawman in Texas is going to know about the guy."

"I'm in the process of researching him and his slave ring, and ran into a few snags." She bit her lip, looked up at him through long, dark lashes. "What can you tell me about him?"

Curious, he shrugged. "Late 40s to 50s, they suspect. Pinning down his identity has been challenging, as the guy has several decoys in various border states. Narcotics and human trafficking, notorious for preying on young girls, or even buying them from desperate parents; usually in the southwest desert."

When he stopped speaking, disappointment filled her eyes and her shoulders drooped.

"Oh, well, then. I got that far. I was hoping maybe you had more information. Of a sensitive nature?"

Gosh, she was either naïve or ruthless. "Miss Newman, files are classified for a reason. Often to protect victims of the bad guy; in this case, the criminal known as El Lobo."

He moved around the desk, hoping she would take the hint that the interview was at a close; but she only smiled expectantly. Jimmy clenched his jaw, and then chided himself. She was only doing her job.

"Miss Newman, I look forward to seeing your report on the news. But as far as other investigations go," he paused, grappling for tact, "I think it wise to remain as far away from that particular subject as you can. Both for your safety and the integrity of the ongoing case."

The reporter pursed her lips. "Thank you for your time, Sheriff Wilson. I'll shoot you a comm and give you a preview of the piece. Work for you?"

He nodded his assent, and ushered her from his office with an extended hand, keeping a full yard of personal space between them. He told his deputy, "If Miss Newman needs a ride, please see to it, Pete."

Jimmy nodded a final goodbye, quietly easing the door closed behind him. He leaned against the door, rolling his eyes heavenward and massaging the triangle of space between his eyebrows and nose. He needed fresh air, the smell of hay and manure, and the feel of pasture beneath his worn work boots. Time to clock out.

He gathered his brown canvas jacket and folded it over his arm; though with the wind kicking up like it was, he should probably wear it. No matter. He could use a cool down after Miss Newman's visit.

Tossing a backward wave at Pete, he said, "Gonna check in with the Cotton Springs office, then go home. You know how to find me."

Pete grunted an acknowledgement, but anything else he might have said was missed. Jimmy felt the fingers of a headache reaching from the base of his neck, entrenching themselves in his skull. Mercy, the last thing he needed today was a tension headache.

Twenty minutes later, he parked his newly issued truck in the lot adjoining the rear of the Cotton Springs precinct.

His head throbbed to the tempo of his heart. As he pushed through the worn metal door, he gingerly rocked his head from side to side, attempting to ease out the kinks.

Wolf whistles and cat calls greeted his quiet entrance. The morons.

"All right, guys. We can't do this every single time I visit," he chuckled.

Bo Simmons, now the lead deputy of this office, kept his dusty boots propped and crossed on the desk top. "But it's so much fun!"

Scott snorted from the corner of the room where the coffee pot rested, and threw a wadded napkin at his coworker.

"Where's Lovelace?"

"Helping Dabney pull his wagon out of a sinkhole," Scott answered. "Don't worry, boss. Small taters out this way. Hardly ever anything exciting happening."

Jimmy eyed his guys in brown. "Let's keep it that way. Quiet and peaceful."

They shot the bull for a few more minutes, until Jimmy's head reached nuclear meltdown level. He said goodbye with a pained smile, and trudged over to Wainwright's Pharmacy. Much of the short foot trip faded into hazy memory, but the tinkling of the bell announcing his arrival revived him momentarily. The lanky red-headed pharmacist waved from the rear counter.

"Howdy, Sheriff!"

"Shhh. Quieter, Nash. Listen, my head is killing me. What is the strongest killer you have that will assassinate this migraine?"

A feminine voice answered from behind, and he grinned. It hurt to grin.

"Just so happens I was restocking my not too famous headache assassin," Cora Tucker said, a hair above a whisper. She handed him a small tub of cream, and held an amber glass vial of pills in the air. "Take two of these, every four hours, and rub this," she tapped the tub, "around the base of your neck and around your ears every hour. Should do the trick. I'm guessing tension migraine."

He eyed his friend through narrowed eyelids. "How did you know?"

"Your shoulders are climbing up to your ears," Cora said with a wry smile. "Not to mention I wouldn't be a good physician if I didn't notice when my buddy's hurting. What's going on?"

New high-ranking, high-stress position. Media trolls. Long-lost love found once more, but she's a person of interest to the federal government. He would lose Elise if he reported her, and his job if he didn't.

"Nothing much."

"Liar."

He glanced in the pharmacist's direction, but Nash had wandered to the shelves behind the counter.

Jimmy added up the cost of the items, laid the coin on the counter, and told the jovial pharmacist to have a good day.

"Walk with me?"

Cora nodded her answer, and looped her arm through his. He smiled down at her, patted her growing belly. "How's my little man doing?"

"He thinks he's a bull rider. I'm convinced. Bucks all night long." She rubbed the small of her back as they walked across. "And Kitty has decided she loves to eat bananas."

"What's wrong with bananas?"

"At two in the morning."

"Ah."

He had forgotten how Cora and Ben's daughter shared a name with Cullen's sister. Fortunately for him, their precocious munchkin had not been able to say her name, insisting vehemently that her name was Kitty. But now that Katherine Miles had interjected herself into his life, the connection between the two was renewed in his aching, pounding head. Which brought him back to the reason the town doc was walking him to his truck.

"What is it, Jimmy?" Genuine concern glinted in her eyes.

He shivered in the brisk March breeze, goosebumps popping up along his forearms. Should have worn the jacket after all, but the headache had kept him from coherent thought. Still was, as he was having difficulty piecing together his thoughts to share with Cora.

"Remember Jo and Cullen's wedding, the date I brought to the rehearsal dinner?"

"Hmph. Yeah, Cinderella, running from the ball. I remember." She squeezed the lower part of his bicep, smiling up at him. "Not sure I can forgive a woman who broke your heart like that."

"Looks like you'll get a chance to test yourself."

She stopped beneath a tall oak in the southeast corner of The Square, her grip on his arm bringing him to a stop. His head raged, a caged lion punishing his skull. He rubbed the base of his neck to relieve some of the pressure. Beside him, Cora waited with a raised eyebrow.

"I saw her. Elise. In Nacogdoches, when I transported an inmate over to their jail."

"She was in jail?"

He shook his head, instantly regretting it. Ouch! "We stopped at Dinah's, and I saw her window shopping."

Cora rolled her hand in the air. "And?"

"And then she showed up at the station today."

The doc slapped his arm. "No way!"

He resumed their stroll, and she joined him. "We agreed to try and work it out between us, try to make something out of the fractured nothing we had."

They crossed Main Street, and he waved to Mr. Mason as he passed by in his horse and buggy. The clip-clop of hooves ricocheted against the brick and mortar storefronts nearby. At the moment, Mr. Mason's rig was the extent of traffic in downtown Cotton Springs.

Cora and Jimmy hung a left, coming in behind the row of businesses where his truck waited in the parking lot.

"Let's just say it's complicated for now."

She remained silent until they reached his vehicle. "I trust you know what you're doing. Is she worth it? She abandoned you once already."

"I know, and I know part of the reason why. But I don't know the whole story, yet."

The wind blew the loose auburn curls hanging below her knitted cap, and with an annoyed slant to her eyes, she brushed them out of her face. "I'm going to give you a piece of advice Mae gave me a few years ago: Guard your heart."

Jimmy rolled his eyes. "How did that work out for you?"

She barked a laugh. "In the end, just dandy. But not without some heartache." Cora rubbed a hand over her baby bulge. "Speaking of which, I should get home. Ben is probably going haywire trying to keep the tiny vigilante occupied."

She gripped him in a side hug, squeezed him tight. "I'll pray for your headache to go away. Now, go take your medicine."

As she disappeared around the corner, and he opened the driver's side door, he could not help but think that his stress was only beginning.

Chapter 13

Elise smoothed the hospital corner fold on the last bedding change of the day, tucking the draped forty-five-degree angle of sheet beneath the mattress with a sigh of relief. She straightened, groaning, the small of her back protesting. Almost done.

A brief gust of air fluttered her dark choppy mop of hair as she threw and centered the clean duvet over the bed. A hazy memory surfaced.

Playing beneath the covers as her mother switched out soiled bedding for clean and crisp. Her hands stilled as she closed her eyes, concentrating on the fleeting piece of a life long-lost.

A white bedspread tent filtering soft light, giggles beneath the fluttering sheets. The scent of linens dried on the line, summer ocean breezes concentrated into the cotton fibers. She knew her mother had laughed, speaking to her, but she only recalled murmurs, indistinct words.

What she wouldn't give to know the words. They were the last her mother said to her.

Her body stood at the foot of a rented hotel bed in east Texas; but her mind jetted to a cottage nestled on the sandy beach of the Pacific. The dunes of Del Mar rolled, retreating eastward toward Oceanside, their progress halted by the abandoned Camp Pendleton military base. Their community had been small, isolated.

The hotel clock above the sink in the kitchenette ticked away the seconds, but Elise heard pounding waves and the laughter of her friend, Ami.

Elise chased Ami over dune peaks and valleys, slashing barefooted through beach grass and sand, trying to snag the scrap of red cotton at Ami's waist. She caught sight of Ami's long golden tresses sailing in the wind and over a dune. In hot pursuit, Elise ran.

Running. Across a wasteland on the border, throwing desperate glances over her shoulder. Dogs braying in the night.

Heart banging against her chest wall.

Ragged breaths.

The dogs, yipping as they caught her scent.

Catching a ripple of light on the Rio Grande river, pushing. Running. Please don't let them catch up.

Plunging into tepid water, its weight pummeling her fatigued limbs.

Lungs burning, straining in a tar-black tunnel beneath the water's surface.

Gasping, and sweet, sweet air.

Her wristcom beeped, startling her back to the present. Her knuckles ached, their skin white from her rigid grip on the duvet. She took deep, jagged breaths, her eyes closed; then tapped the face of her wristcom.

Matthew's face appeared. "Hey. I'm home."

She cleared her throat. Her voice was jagged. "I'll be down in a minute or two."

Her son tipped his head to the side, his brows drawn into a V. "Are you okay? Is something wrong?"

"No." She shook her head, forced a smile. "No, I'm fine, baby. See you soon."

Her boy. The reason she fled El Lobo's captivity at the age of seventeen, after twelve long years of slavery. There were times she could still feel the flutter kicks of her unborn baby, felt his hiccups; she had known when he dreamed. She laid a hand on her empty womb. Time to put those wistful thoughts aside, and finish servicing the room.

When she keyed herself into their apartment in the employee's wing, Matthew leapt off the couch and rushed her.

"Are we leaving? You only have that look on your face if it's time to go."

Her poor child. His life had been filled with such instability. Not anymore.

"Honey, no. We're not leaving. You just caught me in a memory of hard times, that's all. Now," she said, guiding him to the sofa. "Tell me about your day."

He stayed silent, searching her face for reassurance. Finally, he shrugged. "Pretty much same ole, same old. Except, well, I'd like to, um, join the cross country team." He strung the last few words together so quickly, Elise needed to replay them in her mind.

She beamed. "I think that's a great idea!"

Confusion swept across his features. "Really? You never – "

"I know." She laid a hand on his knee, gave it a squeeze. "Before, I haven't allowed extracurricular activities. And we need to talk about something else. Another change."

He rolled his eyes. "Please, Mom. Not that talk again!"

Elise chuckled. "Ha. No, not that one. It's about a new friend of mine."

Matthew opened his mouth to speak, but the door clicked open and Trudy sailed in. She tossed her purse on the couch next to them.

"There's my favorite guy in the world!" She tousled Matthew's hair, and laid a sloppy smooch on his cheek.

"Ugh! Aunt Trudy, come on!"

Trudy flopped onto the thrift store armchair diagonal from the couch, and crossed her feet on the coffee table. "And you?" She pointed at Elise. "How was *your* day?"

Something in her nonchalant tone gave Elise goosebumps. "Fine. You know. Clean rooms, repeat."

"Hmm. Matt, can your mom and I have some privacy for a few minutes? It won't take long."

Her son looked from surrogate aunt to mother and back again; then he shrugged. "Sure. I'll be in my room."

As he walked the short hallway, Elise reminded, "Homework first, then game."

A grunt answered her.

The long-time friends eyed one another. Finally, Trudy dropped her feet to the floor, and propped her forearms onto her knees.

"Why were you in Lufkin yesterday?"

Trust Trudy to be blunt, an arrow seeking its target.

Elise raised a shoulder. "Did a little shopping downtown. Nothing much."

"Did this 'nothing much' have anything to do with a certain new sheriff in town?"

She coughed, thumping herself on the chest. "How did you – I mean, well, maybe I did run into him there. Small town."

"Not that small." Trudy drilled her with a look. *The* look.

"Obviously small enough to get back to you, though. Who?" Elise gritted her teeth, frustrated.

Trudy waved a hand in dismissal. "Not important. So?"

With a huff, Elise rose and strode to the kitchen. The tap filled her glass as she said, "So I saw Jimmy."

She couldn't help the grin that crept along the side of her mouth. From the couch, Trudy rolled her eyes. "I thought I told you to let him go."

"And last time I looked, I was a grown woman and mother who made her own decisions."

"He's the law, Elise."

"He is different. There's something – " She touched her chest, the narrow space at the top of her sternum. "Here. For both of us."

"When he finds out about Matt, he'll run. I don't know why you subject yourself to this."

Her best friend stood and paced the miniscule living area. She continued her rant. "You'll get close, and when he finds out that you're on the run from the feds, he'll have to choose between his duty and his newfound fling."

"I'm no one's fling!"

Trudy flinched. Elise had never yelled at her friend before, not like that.

94

She took a deep breath, dropped her head. "I told him, Tru."

From across the room, the woman she trusted with her life said, "Told him *what*, exactly."

Elise ran her tongue over her top lip, chewed the inside of her cheek. Then she faced Trudy straight on.

"Matthew, first of all. And that I'm a person of interest. Which he already knew, by the way."

It was Trudy's turn to shout. "What?"

Elise ignored her. "And I will tell him the rest in two days. We're going out Thursday."

"So you just hop a train, waltz into a law enforcement office, throw yourself at a man you spent all of two hours with, and expect nothing will come from it? You are not this naïve!"

Forcing herself to unclench her jaw, she jammed her hands onto her hips. Enough was enough.

"Trudy Blue, you have been my best friend for twelve years. You have fled numerous towns and cities, supported me and Matthew every day. But that does not give you the right to run my life. I'm done!"

"With what? Us?" Trudy's eyes showed surprise and hurt.

"No." Elise calmed, shook her head. "I'm done running. Jimmy and I will face whatever comes head-on, including Katherine Miles."

Her friend threw her hands in the air, then rested them atop her head. She mumbled and paced the room, throwing accusatory stares at her. "You. And Jimmy?"

"Yes."

She crossed the handful of feet to put her hands on Trudy's shoulders. "I want this. Him." Then she quietly added, "A normal life."

Trudy drew her into an embrace, smoothed a hand over Elise's cropped hair. Elise felt her best friend's chest move in and out with slow, deep breaths. She even knew the moment acceptance washed over Trudy.

"Okay, then. But I need some air. What does Matthew think of all this?"

"You walked in when I was about to tell him."

Reluctantly, Elise dropped her arms, freeing Trudy. Her near-sister eased her way to the door.

"I'll be back. I just – I need to breathe."

Elise nodded.

Trudy slipped through the door without a backward glance. Something niggled at Elise's memory; something Trudy had said.

Went it hit, her stomach thudded to the floor.

How had Trudy known Elise had gone to the sheriff's office?

Chapter 14

The rising sun yawned behind him as he pushed through the glass door of Dixie's Café. Old timers and early risers warmed bar stools and booth benches, and cups of coffee warmed their hands. A handful of them raised a hand in greeting. Jimmy plunked down on a stool just as Dixie slid a hot mug of coffee into his hands.

"Thanks, Dix. Busy?"

She shrugged. "About the usual. You're in early."

He took a good, long look at her. Blonde hair was pulled loosely into a ponytail, and she wore her normal jeans and a t-shirt. He narrowed his eyes, and pointed a finger at her.

"Why were you out late last night?"

The striped cotton terry towel halted in mid-swipe, and gave a lopsided grin. "Who says I was?"

"Those two black shopping bags beneath your peepers."

Snorting, she replied, "Sheriff, telling a lady she looks tired isn't exactly a compliment."

Jimmy smiled over his steaming mug. "So who was it?"

"Winston."

"Winston Frost, the dentist?"

Dixie nodded, and then covered her yawn with a quick hand. He slapped the bar, and barked a laugh.

"About dang time that man got up the nerve to ask you out."

She turned to snag a plate from the kitchen pass-through at Mack's shout of "Order up!" The white porcelain thunked hollowly in front of him.

"He didn't."

He choked on the bite of cheddar scrambled eggs, thumping his chest with a tight fist.

"You asked him out?"

"And why not? He's been coming in the same time every Tuesday and Friday for months now. I knew he was sweet on me, and I guess he won me over."

They chatted between bites and customer demands, until he wiped his mouth and chin, satisfied.

"You made me fat and happy, girl." Two silver coins clinked on the bar top.

Dixie flicked her towel playfully at him. "The day you're fat is the day I'm ugly."

Chuckling, he was halfway through the glass door when he turned to his friend. "Dixie?"

"Hmm?"

"You look happy, hon."

She grinned, and said simply, "I am."

Her words reverberated with him off and on throughout his drive to Lufkin. He missed the rocking cadence of his horse, Clarence, and the routine of saddling him in the tack he had inherited from his father. The days of being a junior deputy and riding the two miles into work, rather than driving a cruiser, had passed. Jimmy had given up his preferred ride when he had become a senior deputy a couple years ago. Now the sheriff, he maneuvered a new high-tech, federally-issued pickup along the nearly deserted highway from Cotton Springs south of Lufkin, into the county seat city. Running alongside the paved highway stretched the hardpack dirt horse path; he traveled past a dozen single horse riders, and three horse-and-buggies.

The sky overhead shone blue, renewed and hopeful, tickled by puffs of whitish-gray clouds on the horizon. Bright, brilliant, the sun hovered behind the tips of the tallest trees. The March morning air was warm, promising; the kind of day in which he longed to be working his horses in the pasture, instead of manning a desk under an artificial sun.

He hadn't mentioned Elise to Dixie, or their date this evening, though he had begun to. At the last second, he held back, suddenly wary. It wasn't that he didn't trust his long-time friend; it was more of not wanting to drag her into the unknown, the uncertain situation surrounding Elise and her son.

Her *son*. Elise was a mother to a boy more grown than not. The knowledge had been so new, so raw when she told him that he hadn't the opportunity to fully process it. How would the boy – no, Matthew – how would Matthew react to Jimmy's interest in his mother? Was Jimmy's affection for Elise enough to encompass a child as well? He barely knew her.

As the earthen surroundings whizzed by outside the truck, he lost himself in thoughts of a woman who was more of a mystery than anything; and before he knew it, he mechanically walked through the doors to the sheriff's office. He nodded and waved to coworkers on autopilot.

It was nearly lunch before he realized what was really bothering him. He was nervous. As in schoolboy with a crush, sweaty-handed, chest-pounding, awful case of the jitters kind of nervous. It disconcerted him. He had been confident and secure, easy, with her from the first second in her presence. Had discovering the existence of a son in the picture affected him more than he realized? Certainly seemed the issue.

It had been years since he was jumpy before a date. High school prom, over twenty years ago, with Nelly Jean Weeks, the prettiest girl in the senior class. She had replied a shy yes when he had asked her, and he could still recall the heart-thumping in his chest. They had shared a fun evening among friends, and a chaste kiss on her doorstep at midnight; but the infatuation fizzled shortly thereafter. Nelly Jean had married a man she met in college and moved away.

But Elise? She was woman, where Nelly Jean had been girl.

He rubbed damp palms across his jeans and flicked a glance at the clock on the wall. Four hours until he met Elise at the train station. A borrowed picnic basket laden with cold sausage, a few cheeses, crackers, and crisp apple pie waited in the refrigerator. He planned to take her out to the willow pond on the rear half of his property. The view of the sunset would be spectacular if the weather held, and he could picture the reddish glow painting her tawny face with warm fire.

On Tuesday, Elise had promised to notify him if she wasn't able to get a sitter for Matthew. As of now, she hadn't called, so he assumed everything was a go.

Now to get his nerves under control.

***

Matthew stared at her, vacant-eyed. Stunned.

She stopped pacing, and sank into the worn sofa beside him, laid a hand on his shoulder.

"Is he nice? This cop."

"Well, yes, he is. And he's the Angelina County Sheriff."

His gaze remained locked on the generic stock framed poster adorning the opposite wall. She knew firsthand the print of a worn statue in a garden wasn't all that interesting, so her son had to be deep in thought.

"I thought you said to avoid the police," he said, monotone.

Elise inhaled, focused on easing the tension in her shoulders. This wasn't going as well as she hoped. "I did. I know, it makes me seem like a hypocrite. But he's different. There's no way for me to logically explain it. I have a feeling it's *right* for him to be in my life. In yours."

He shot up from the sofa, fairly vibrating. "So you're going to put us in danger because you *like* a guy?" His voice rose with every word, emotion jolting it between high-pitch and fledgling bass.

"Hey, take it down a few levels, buddy. I know it doesn't make sense to you now, but – "

101

"Doesn't make sense?! How many times have we left town in the middle of the night with what we can fit in Trudy's car? Why is this different? Mom! Come on!"

"Matthew, please, can you trust me?"

Her son strode the half dozen steps across the room, braced himself on the end of the kitchen countertop with his head lowered between his arms. He had grown. Ropy muscles lining his forearms trembled. His maturing body had lengthened, and the breadth of his shoulders stretched wider than before.

"Can *I* trust *you?* It's all I've done, forever! How about you trust me this time? Tell me why we run!"

"Matthew, when you're –"

"Yes, older. I know the excuse. I'm sick of it, though. And now you say we're making a stand and this man, this sheriff, is going to be part of it? You don't even know the dude. How can you possibly trust him?"

"I don't know!" she yelled, her patience snapping like a severed rubber band. Once she regained her composure, she continued. "Honestly, it's just a hunch. But one I've never had before. I learned to rely on my instincts years ago, and it's how I have kept us safe."

"Tell you what, Mom. I'll trust you about the sheriff when you finally trust me enough to tell me the whole story."

The glare in his eyes stabbed her chest wall, embedded in her heart. "Honey, I – "

His hand slashed through the open space between them. "No. I – I need some air. I'm going for a run."

Matthew slammed the door, rocking the frame, and Elise crumpled to the floor. Was she doing the right thing? Her interest in Jimmy was already a wedge between her and Matthew, and they had not even begun to build a relationship. Was she being selfish, to want a different kind of love? Or, at least, the smallest chance to find it?

Flustered, weary, she shuffled to the shower. Ten steamy minutes later, Elise emerged from a hot, misty cloud wrapped in her plush robe. Unshed tears filled her eyes.

She sat on the edge of the queen-sized bed, despondent. Elise knew her son, knew he needed time to puzzle out this new development. Still, she was restless. He had never been allowed to leave the house unattended, let alone go for a run around the unfamiliar streets of a somewhat new town.

The clock on the bedside table showed she had a couple more hours until she boarded the commuter train to Lufkin. Before the emotional conversation with her son, Elise had been excited, giddy, to see Jimmy tonight. Their first official date. Even Trudy had grudgingly agreed to bring pizza and a movie over, and stay with Matthew, though not without a lecture on how irresponsible she was acting.

The nightstand drawer gaped open an inch, enough to ignite her compulsion to close doors and align pictures on the walls. She reached to shut the drawer, but found herself opening it instead. Nestled deep inside, with only the corner visible in the light, was a book. Elise withdrew it, surprised by its solid heft. The words 'Holy Bible' were embossed in gold leaf on the front cover.

From deep within, she heard an old woman's departing words: *May God bless you and keep you, child.* Elise shivered, and it had little to do with being chilled from the recent shower. Mother, the wizened old lady from Tent City all those years ago who helped her escape.

Hesitantly, she let the book fall open where it may. She blinked twice when she saw her son's name at the top of the page. Matthew. Elise flipped the onion skin pages, through the names Mark and Luke, and ending up with John heading the page. The first sentence she read was, "In the beginning there was the Word, and the Word was with God, and the Word was God."

Intrigued, she continued to read, and the tension of her argument with Matthew ebbed into peace. A quiet voice seemed to whisper to her troubled mind.

My peace I give you.

Chapter 15

In the leafy canopy backdrop, mockingbirds mimicked the crows. Their raucous laughter joined a chorus of frogs near the pond. The evening air swept through the delicate tendrils of the weeping willows surrounding the far sweep of the nearby pond, carrying the scent of manure, new grass, and Jimmy's faint aftershave. She inhaled the smell of east Texas in the spring, hoping it would ease her racing heart. But they sat side by side; and when he shifted his arm brushed hers, or his thigh rubbed lightly against her knee.

They sat on a plaid woolen blanket at the edge of the tree line, on the back half of his land. With mincing steps, Elise had joyfully maneuvered bare patches of pasture, laughing with each hop-step around horse apples, to arrive at their picnic spot. Obviously, he had been out with a shovel. Their square of earth was blessedly free of dung.

Jimmy had laid out the finger-food feast with a meticulous hand, impressing her with his thoughtfulness. Crackers and flatbread, hard and soft cheeses, plump red and purple grapes, and two choices of sausage. And the apple pie! A perfect lattice top, golden and sugared, its aroma enticing. She wanted to dig into it first, and skip the rest.

But as tempting as it was, the pie held less appeal than watching Jimmy's mouth as he told her about life in Cotton Springs, and the antics of the townsfolk. His nearness intoxicated her. Elise almost pinched herself to make sure she wasn't dreaming. A sunset picnic with a man who made her tummy flutter, and no demands on her attention, no looking over her shoulder. When he smiled, the minute lines around his eyes sprung to life. Her fingertips tingled with the desire to trace them. The butterflies beat a raucous rhythm beneath her sternum. She was here, with him.

A few seconds passed before she realized he had stopped talking, and was staring at her just as intently as she returned his gaze. How could he not hear her pulse thudding in the silence? His glance flicked to her mouth, and she bit her bottom lip. Whoa, boy.

To their right, a flight of doves took wing, beating the air. Elise jumped, a hand flying to her chest.

"Oh!" she exclaimed. Perfect, imperfect timing.

He chuckled and shifted, clearing his throat; the moment blurred. That potential energy, the tug between his skin and hers, buzzed unsatiated. But the kinetic moment passed, waiting to be kindled. Jimmy busied himself fixing a plate. He held it out with a questioning rise of an eyebrow. She nodded, taking the dish, but not trusting herself to say anything.

They nibbled in silence, and her thoughts wandered along country backroads. The sleepy sun slid down the sky's round slope, inexorably reaching for the horizon, yearning for its slumber. She sat cross-legged on the plaid covering, hands clasped in her lap and crumb-laden plate at her side, while she wondered if Matthew had cooled off enough for a rational conversation about the man sitting beside her. Or had the time spent running only angered him more? Elise had hated to leave for her date under such heavy circumstances, but Trudy had reluctantly insisted.

"Jimmy will be waiting for you at the station, and it's not like you can call him," had been her friend's argument. "At least, you shouldn't. You are already taking huge risks with your safety without establishing a traceable connection between the two of you."

The recalled admonishment overshadowed her thoughts, and she jumped when Jimmy's warm hand covered her clenched fists.

"Where are you, Elise?"

His smile was kind, concerned, drawing down his brows. Here he was giving her his complete attention and she sat here, her mind wandering all over the place.

"I'm sorry. It's just," she began, running a hand across her face, "Matthew and I had an argument before I left. He wasn't home when it was time for me to leave. I'm sure Trudy has it under control, though. He was only going for a run to clear his mind."

He patted her knee, gave it a squeeze. "More tea?"

She nodded her assent. Ice cubes clinked against the glass, falling with the chilled amber sweet tea.

"Want to talk about it?"

Elise sighed, accepting the offered drink. "Sometimes motherhood is just downright hard. He is my greatest joy, my pride; and my greatest challenge. The will of a teenage boy is nothing to be trifled with."

"I imagine he's a good kid."

She grinned, despite the heavy heart. "He is, in spite of his unstable life."

Elise told him of the confrontation earlier in the afternoon, of Matthew's reaction to her interest in a man. Jimmy frowned in consternation, his mouth clenching so tightly she could see the outline of jaw muscles. In the end, they both gazed at the distance, not at each other.

"Look, I know Matthew is a complication you weren't bargaining on," she explained, a sad smile sweeping up a corner of her mouth.

He stopped her by grabbing her hands and turning her face to meet his. His calloused thumb grazed the hollow below her cheek. His tousled honey-shaded hair lifted in the breeze, and the dying sun glinted off the silvery brown stubble on his face. Faint laugh lines creased around his eyes.

"No," he said, intense. "I hadn't planned on you having a son. But that's not what bothers me."

"It's not?"

He shook his head, still anchoring her face to his palm. "I'm sad that your son has had to live day to day without knowing if it was the last time with new friends, whether you would flee in the night, or whether he could trust another person outside of you and Trudy. That's not living. It's barely surviving. I feel sad for the man he'll become if this continues."

His scrutiny threatened to overwhelm her. She stood abruptly, the fight-or-flight rush of adrenaline coursing through her veins. Elise argued with herself. He needed to know everything, but could she honestly trust a man in law enforcement, one who was under orders to report her presence to the Federal Prosecutor? Even her son didn't know the whole truth, only a sliver of it.

She wrung her sweaty hands, unable to meet Jimmy's stare. Stay or go? Confess or hide? Ah, it was too much! She rushed beneath the sheltering umbrella of foliage, into the cool shadows where the earth saturated the air, permeated her lungs with the land. With a furtive glance, she made sure Jimmy stayed behind, and he had.

He was a good man, of that Elise was sure. It was his honesty that threatened her though. So much for being brave. She wanted to spit the false courage into the nearby bushes. It was now or never, ultimately. Another cautious glance at the man on his knees with the wool blanket beneath him. Waiting for her. Giving her time.

She stalked to the open air, to the cleared pasture, and fell to her knees in front of him. "Have you told Katherine Miles you've seen me?"

"No," came the simple reply. She read truth in his eyes.

With a silent plea to the air around her and a deep breath, she told Jimmy the story of her past.

Goosebumps rippled across his skin as she dully recounted her life as a slave. He tried to focus on the warm timbre of her voice, rather than on the bitter, deplorable existence she escaped that moonless night at the New Mexico and Texas border. Like water tumbling over rocks beneath the rapids, her voice flowed, shuttered, rushed. It crashed against his soul and drew him in, pulled him under. She destroyed him.

Jimmy wanted to hit something, needed to pound out the injustice done to the sweet woman who held his heart in her fragile hands. No, her tough hands; hands that had clawed up from the forgotten depths of hopelessness, cracked and bleeding and scarred. But fragile nonetheless.

He rocked her as the sun sank below the hemorrhaging horizon. She lay locked in his unflinching arms, snug on his lap, with her head resting in the thudding hollow between his chest and neck. Eventually, she settled, and her breathing joined the chorus of crickets and frogs serenading the dusky evening. He soothed her as though she were a timid filly, with quiet shooshing sounds and soft caresses along her arms. Every once in a while, she swiped away a tear. The widening puddle on his jeans told the tale of the ones she missed.

She sniffled and tried to pull away, but he clamped down, holding her close to his heart. How had a five-year old girl been able to survive, to learn to adapt to captivity? While Elise cried, he replayed her story across the widescreen of his mind.

Her mother had been changing the linens on the bed while Elise played beneath them. There had been a knock at the door. She remembered her mother sighing as she left to answer it. Elise had remained beneath the spread, pretending she was in an exotic cave, barely registering the muffled voices in the front of the house. But as the voices grew louder, accented by crashing and thuds, she had known something was amiss. She had hidden beneath the bed, shivering, understanding the situation was grave while not knowing exactly how.

Then flashes of memory, like strobes. Black, dusty boots, with the leather of the toes worn to dull patches, appearing beside the bed. Hands yanking her across the sandy, wood floor. Screaming. Being thrown over a tall man's shoulders, his bones digging into her abdomen, and then seeing her mother in a pool of blood as her abductor carelessly stepped over her. Elise had fought, then, kicking and bucking. Then a fist connected with her face. Waking in a wagon, bumping along the weed-strewn desert hills of southern California, with the sun sinking blood-red into the ocean. Everything had shimmered in psychedelic waves. Shapes morphed and colors clashed, and she was so nauseated that she vomited all over herself. They beat her for it.

The first weeks were spent fetching items for the mid-level bosses, and being clouted on the head when she didn't move fast enough. Her motions were deliberate, yet slow, because of the drugs coursing through her veins. If she had the presence of mind to refuse, they lashed her with a split leather strap. She had lain on a ragged cot, recovering, for three days in a makeshift hospital tent a month into her captivity, for spitting in a boss' face. Her childhood friend, Ami, had mopped her tears and cleaned her festering lash wounds. It was the first time she knew Ami had been taken as well.

Sixth months later, she was assigned to the burial crew. By then, her captors had lowered the drug dosage. She no longer experienced the hallucinations, but was fully addicted to whatever they injected her with. Elise had been the youngest on the grave detail; most of the others were in their teens, boys and girls alike. All had empty, vacant eyes, and moved mechanically. It was when they brought the bloated, foul-smelling bodies that Elise understood her crew assignment.

On her second day of grave diggers, she buried Ami in a grave with eight other children and one woman. It was the last time she saw her friend.

For ten years, Elise rose with the sun, worked 'til sundown, and never questioned authority again. Drugs no longer subdued her. Fear took care of that. Through torn and bleeding blisters turned callous, broken bones, and painful whipping, she worked. Each time she thought of confrontation, the specter of Ami's face rose from a shallow grave in the foothills of the Colorado Rockies.

Until the time she came into womanhood, or the physiological version of it. Once her monthly courses began, Elise found herself in another, nicer tent. The girls occupying these quarters were cleaner, better-clothed; but if possible, their eyes were more haunted than Elise's own. The girls were fed more rations, having curves where she was skin and bones. She had heard rumors, she explained, but seeing the Candy Girls firsthand – well, Elise learned soon enough what it meant to be Candy.

Though she hadn't gone into detail, Jimmy knew. She was property, chattel, and now had come into the stage of earning her keep. Regularly threatened with fates worse than death, she had chosen to comply. The bosses, men and women, were armed and malicious. The new girls were instructed to be obedient, give pleasure, submit; and above all else, make sure the patrons of the Candy store were satisfied enough to return.

She glossed over the two years as a sex slave in the telling of it, and he did not blame her. He possessed enough knowledge and sense to know what went on, and there was no need to expound. Elise had sunk into his rocking arms. To be held, without the expectation to return a favor. Simple comfort he could give her. In time, he hoped he could help her heal.

The chirping crickets had grown quiet. The frogs acquiesced as well, with only the breeze whispering its ageless secret through the leaves and needles on the trees. The darkened sky, midnight blue and star-dotted, cocooned them in a peaceful nest.

Jimmy thought she had fallen asleep, until she stirred. She withdrew, looking at him with unshed tears. "There's more."

"Elise, honey, you don't have to – "

"But I do," she interrupted. "It's the reason I run, the reason why Katherine Miles wants you to turn me in."

A solid lump of dread settled in his stomach. Her tale was wretched enough to leave scars on his soul forever. What else could possibly overshadow it?

"Five months before I escaped," she began, head down, speaking to her clasped hands, "I was commended for my, well, *performance.*" Elise shuddered, and he tightened his hold on her, resting his chin across the short, silky locks atop her head.

"Pleased with my reports from customers, I had earned a trip to the Big Tent."

The way she emphasized the words led him to the conclusion that the Big Tent housed someone of utmost importance. She confirmed his suspicion.

"They brought me to him. El Lobo. We had heard rumors, of course. From day one, they threatened us with The Wolf. That he would find us in our sleeping sacks and rip out our throats if we were bad."

He tried, unsuccessfully, to block out the images coming to life in his head.

"He's short. That was the first thing I noticed, that I could almost look him in the eye. But those eyes. Hooded and gray, like quicksilver. Even in the lamplight I saw the evil lurking behind them."

Jimmy felt the rage clawing to escape as she told of the encounter with El Lobo, the ringleader of the largest slave trade organization in North America. Tears fell onto his lap once more. She let them fall.

"They brought me to him a few times a week. It was two months later that I realized I had missed my period," she said quietly. "I knew they gave all the Candy Girls a form of birth control, in the water we drank. The lady boss had grinned when she told me I hadn't been given it in three months."

Elise gave voice to the unsaid. "I ran because I was pregnant. Matthew is the child of The Wolf. Katherine Miles knows, as does the whole judicial branch of Texas. They want me in custody, so that I can testify against El Lobo when they catch him."

Jimmy nodded, slowly. "And they plan to catch him –"

"Yes. With me." She took a deep breath. "I'm the bait for the wolf trap."

Chapter 16

The gusty gales of March tormented the citizens of east Texas until at last, their ears frozen and noses running, they applauded the April deluges mucking up the horse paths and pastures. For the first seven days of the new month, it rained. Constantly. From horizon to heavens, gray permeated the skies. When one cloud exhausted its water supply, another seemed to magically take its place. Puddles turned to ponds, and ponds transformed into brackish lakes. Soon the voices moaning about the March winds complained of the unceasing wetness.

Jimmy had become so accustomed to waking up and slogging through interminable mires to feed the horses, that he hardly registered the sun shining through the east-facing windows. Giddy like a child on the first day of summer, he threw his boots on and tackled his outdoor morning chores with gusto. Even the horses shared his enthusiasm. They nickered and tossed their heads, despite mud-caked hooves and fetlocks.

His good mood stayed with him throughout the short drive to Lufkin. The sun slanting through his office windows bolstered him through monotonous morning paperwork and scheduling. The tall cup of

Pete's stout coffee warming his hand helped as well. He pushed aside the white wood blinds, shading his eyes against the glare glinting off puddles on the street below. A little boy, maybe three years old, jumped smack in the middle of one such puddle, and his mom leapt back, shouting. Jimmy grinned, and turned back to his desk. They reminded him of Elise and Matthew, though her boy was closer to man than toddler.

Over the last three weeks, they saw one another five times. With each date, the meeting was sweeter and the parting more difficult. He lost himself in her easy smile, the one which brought out the tiny parentheses around her dark brown eyes. Her scent intoxicated him, left him craving more. They simply ignored the lurking cloud of her past, choosing to instead focus on getting to know one another. But every time they met, she came to him. He had yet to meet Matthew in person.

He sighed. Enough daydreaming. Time to get back to work or he would never leave the office.

The jail schedule beckoned. Forty-five minutes later, after a glance at the clock, he rose and stretched. He had a hankering for a meatball sub from the sandwich shop down the block. Jimmy strode through the door, pulling on his lightweight jacket, when he noticed three of his deputies gathered around a viewscreen.

Pete saw him first, and waved him over. "Check this out, Boss."

The deputy increased the volume.

"... *details about the notorious El Lobo crime syndicate have come to light, particulars known only to law enforcement agencies. My confidential source reports that The Wolf has migrated to the Arkansas District, near the Texas border. Though still unconfirmed, citizens need to ask themselves if either Texas or American law enforcement agencies are doing their best to capture the elusive El Lobo. Stay tuned next week, as I reveal the identity of the person residing in Texas who is the key to unlocking this mysterious organization, in this ongoing investigation into human trafficking, and the man named The Wolf. This is Tandy Newman, East Texas News."*

His cheerful mood vanished. Mind racing with questions, possibilities, doubts, and fear, he paced the room.

"Turn it off!" he barked.

Heat flared, reaching, grasping up from his collar toward his hairline. The nerve of that reckless, immature, naïve reporter.

His deputies considered him through slanted eyes and covert looks as they hurriedly bustled to their desks. Jimmy had been careful. After the first time Elise had appeared at the station, they had both concluded it better to meet in neutral places – a park across town, or the walking trail that snaked around the more bucolic parts of the city. He insisted the danger was too high for her to be seen downtown. The guilt of not obeying Katherine Miles' court order weighed on his conscience, but not enough to either turn her in or stop seeing her altogether.

No, Elise was worth it. He thought at first she was like a beacon on the edge of a rocky sea cliff, bringing him safely ashore. But honestly, he was the moth to her flame. One of them would burn, if not both, before it was all said and done.

As the men in brown and khaki shuffled to and fro, doing their best to give the sheriff a wide berth, Jimmy considered his first and only interview with Tandy Newman, East Texas News. He sorted details, replayed questions asked and answers given, reviewed her tone of voice and mannerisms. Obviously she had tried to use her feminine wiles, for lack of a better description, to extract information. He felt positive he had not revealed any detail unknown to the public. That left the question of who was her source, her inside man?

"Pete!"

Movement around the office halted, but only for a split-second.

"Yeah, Boss?" The officer rose, ambling over to where Jimmy stood by the blind-shaded bank of windows. He hooked his thumbs in his pockets, but kept his wide shoulders pushed back, formal.

"When Miss Newman was here for that interview awhile back, did you take her home after?"

Pete shook his head, chewing on a nail. "Naw, said she was taking the bus."

Jimmy faced his assistant, locked his gaze on him. "Do you know anything about this inside source?"

Pete's eyes widened, then blinked rapidly. "No, sir. Honest. I didn't say nothing more to her than to ask if she needed a ride."

"And you didn't see her speaking to anyone else?"

His officer shrugged, lips pursed. "Nope. Far as I remember, we was the only ones here."

He trusted Pete, felt the ring of truth to his words. Jimmy, too, remembered there was only the two of them in the office that afternoon.

The next question was interrupted by the vibration on his wrist, an incoming comm. He mumbled an excuse to Pete, and stalked to his office, shutting the door behind him.

"Hello?"

Elise's frantic speech filled the silence; half Spanish, half English, and total panic.

"Elise? Honey? I can't understand –"

"Matthew! It's Matthew!" Then another mixed string of words. He pieced together a few, and his heart began to race.

"Where is he?" Jimmy interrupted, fear clutching his throat with an iron hold.

"I don't know! I came home from work, and the school called to say he hadn't returned to classes after lunch."

"Calm down, honey." His soothing attempts failed, as Elise sniffled and cried on the other end. "Do you know where he might have gone, or why he skipped class?"

"No. I mean, I don't know where he is. I told him."

"Told him what?" The fearful chokehold made swallowing difficult.

The line fell silent, except for muffled sniffles. Then she cleared her throat, and spoke the word he knew was coming.

"Everything."

Chapter 17

Emotions ripped through his barriers like floodwaters bursting through levies. Fear, apprehension, and dread clung anchor-like around his shoulders. He replayed the news report about El Lobo, and wondered if the ringleader was closer than Tandy Newman's so-called sources indicated. Had they had a hand in Matthew's disappearance? If so, how did he break the news to Elise?

Wave after wave of speculation washed over him. Jimmy utilized his vehicle's emergency strobes and siren on the highway between the two cities, but it wasn't until he reached the outer loop around Nacogdoches that he silenced them. The last thing he wanted or needed was undue attention inside the city limits. He cruised by more horse riders than drivers, sliding by in a quiet hum as the electric motor purred.

The call came as he turned onto Hospital Street, the Fredonia in sight. He didn't recognize the number.

"Wilson here."

"Jimmy?"

"Elise? I'm nearly there. Just hang on, honey."

"Trudy found him."

Breath he was unaware of holding exploded into the quietude of the cruiser's cab. "Thank God. Where?"

"He's at the University stadium."

He pulled into the semicircular drive in front of the historic hotel. Elise waited under the white-columned awning, wringing her hands. She still wore her housekeeping uniform. Before he could exit and open the door for her, she slid into the passenger seat. He gripped her hand, squeezed.

A hint of a smile ghosted across her face. She whispered, "Thank you for being here."

"Where else would I be?"

The stadium parking lot was eerily vacant, with the exception of Trudy's dark sedan. Behind the silhouetted tree line, the sky glowed the orange and yellow of a great bonfire. Cooling shadows laid across the pavement, and swallowed the sizeable horse paddock set into the trees. The solar lights flickered on as he and Elise walked toward one of the darkened entrance corridors to Homer Bryce Stadium. From the outside, it resembled a giant concrete maw with obsidian teeth.

Jimmy had attended quite a few football games here over the years, had played even more. Still, the unoccupied facility took on a whole new stark personality when not invaded by purple-clothed fans. Rather than cheers rumbling through the stands, the high-pitched screech of a handful of bats near an end zone welcomed him to his alumni home; he couldn't help but shiver at the unnerving transformation.

They emerged in the stands, at the midway point between the upper and lower decks. Her hand gripped firmly in his, she quite nearly dragged him down the concrete molded steps toward the orange rubber track encircling the football field.

Matthew and Trudy huddled where the 50-yard line met the track. They sat cross-legged; him with his tousled head lowered, but gesturing with quick, sharp motions. Trudy listened with an arm draped across his wide, lean back. Elise called out, dashing down the last flight of stairs connecting the stands to the field. Cool air kissed his warmed hand, once joined but now alone. He sighed with regret, even as his heart smiled watching Elise tackle her wayward son.

Suddenly an outsider, he retreated to a cold, aluminum bleacher. If he closed his eyes, pushed aside the reunion below him on the field, he was 21 again. Like spectral mist rising from a pond in the cool hours of the morning, the remembered sounds of a crowd cheering filled his mind. The thump of the drums, the battle call of the horns, and storming the green, hash-marked field with his teammates. He felt, more than remembered, the crowd's roar in his bones crushing the butterflies that were always fluttering before a game.

But when the whistle blew, and the team huddled, the fans vanished, muted, beneath the challenge before him. Nothing else mattered except his teammates, and the leather football. Play after play, bone-jarring tackles, and the ball locked against his gut as he ran, dodged, sometimes leaping across white line after white line. Down by down, advancing and retreating. The roar around them was nothing more than background noise. Time both raced and crawled in that mysterious dual existence. Then, after hours of battle, the whistle blew and time engulfed him once more. Thousands of voices soared, merged, rumbled through his chest amidst the jostle and congratulatory thumps of teammates. Or the heavy weight of devastation, of loss, crowding the space between stomach and throat, heads held low and mental replays of the should-haves and would-have-dones.

A hand alighted on his shoulder, and he raised his head. Elise smiled through happy tears glistening in the corners of her eyes. So involved in the past, he had lost track of the present. Trudy sat with Matthew on the field. Elise took his hand in hers, gave a little tug.

"Will you come meet my boy?"

"Lead the way."

Not the best circumstance in which to introduce himself, but would there ever be the perfect time to do so? After all, he was most likely the source of the angst that drove Matthew to run, to hide. Jimmy shrugged off the gnawing dread and uncertainty. If he dealt with criminals on a daily basis, then surely he could interact with one teenage boy.

A thousand thoughts and none at all raced across his brain. He couldn't shake the feeling that this moment would direct the course of his relationship with Elise.

Matthew glared at him, jutted chin defiant. Trudy kissed him on the cheek and ruffed his hair, to which the boy rolled his eyes. A hint of a grin appeared and faded, to be replaced once more by lips slashed with distrust.

Jimmy thought he'd prefer a criminal at the moment. At least he would have been on familiar terms with the situation.

As it was, he tipped his head to the side and asked, "Wanna take a walk?"

Matthew shrugged, and his mother whispered gentle encouragement. She squeezed his shoulder, nudging him forward. Matthew grunted and rolled his eyes again.

"Whatever," he mumbled.

The boy's shuffled steps *shooshed* in the cool, quiet evening. The crickets had begun their symphony, muted by the urban surroundings, but present nonetheless.

"Feels like rain, doesn't it?"

Matthew cocked his head, and raised his brows in question, but remained silent. He walked with back hunched, hands shoved into the pockets of his running pants.

Jimmy pointed to the wooded area at the skinny end of the giant oval bowl of the stadium. "When we get out of here, check out the leaves. They'll be bottom's up, kind of waiting for the moisture."

His observation was met, once more, with silence. At least there was no hostility. Yet. Jimmy switched strategies.

"She told you? About El Lobo?"

Matthew halted, mid-stride, then resumed their trek. The rubbery track absorbed Jimmy's measured progress.

The teen answered low. "Yeah, she told me."

Silence was their companion for another dozen paces. Then Matthew cleared his throat.

"What are you gonna do about it?"

"Protect you, and your mother. Whatever it takes."

More shuffling, more silent rebuke, another quarter distance around the track.

He felt the shift. Whether it was a surrendering sigh, or the subtle posture change of his young companion, or the gentle guidance of the Holy Spirit, he didn't know. Yet, there it was.

They stopped simultaneously. Hesitantly, Jimmy reached out a tenuous hand.

"Will you help me?"

Matthew's eyes sprang wide. "Me? How could I do that?"

Jimmy locked eyes with the young man. "By never doing this again. Running away. You scared your mother senseless."

Matthew caught his lower lip between his teeth, cast his eyes to the ground. "Yeah, I know. I apologized. I was just so – so angry. And hurt. Why didn't she tell me sooner?"

"To protect you, most likely. Mothers are like that."

The teen grunted, ran a hand through jet black hair in need of a cut. "I can take care of myself."

"No," Jimmy insisted. "Not from that man. He's evil, Matthew, and he'll cut down anyone who stands in his way."

As though the words were ripped from his soul, Matthew agonized, "He's my *father.*"

Unable to help himself, Jimmy wrapped an arm around Elise's son. "No, not really. He helped make you, true. But he is no father. Your mother has shouldered both roles for so long. To show you right from wrong, to teach you to be a man worthy of respect."

They took up their walk again, this time linked by Jimmy's sheltering arm. As they neared their starting point, Matthew nodded.

"Yes. I will help you. But," he said, halting and facing Jimmy.

In that instant, he saw the man Matthew would become. In the set of his shoulders, the depth of his words, the hardened grim lines surrounding innocent eyes.

"Do not hurt my mother."

Chapter 18

The doorknob bolt slid home with a soft click. Elise took two deep, shuddering breaths away from Matthew's bedroom door, closed her eyes, and coerced her knotted jaw to loosen. What an afternoon and evening.

It was quiet in the hotel room turned apartment. Three steps through the tiny hall brought her into the spartanly furnished, dim living room. A single lamp bravely fought the darkness outside the window. Her stomach growled. A quick roast beef sandwich and some carrots, then, since she missed supper. Food, a tall glass of iced tea, and a long, hot soak in the tub were what she needed right about now.

A head rose above the back of the sofa, and a high-pitched squeal escaped before she could clamp a hand across her mouth.

"Oops," he said. At least he had the courtesy of looking sheepish. "I thought you knew I had stayed."

Her heart beat slowed from oh-my-goodness-I'm-gonna-die speed, to just over a rapid staccato. "You scared me to death! You're smiling. Stop that!"

"I'm sorry," he laughed. "But you're adorable. All big brown eyes."

A flush crept into her cheeks as she waved him off.

"Why are you camped out on my couch?"

"I wanted to talk to you about something, and you were talking to Matthew. I didn't want to interrupt. Trudy offered to stay, too, but I told her I would stand watch."

In the kitchen, she grabbed a glass tumbler from the cabinet. The refrigerator glow lightened the room briefly as she poured from the tea pitcher. Elise knelt to retrieve the leftover roast. She called over her shoulder, "Want something to eat?"

"No," came the response directly behind her.

She jumped. Again. And knocked her head on the freezer handle above her, nearly dropping the roast on the floor. She growled under her breath, and rubbed her head with her free hand.

"Here," he offered with an outstretched hand. "Let me help before I end up killing you."

"You need to stop sneaking up on me." She had to fight off the giggles, though.

"Carrots?"

"Whatever you're having."

They worked in silence, prepping the sandwiches and peeling carrots. He peeled, and she sliced, working seamlessly together. His sly glances pitter-pattered in her chest, and more than once she narrowly missed her finger with the blade's sharp edge. The ding of the convection oven announced the beef was warmed, and she slathered mayonnaise on the sliced bread. Satisfied, she plated both meals, and invited him to the bar of the island with a jerky nod.

She liked that about him, that words weren't necessary. Some people felt the need to constantly shatter the fleeting silence found in the pockets of an otherwise busy existence. Jimmy seemed at peace with stillness.

They sat on the wooden stools, and Elise was acutely aware of the nearness of him. Their knees touched, worn denim brushing lightweight linen. Little jolts of electricity arced at his touch. Did he feel them? A covert glance revealed a slight grin on his face, right before he shoveled the last bite of sandwich into his mouth.

She dipped a carrot into some ranch dressing. "Want some dessert?"

"Mmph," he nodded.

"Look in the breadbox," she said with a pointed finger. "There are some strawberry tarts in there."

He swiped a napkin across his mouth, and stood. She tracked him as she crunched on a carrot, careful to guard her face. The space next to her felt empty, expectant. Elise lowered her eyes to focus on the single carrot remaining as he returned to his barstool. His leg brushed against hers, and the butterflies fluttered and fell, tightening her chest and tingling her fingers. She turned to watch his reaction to the pastry, curious.

His brows climbed high. Around a mouthful he mumbled, "Wow." Then he swallowed, wiped his lips with the crushed napkin. "That's delicious. Did you get those from Dinah's"

It was her turn to grin. "Nope. Made them myself."

Without a word, he hurried around the island to the wooden breadbox again, then returned with half a dozen more.

She barked a laugh, then remembered her son in the other room. Shoulders shaking, she asked in a hushed voice, "So they're okay, then?"

"Moh van okay." His Adam's apple bobbed around the bite, and he added, "They're amazing."

Her cheeks flushed again. "Gracias. Manny, the pastry chef, lets me help him on the days I finish my rooms early. I love baking."

He appraised her with narrowed eyes, and popped another tart. "Now that's a gift, girl."

She gathered their plates, unaccustomed to such admiration, and carried them to the sink.

"Thank you, Jimmy." Elise cleared her throat, suddenly nervous. "Uh, what was it you wanted to talk about?"

"Oh, well," he stuttered, crumpling the napkin in his hand. "I, uh, have some unsettling news. The, uh, Syndicate has been located up near the Arkansas District and Texas border."

Hundreds of miles, far enough away. Her eyes must have revealed her thoughts, though.

"Not far enough for my comfort, I'll tell you that much right now," he added. "So, I – well, I've been thinking."

The clock on the wall ticked into the silence. "Yes?"

He stood, abrupt, and ran both hands through his hair. His eyes settled on her and he smiled, a hesitant pull of the mouth that spoke of shyness and reticence.

"I want you to move to Cotton Springs." The words strung themselves together in a rush. He held up a hand. "Before you protest –"

And she was about to, at that.

" – I know I can find a job for you there. I know everyone in town. And I, I can keep an eye on you better there."

She stared, letting it wash over her. Move, again? They haven't even lived in Nacogdoches for nine months yet. Then again, she had spent less time in a few other map dots.

Elise must have shown a few cracks in her resolve, because he spoke up again. "There's a reporter. Tandy Newman. Ah, I see you've heard the name."

She nodded, clicking her teeth shut again.

"I don't know for sure, but I think she has a mole in my department. She says ..." He paused, licked his lips. "She says she is going to reveal the name of the person who is the key to the El Lobo case, that she knows who it is."

Impossible! They had been so careful. Until the day she went to Jimmy's office in Lufkin that one day. Had she been seen? But how would anyone know her from any other normal citizen? It wasn't as if she wore a flashing sign across her back: Key Witness in Slave Ring Case.

Jimmy was nodding. "I don't know how she knows, but I suspect she knows who you are, and where you live. It's not safe here anymore, Elise."

She paced to the window, stared at the glow of the streetlamp alight at the end of the block. Elise caught his reflection nearing her in the glass, and stiffened. His arms slid around her in a gentle embrace, and he laid a chin on her shoulder. Exhausted, mentally and physically, she relaxed, melted into his arms.

"I said I would never run again," she whispered to him, to the night, to whatever force was shaping her life. "I promised."

"I will protect you. No matter what."

She leaned her head back, exposing her neck to his breath at her shoulder. Attraction trickled over her body in waves.

"You'll lose your job, Jimmy. You're not even supposed to be with me without reporting it."

His breath was hot on her neck. "I don't care."

She spun, shoved away the magnetic pull she felt toward him. "I won't ask you to do that."

"You're not. I know the stakes. And you, honey," he whispered, gathering her in his arms once more, "are worth the price."

"I'm not running away from him again. I'm done!"

She laid her dark head on his chest, listened to the reassuring, steady thump of his heart. He reached a finger under her chin, tipped it up toward his unshakeable gaze.

"This time is different."

"How?" Her voice shook on the single word.

"Because this time, you're running toward someone."

He lowered his head, and their lips touched. Sparks, sharp and bright, flowed through her body, racing from the center of her soul to the very tips of her extremities. His kiss was gentle, yet it claimed her. Her toes curled in her socks, and her breath came in short gasps. Elise slid her hands to cup his face, pull it toward her.

It was a long time before she came up for air.

Chapter 19

"You can't seriously be considering it!" Trudy's wide eyes shined through a mask of confusion and indignation.

Elise glanced at Matthew. Up early on a Saturday, he was engrossed in his virtual world in the living room. His arms and hands thrust, flung, and chopped at invisible enemies, and he ducked and weaved like a boxer in the ring. One of his martial arts games, then. Not a favored chosen pastime for her son, but at least he could work off angst and frustration in his own world, in his own time. She sympathized with him, though. It seemed that her whole life had been a massive contest with one enemy or another, seen and unseen.

Over an early morning of blueberry muffins and orange juice, she had spoken at length with her son about Jimmy's offer. At best he was resigned, although he hadn't seemed as distrustful of him as he had been before the incident at the stadium. Maybe meeting him in person helped shed some light on the unknown. Who knew? Surprisingly, Matthew had simply shrugged his shoulders, saying it would not be the first time they moved.

For at least the millionth time since her son was born, Elise chewed on the decisions and choices she had made during the last thirteen years. The constant upheaval, fleeing one compromised town for the secluded safety of another. New names, new identities. Constantly doubting, wondering, questioning if running was the answer, or should she stand and fight. In the end, though, caution won every time. She would protect her son from *him*. The enemy. The Wolf would never claim her son. Elise had held her newly delivered child and pledged her body to protect his, no matter what.

Now? The deep, hidden secret place that was *her* knew the time for vanishing was over. She couldn't pinpoint it, could not place a short, manicured nail tip on the certainty, and yet it existed.

"Yes," she answered, meeting the full force of her best friend's glare. "I am. I told you, Tru. I'm done running." Elise sliced a hand through the air.

"This is not like you, Elise. I – I don't even know what to say."

She laid a hand on Trudy's forearm. "You don't need to say anything. Listen. My instincts are finely honed. They led me to you. Now they are leading me to Jimmy."

"So you'd rather climb into bed with the law, than let me protect you? You'll just abandon me?" Tru's eyebrows climbed aboard her hairline.

Gasping, Elise hunched reflexively, shooting a look toward the living room, but Matthew only had eyes and ears for the game. With a glare, she faced her friend. "I am most certainly *not* climbing into bed with anyone, thank you very much."

Trudy waved a hand in dismissal, her short curls bobbing ferociously. "Literally, figuratively, whatever."

"I want you to come, too. We can find a cute little cottage or something. Cotton Springs sounds – I don't know – like home."

"Your hormones are talking, not your brain."

Elise inhaled, an attempt to calm her chattering nerves. On the exhale, she pushed the frustrations away, down through her trunk and out through the tips of fingers and toes. She loved Trudy, but she could slide head first into overbearing at times.

Her friend had turned, watching Matthew maneuver in the living room, and it occurred to Elise how much Tru loved her son. He was almost as much a part of her, as he was of her own flesh and blood. She fed him bottles of pumped breastmilk as an infant, to allow Elise a few hours more of precious sleep. She changed diapers, and wiped snot. Saw him through the crying, drooling nightmare of teething. Trudy waded into numerous colds, illnesses, and a broken arm like a general overseeing her troops. She held Matthew's hand as he crossed busy streets, and lent her shoulder when he cried each time they moved.

Matthew may not be the child of her body, but he was the child of Trudy's heart. How could she not be worried or concerned?

She embraced Trudy from behind, her face lying against the flat bone of her warm shoulder blade. Elise squeezed, and felt Trudy's hand cover hers, a gentle pat of reassurance.

"You're sure?" she whispered.

Elise grinned against the soft cotton of Tru's shirt, shook her head fractionally. "One hundred percent? No. Who could be? But I am sure that I want to try. Will you come with me?"

The silence stretched, interrupted only by the grunts and growls emitted by the teenage boy across the room.

Finally, Trudy said, "When?"

Elise released her hold, and wiped a hand across her face. "He wants us to come out today and look at a cabin. You up for that?"

"I guess we'll find out."

***

The rough-hewn log cabin sprouted from the fertile, weedy earth surrounding it. Worn cedar siding, gone grayish-white with age, shielded the walls. A metal roofed kissed by patches of rust sheltered the structure. Empty planter boxes adorned the space below the grimy windows. Shadows cast by the overhanging trees danced and swayed, covering more than half of the home in cool shade. The cabin itself rested in the rear, forested corner of Jimmy's property. Several yards to the left of it, a fence in need of some careful care enclosed what appeared to be a fallow garden; behind it crouched a small, worn shed, its door hanging from the top hinge.

Beside her, Trudy snorted. Jimmy glanced her way with a twist of the mouth.

"Don't let it fool you. She's solid, and in good shape. Just needs some cleaning up. A little elbow grease, and she'll be move-in ready. Might need a couple of mouse traps." He rocked back on his heels, nodding to the old place. "This was my great-grandparents' home. Been in the family since before The Secession. I've done some work on it. The plumbing is mostly new, and the well and septic are in good shape."

Curious, open to possibilities, Elise slowly paced the perimeter of the house. "You said it's three bedrooms?" She couldn't keep the disbelief off her face.

"Well, yes," he hedged. "Three *small* bedrooms, but hey. It's privacy, right?"

She nodded, slipping into the moist, cool shadows of the end nestled beneath the tall oaks and yellow pines. Songbirds trilled in the understory, ignoring the chirping of a somewhat annoyed squirrel. A scarred brick chimney climbed the weathered walls, reaching for the sky. Serenity lived here, a sense of calm confidence. The home seemed to say, *I have withstood the storm, and am here to stay.* Elise caught her lower lip in her teeth. She imagined a bench, just there, in the center of a dogwood stand. Hundreds of shed white blossoms littered the fecund ground below the trees, while they selfishly clung to half of the remaining blossoms, seemingly determined to hoard their beauty for as long as possible.

"Mom!" Matthew shouted from somewhere further into the trees. "Check this out."

She grinned at the unabashed enthusiasm in his voice. "Be right there!"

Overwintered leaves and pine straw crunched and shifted under her tennis-shoed feet. With each step, she brushed aside branch or briar. A bird flushed from its cover, startling her; but she had to laugh as a nearby squirrel reprimanded her. Ahead, through a break in the trees and scrub, she caught a glimpse of Matthew's red hooded sweatshirt. While it was warm in the sun, the forest cooled the air by at least ten degrees, and she was grateful for her lightweight cardigan. Her "granny sweater," as Trudy called it.

Matthew waved, and jogged over to her. A path materialized, and she joined him on it.

The treehouse at the end of the trail was impressive. It sat amidst the thick, twisted trunks of an ancient oak tree, fifteen feet above the ground. A raggedy rope ladder hung from the open trapdoor in the floor of the treehouse.

"Please tell me you didn't go up there? It's ancient!"

He nodded, a smile stretching from ear to ear. "I did! It's fine, Mom. Solid as a rock. See?"

Even as she protested, he shimmied up the ladder, his weight creating squeaks at the joints where the rope was tied to form rungs. Her son was fearless, and would likely give her a heart attack one day.

His head popped out of the open window like a jack-in-the-box. "Isn't it the best?"

Happiness was contagious, and she smiled with him. "You're not going to fall through the floor, are you?"

"Mo-om!"

She laughed and twirled, enchanted by the woods, the dappled light, and the dancing shadows. Clouds winked through the leaves above, and birds swooped and dove close enough for her to reach out and grab one.

Elise turned at the sound of muffled leaf crunching behind her. Jimmy materialized from the other side of a wide yellow pine with a brief wave.

"Thought I might find you out here."

"Boys have a magnet for this sort of thing." She gestured to the tree house. "Yours?"

"My dad's first, then mine," he corrected. "Don't worry, mama. It's safe."

"Mamas always worry."

"Hmph. Well, what do you think?"

"So far, I love it. It's like a slice of paradise. But," she said with a wry twist of the mouth, "I need to see the inside of the house."

Jimmy angled his head toward the sunny edge of the trees. "Trudy's been through while you were playing. Let's take the grand tour, shall we?"

Matthew reassured her that he could find his way to the cabin. Hand in hand, Jimmy and Elise strolled down the leafy path. Her hand tingled in his.

"I played out here all the time as a kid. This was a deer path at one time. Not sure I could count the hours I spent out in the woods." He inhaled, a content sound. "It's peaceful, like the world faded away and all there was to the world was the forest and its inhabitants."

She hummed agreement. It was true. Elise felt a symbiosis here, as though she were a prodigal coming home after a long journey. If there was a God, she admitted ruefully to herself, surely He existed here.

As though he heard her thoughts, Jimmy said, "God's creation amazes me with its sophistication and simplicity. I feel it the most out here, or in the pasture with the horses. Know what I mean?"

"I like the idea that God is real, but I admit, I haven't thought about it too much. When I was running for my life, the first time near El Paso, an old woman helped me. Everyone called her Mother. I'll never forget her last words to me. '*May God keep you and bless you, child.*' It was the first time I ever heard anything like that, but it stuck with me. I don't know why. I found a Bible in the apartment. I have read some of it, but it gets confusing at times. I still wonder if He exists, though."

He squeezed her hand, a gentle pressure. "God is most definitely real, and He has kept diligent watch over you."

"You think so?" It was a grim chuckle that escaped her lips. "Sometimes, I don't know."

"You're here. You eluded a man no other person has, and have survived for nearly fourteen years! On top of that, you have a fiercely loyal best friend who has waded through thick and thin with you. I'd say that's plenty evidence that He exists, honey."

His words lodged themselves in her heart, and burned like hot coals. Truth had an undeniable resonance to it.

They remained quietly joined at the hands until they reached the diminutive cabin. With an outstretched arm, he ushered inside.

Primitive. Primitive, yet tranquil. An L-shaped kitchen with an open eating area greeted them to the left, with a moderately-sized living room spreading outward from it, the space wide and open. A bank of windows opposite the kitchen brought the forest inside. She could imagine warm spring days, the windows sashes up, and birdsong in the air. A stubby hallway held doorways leading into the three tiny bedrooms, each barely large enough to hold a full-sized bed. But she gasped in pleasure when she opened the door to the bathroom.

"A clawfoot tub!" she exclaimed. She walked forward, ran a finger along the chilly white porcelain. "I have always wanted to bathe in one."

"I used to call it Granny's swimming pool, when I was a kid," Jimmy admitted with a smile.

Small, yes, but the charming home at the edge of the woods beckoned her, as though it were a living, breathing entity. She could see early morning cups of coffee outside, gazing over the pasture and the horses. Picnics under the leafy canopy, Matthew having friends over and hanging out in the treehouse. A garden, all her own, with bursts of greens, reds, and yellows.

"You can decorate however you want," Jimmy pointed out, breaking into her reverie. "If you want it, that is."

Did she? Yes, very much so.

"I need to talk it over with Tru and Matthew, but ..."

He leaned against the doorway, silhouetted by the afternoon sun, his thumbs hooked into the pockets of his jeans. The sly smile was barely visible in the shadows. Oh, he knew she was hooked. She could see that in his teasing eyes.

"Yes. Oh, Jimmy. I really want to live here."

He bolted forward, and swept her up in a spinning hug. When he lowered her to the wood-planked floor, Jimmy kissed the end of her nose, and pressed her ear to his chest. His heart thumped wildly beneath the cotton shirt.

"Good, because I wasn't going to take no for an answer."

She smiled against his shirt, and relaxed.

She was home.

Chapter 20

Packing had never been the issue.

The mechanical act of boxing their scant personal belongings in used cartons, taping the hungry flaps, and loading them was second-nature. The cardboard containers, a meager sum of their material lives, were stacked in the tiny living room of the hotel apartment, awaiting transport to their next home. A handful of bags leaned haphazardly against one another, as though for emotional support. They sagged and bulged, full of hygiene items and the odd memento collected along the winding path of their transient lives.

Elise swiveled a melancholic glance around the apartment. In removing a few collectibles, the apartment assumed the generic appearance it had possessed in the beginning. The trio of framed photos no longer adorned the mantle, and the tiny shell collection from their migration along the Gulf towns was wrapped snug in an old cotton t-shirt, tucked into the navy blue rucksack by the door. A crocheted afghan, Trudy's Christmas gift from three years ago, huddled folded and hidden, awaiting the unpacking in its new cabin abode.

No, the packing was not the problem. Not really. Wistful, she turned in a slow circle, and her gaze returned to the young man curled up in a lanky comma on the worn sofa, his attention on the book in his hands. Another western novel, she thought with a smile. Her reticence revolved around Matthew. Finally, at a time when he had begun to emerge from his introverted shell and join the cross-country running team, they were moving. Again. Anger, frustration, sadness. She bundled them up in a spiky emotional ball and shoved it to the recesses of her mind, choosing instead to focus on the positives to be found in moving to Cotton Springs.

The last move, if she had anything to say about it.

Jimmy's revelation about the local reporter's so-called breaking news set her on edge. Yet the part of her soul labeled *Instinct* told her the move was right, necessary. Elise had been sincere when she told both Jimmy and Trudy of her intentions to stop running from The Wolf. Whatever the journalist – curse her vulture eyes – had in the way of information about her, it would no longer determine her course of action. The cabin nestled in the far tree line of Jimmy's property, the home of his great-grandparents, would be her shelter. A home, at long last.

Jimmy called last night, contacting her through Trudy's secure line, to tell her that the town's doctor, Cora, had need of an assistant in her expanding medical practice, in light of the retirement of the other physician in town. Not to mention that Doc Tucker was reportedly near delivery of her second child, as well. Home and employment, falling into place.

An image of the leather-bound Bible, shrouded in the confines of the nightstand drawer, flickered in her mind's eye. Should she? It felt like stealing. As she walked past Matthew, she ruffled his hair and smiled at his grunt.

The drawer slid open with a slight friction squeak of wood on wood, swollen with the ever-present humidity. The simple book beckoned her, and she lifted it. A bookmark held the place where she left off days ago. Drawn, she opened the front cover, and her eyes landed on a sentence at the bottom of the title page.

This Bible belongs to you, courtesy of The Gideons. May God bless your steps as you journey through His Word.

Solved that problem. Elise tucked the Bible between her elbow and side, and returned to the living room to kneel beside her son.

"Trudy should be here any minute to pick us up, kid. You ready?"

With his eyes glued to the page, he answered with a sigh. "Yeah, I guess." He dog-eared the page and rose, stretching long, slender arms toward the ceiling. Nodding at the book under her arm, he asked, "What's that?"

Suddenly shy, she waved a hand. "It's a Bible, actually. I started reading it a few days ago." She showed him the Gideon's inscription, and he responded in true male fashion.

"Hmph."

Elise grabbed her son, and pulled him in to a squishy hug. He had been two when he first called it that, a squishy hug. Then, she had to kneel to be at his level. She let go and realized she could look him in the eye.

"Well, kid. Let's go home."

With greater wisdom than his years, her thirteen-year-old son shrugged his shoulders and whispered, "As if we've ever had one."

He threw a knapsack over his left shoulder and hefted two boxes. She held the door open for him with her foot, juggling her purse, the two other canvas bags, and a heavy box in her arms.

Trudy waited beneath the white-columned awning, the trunk lid ajar. She and Matthew loaded their boxes and bags in jigsaw puzzle fashion. Two more trips using the hotel's luggage dolly, and all their belongings were snug in the confines of the trunk and back seat with only enough space for a man-child.

"I'm going to make one last sweep," she told Trudy, who nodded and slid behind the wheel. Matthew sat in the back seat, intent once more on the western novel.

With each room explored and cleared, she stood at the door. She laid the key on the coffee table. It already felt vacant to her, a shell.

To the empty apartment, she whispered, "Next stop: home."

***

Tandy squashed her eyes shut, squeezed like she was a kid again playing hide and seek with her cousins. A rectangle glowed behind her lids, black with neon yellow around the edges, an afterimage of the viewscreen in front of her. Slowly, she opened one eye into a slit. Yes, it was still there, the communication in her inbox. Baffled, but relieved she was not imagining it, she focused on the text of the missive from an anonymous sender.

"If you want El Lobo, follow these steps exactly. Send a comm to the address below. The message must be three lines only, and you must use

these three words: burro, candy, and canyon. This code is only good until midnight tonight. They will contact you."

Her rudimentary tracing skills were insufficient in identifying the sender. Whoever it was, she was positive the hidden source had ulterior motives, and Tandy would use it to her advantage as well.

Her heartbeat fluttered beneath the fair skin of her neck, thumping wildly. She swiped sweaty palms across the thighs of her gray linen suit pants, and cast a nervous glance around the office. Only a few station employees floated around, and all of the other reporters were out on assignment; but they were due back any minute, she thought, noting the time on the wall of clocks at the far end of the room.

She stood abruptly, dashing her wheeled chair into the one behind her with a clatter. Her fingers tapped and flicked, locking the screen. Tandy needed air, to pace. To jump up and down in glee! This was it. Finally! Her break, the story of a lifetime. Her edgy piece on the mysterious woman occupying Sheriff Wilson's time would carry more weight if she had the inside track.

She clacked down the tiled hallway in three inch heels. Dozens of framed photographs flanked the cream-colored walls, portraits of employees and stories over the years, but she paid them no mind. She pushed through the double glass doors, and into the courtyard. Overhead, clouds amassed, a study of the color gray, thick and menacing. Leaves shimmied in the fickle wind, their bright greens waving like thousands of frantic flags. While she circled the paved courtyard, her mind raced ahead.

Tandy Newman would be a household name, her face framed in the hallway, blasted across screens in every home. If she could get close enough to El Lobo, maybe bring his organization to heel, she would get credit for bringing down a monster. Book and movie rights, and oh the awards. A place on one of the national network teams. Her insides danced and leapt like the shivering oak leaves surrounding her. She could do this.

Get inside, infiltrate the organization, and then lure the mastermind into a trap. The prospect had its dangers, but the end would justify the means. For now, she would hold off on releasing the photos of Mystery Woman, until she gathered more intelligence.

From inside The Wolf's lair.

Chapter 21

An east Texas spring glowed. Pollen coated every available surface in neon yellow, and runny noses and sneezes frolicked alongside the various breeds of flirtatious songbirds and chirruping squirrels. The woods outside Doc Cora's little clinic bustled with a cacophony echoed by the constant influx and departures of allergy-smitten patients.

Yesterday, Elise busied herself in washing linens, sterilizing equipment, wiping toddlers' noses, and serving water to the men, women, and children seeking care. Mondays were hectic, Doc Cora had said with a shrug, and leaned over her burgeoning belly to wash her hands and arms once more. Elise barely had time to breathe, much less manage to eat a meal. Conversation with her new employer was limited to professional acknowledgements, grunts, nods, and the odd non-medical sentence or two.

Today was slower, and Elise returned to the waiting room – also known as the dining room – to find it blissfully vacant. She eyeballed the askew ladder-back chair longingly, sighing with the sense of duty that prevented her from collapsing into its stiff wooden embrace.

Doc Cora had no such compunction. She poked her frazzled curly red head around the hallway corner, and with an outrush of breath akin to that of a blacksmith's bellows, waddled around to the plush sofa in front of the tiny fireplace and surrendered herself to its depths.

"Sit," Cora advised. "Now." She pointed to the comfy-looking armchair forming the short side of the L-shape positioning of the furniture.

Not needing further convincing, Elise plunked her feet perpendicular to Cora's clog-shod ones.

Her head lolled into the softness behind her shoulders and she murmured to the ceiling, "How do you do this every day?"

A content chuckle answered. "It's what I love. But I have to admit, I am happy for the lull in action. My toes feel like fat sausages shoved into my shoes."

Elise's stomach grumbled in protest, the result of focusing on the sausage comment. She covered her abdomen with a giggle as it gurgled once more.

"Borborygmus."

Elise flopped her head to face Cora. "Hmm?"

The doc pointed to the general vicinity of Elise's hungry organ. "That's the technical word for a rumble in your tummy. Borborygmus."

"Huh. Interesting." Assessing the time, and the lack of clientele, Elise grunted and rose, intent on feeding herself and Cora. "I can make lunch, if you like."

Cora muttered, an unintelligible reply, and nodded assent. Elise grinned, stretching her sore shoulder muscles as she crossed the short distance to the galley kitchen.

Not only had she started a new job with the doc, but she also had spent the last few days scrubbing her new cabin from top to bottom. She peeked out the window framed above the sink, and was reassured by the clear, azure sky. She had linens and coverlets drying on the line at home. Hopefully Matthew would remember to bring them in and fold them, along with doing his other chores and homework. With Trudy commuting to Nacogdoches and back every day, her best friend had little time to spare for the mundane cleaning and updating the older house required. Elise snorted. As if she had the time, either. It wasn't the first time she felt resentment creep up and bite her. She slapped the emotion down, admitting that Trudy had been through the trenches with her, and had provided monetarily more times than she could count.

Elise hummed as she pulled the wrapped sourdough loaf from the rucksack she brought along. After a patient vomited on her yesterday, she saw the need to bring along a change of clothes, in addition to her lunch. She opened and closed a couple of drawers before finding a bread knife, and sliced the bread in thick slabs. A search of Doc's refrigerator yielded a head of romaine lettuce, and thin-sliced deli meat. She gave it a sniff. Chicken, then. She eyed the tomato, then decided against it. Elise despised the red, plump fruit, and had no idea if the good doctor shared her animosity.

Soon the smell of bread frying in butter permeated the air, and her stomach made itself known once more, this time with more gusto. Once the panini-style sandwiches were toasted, she plated them, and added an apple tart on the side, also from her packed stash. It took quite a bit of self-control not to gobble it up before serving her employer, but she made it to the living room. Barely.

Elise extended the loaded plate toward Cora, who opened one blue eye in curiosity.

"Food. Yes." Cora balanced the white ceramic plate on her baby bump, securing it with one hand and grabbing the sandwich with the other. Elise dug in as well, moaning around the first bite. The sounds of concentrated mastication harmonized with the ticking of the clock and the song of the chickadee outside the opened windows. The dish on Cora's belly shifted, like a boat rocking with a wake.

Her own stomach tightened with wistful muscle memory. No turn of phrase, no physical description could adequately describe the feeling of nascent life stretching its limbs, reaching and pushing to make itself known, to stake its claim and say, "I am here."

"I love watching him move," Cora said, echoing her thoughts. Elise realized she had been staring, the sandwich hovering inches below her mouth. A rush of red flushed her face, and Cora waved a hand in dismissal.

Elise cleared her throat, still embarrassed. "I remember the feeling. I miss it. Some days."

Cora chuckled around a bite, hastily dabbing at the corner of her lips. She swallowed, and said, "I'm surrounding by moving children."

"How old is your little girl?"

"Nearly three. Kitty's our May Day baby. Yours? His name is Matthew, right?"

Elise nodded. "Thirteen going on thirty, most days."

The doc dropped her feet to the floor, and rocked side to side to get to a sitting position. Elise raised a questioning eyebrow.

"One month left," Cora answered. "Demands of the bladder." She shoved the last bit of meat and bread into her mouth, and stood, not without some groaning.

The physician waddled off to the kitchen, and then Elise heard the bathroom door shut with a soft click. She took in the homely feel of the room around her. Her eyes alighted on a nondescript brown leather book on the end table. Worn gold-gilded words proclaimed the title: Holy Bible. Before she knew what was happening, the hefty tome was laid open, the binding cool in her palms. Onion-thin paper crackled as she quietly thumbed through the pages. It contained the same stories as the one in the hotel. When Cora spoke behind her, she jumped, juggling the book.

Guilt spread across her face. "I'm sorry," she mumbled, "I saw one of these before, in my last apartment. I was just curious."

Cora, revived by the brief rest and lunch, marched across the room and laid a kind hand on her shoulder. "Never feel guilt for being curious about God. Ever."

"Your kids are lucky, you know," Elise surprised herself by saying. "To be raised in a loving home. I've only read a few pages, but it seems to mostly be about love." She ran a slow, careful finger over the words, as if absorbing them somehow.

"That is the best part about God. He offered a way for us all to belong to something larger than ourselves. To have a family."

Family. Love. Two things she lacked in her youth, but she made sure to give her son. But if *she* could have it too?

The emotion must have been written plain as day across her face, because Cora gripped her in a fierce hug. She held her as the clock above the mantle ticked, until a familiar jab nudged her in the side. Elise laughed, pulling away.

"Looks like Eggbert agrees," Elise said in a quiet voice, wiping a fugitive tear.

Cora's mouth pulled to the side, joined with a tiny laugh line around her eye. "All I need is another opinionated child."

The screen door screaked the arrival of another patient, and the comradery shared between them slunk away in the name of duty. Minutes crept and hurried in fits and starts, until once more Elise lost herself in the care of strangers. But when time allowed, she read a verse or two of the strangely familiar prose-poetry found in the Bible's pages. Could words on a page offer something she never had before?

She bandaged appendages, folded linens, refilled Cora's homebrewed herb concoctions, and dreamed of sanctuary.

Chapter 22

For the tenth time in as many minutes Jimmy brushed moist palms over the thighs of his crisp, starched jeans, and checked the armpits of his pale blue button-down cotton shirt for sweat stains. He shouldn't be nervous. Heck, he moved the woman here. So what was with the jittery sweat fountain impression?

The late afternoon air held promise of a warmer day tomorrow. Worn leather straps that smelled of linseed oil and old horse lay limp in his calloused hands. Thankfully, the recent rain helped tamp down the red clay dust that normally would have accompanied the horse and buggy on the winding road meandering through his property. Out of principle he flicked the reins. Clarence, the gelding on the right, tossed an annoyed look over his long, chestnut shoulder, and then bobbed his head and snorted; nonetheless, he increased the pace. Dolly, the dun mare quarterhorse hitched to the left, playfully lifted her lips and bared her teeth at Clarence. Those two acted like teenage siblings.

"All right you two, knock it off. Git up!"

He had just under a hundred acres, left to him by his paternal grandparents. Or, rather, the old place was left to his dad, who quickly signed it over to Jimmy. His father and mother, David and Evelyn, preferred a somewhat nomadic way of life. After his mother retired from thirty years in nursing, their passion became exploration; and they put thousands of miles a year on their modest recreational vehicle. Where were they now? South Texas? The Gulf? No matter. Safety and precaution prevented Jimmy from even mentioning Elise's name to them, much less introducing her. Being an only child also simplified things. He uttered a rapid-fire prayer that his parents would give him a few days' notice before maneuvering their shiny retrofitted Airstream down his driveway. Might be awkward explaining the new family settled into the cabin. Thankfully, when his folks were in Cotton Springs, they parked and leveled the spaceship-looking motorhome behind his home.

Jimmy's place, a traditional two-story farmhouse with white wood siding and charcoal gray trim, rose from the hilly ground on the opposite side of the acreage from where the little cabin squatted near the far trees. In between, a verdant grassy sea rolled, dotted with scattered stands of oak, willow, and pine, and dipped around a handful of brackish ponds. A brilliant blue, the color of swooping jays, exploded upward from the horizon line, fading to cornflower overhead. Fluffy white clouds, lined with silver, hovered contentedly. It was a beautiful day for a carriage ride.

Jimmy had kept tonight's festivities a surprise from Elise and Matthew, and he hoped Trudy had maintained his confidence. It was her duty to come up with a reason for Elise to forego cooking this evening, as he had put together a little welcoming barbecue in The Square. While the main point of the get-together was to introduce her to a handful of local families, businessmen and women, the other was less tasteful.

He was hunting moles.

The carriage crested a little hill, and the old cabin came into view. He'd spent magical summers there with his grandparents. He remembered ripping and roaring over the hills, skinny dipping in the nearest pond, and adventuring into the woods with the tree house as home base; then reluctantly returning to the cabin for food, sustenance, and to have the mud and grime sprayed off him with the old garden hose before Grammy would let him in the house.

Would Matthew find the same freeing spirit among the towering pines, the ancient oaks? He hoped so, more than anything. Elise's son was nearing the age when he needed time alone, to process all the changes happening to him in body and soul, or simply to vent and take his frustrations out on the unyielding bark.

Jimmy rubbed a knuckle, feeling the ghost ache of a sore hand, and his mouth turned up in a wry grin. He'd punched a few trees as a teen himself. The tree always won.

"Whoa!" He pulled back on the reins, and the horses came to a halt.

Out of habit, he looped the reins around the weathered hitching post. Though not the original one, this forlorn post had seen at least as many years as he had. He had braced himself against it for more than one whoopin' at the hands of his Papa.

It was strange to knock on a door once always open for him. He reminded himself of the good purpose this longstanding house had at the moment.

A muffled, "Coming!" answered his knock, and then three seconds later, Elise's raven-haired head peeked around the corner of the partially open door.

"Jimmy!" she yelled, a broad smile on her face. "Come to check up on us, already?"

He reached out and cupped her chin. "You're always on my mind, honey. Now," he said with a shooing motion, "go get yourself ready. We're going out on the town."

Elise pushed wide the door, while looking down at herself. Her t-shirt, faded red with a tiny pocket near her heart, was stained; her jeans dusty and torn. A red bandana was tied around her short, elfish hair with a knot on top. He wiped away a dirty smudge on her cheek.

Gosh, she was beautiful.

"I can't go out like this!"

He kissed her on the end of the nose, suddenly forward. "I'll wait. But you're gorgeous just the way you are."

"We were just going to have a sandwich night. Tru's idea, since we've been working so hard around here," she said, waving an open hand around her head. "Plus, she's working late and can't be here to watch Matthew."

From down the hall, a muffled voice exclaimed, "I'm too old for babysitters, Mom!"

Trying not to laugh, Jimmy shrugged. "Bring Matthew. I'd love to have him along."

Was that a snort from the boy's end of the house? Hmm.

He and Elise stared at each other. His amusement must have won over her consternation and exasperation, because she threw her hands up in the air.

"Oh, why not? I need a shower, though."

"I can wait."

Shaking her head, and casting eye-rolling glances over her shoulder, Elise tipped a head through Matthew's partially opened bedroom door down the hallway, presumably to tell him to get dressed. A mumble, the dull thud of one door shutting, and a politer click of another. At the sound of falling water, he made his way outside the cabin and into the late afternoon sunglow.

As he walked around the cabin, checking the exterior, making mental notes on repairs, he pondered the identity of the informer within his precinct. But he continued to hit the same block he invariably came back to: motive and opportunity. He had been diligent in observing each of his deputies, careful to spend time with each of them, paying close attention to open investigations in addition to his regular scheduling and oversight duties. No matter what angle he attacked the predicament from, though, it never felt quite right.

He was missing something. But what?

Jimmy was in the process of checking Dolly's front right hoof when the rickety screen door banged shut. The mare snorted, yanking the foot out his grasp in response, tossing her head and blonde mane.

"Oh, thank goodness, a buggy!" Elise's sincere gratefulness surprised him, but his heart swelled a little with the thought he had pleased her.

She wore dark denim jeans and a billowy white shirt. Dangly pearl earrings jiggled below her ears, and her fresh face captivated him. The woman could make a gunnysack look gorgeous.

He tucked his head to hide the proud grin, giving her a hand up into the battered, but serviceable carriage. "Seemed like a nice night for an open-air ride."

Jimmy glanced up to find her surreptitiously rubbing her backside. Her cheeks flushed red when she noticed him noticing her. "I, um, am still getting used to horseback transportation," she admitted. She jutted her chin past him, to the pasture beyond. "Windy's a good girl, though. Very gentle."

As Matthew clambered up the haphazard ladder on the opposite side, Jimmy glanced out across the one-acre separation between the cabin and the red-sided barn. Sure enough, his sorrel mare, Windy, lazily munched fresh spring growth in the wood-railed paddock attached to the barn. As though she sensed they were talking about her, the horse raised her head and tossed it with a nicker. At his side, Dolly answered with a spirited neigh, and Clarence tossed his head, grinning toothily. Jimmy snorted himself, and climbed up to plop on the seat next to Elise.

Leaning over he asked Matthew and his mother, "Ready?"

Jimmy was right. It was the perfect day for a buggy ride, and she swore even Matthew enjoyed himself. They pulled into the central downtown horse lot and piled out. Jimmy enlisted Matthew's help in unhitching the horses. Watching him interact with her son grabbed her heart and squeezed out a comforting ooey, gooey warmth. The guys led Clarence and Dolly over to the paddock. Several other horses were in residence, placidly chewing hay and slurping water. Jimmy slapped the gelding on the rump to urge him in, shut the gate, and he and Matthew returned to her side, a slight haze of dust kicked up behind them.

"So we're eating at Dixie's?" One meal in there had had her examining her waistline in the dim light of the full length mirror at the end of their new hallway.

"In a manner of speaking," came the mysterious reply.

Elise used her most formidable mom-stare on him. Something was fishy.

Jimmy laughed, wrapped an arm around her shoulders. "Wait and see. Ready, kid?"

Matthew shrugged and grunted, but at least his face remained frown-free.

The main horse lot in Cotton Springs was situated behind the row of interlocked storefronts which included Dixie's Café, among other things. The trio rounded the corner, and crossed Main Street. Three vehicles occupied parking slots on the thoroughfare, and jazzy music lilted in the air. The Square was filled with people, at least three dozen. Kids zipped and darted around the trees, their laughter trilling behind them. Adults gathered in small groups, chatting and laughing along with their kids.

Enchanted, Elise could only stare, a bewildered smile on her face. "It's so perfect."

At her side, Jimmy replied, "Hmm?"

"The party going on in The Square. That must be something special, a birthday or something. It just looks so cheerful. Like a movie, or a scene from a book," she laughed. "You must think I'm silly."

"Not at all."

He led her and Matthew along the sidewalk forming one end of a cross of sorts, which divided The Square into four chunky park-like areas. Old fashioned gas lamps lined the walkways. Barbecue filled her nostrils, and she found her fingers tapping against her thigh along with the music. Wistful, she shyly glanced around, careful not to draw attention to herself. She was just about to ask Jimmy where he was taking her when they rounded the bend, and came face to face with a giant banner strung between two expansive oaks.

Welcome Home, Elise and Matthew.

Elise froze, gulping like a goldfish for about three seconds, and then she found her voice. "What did you *do*, James Wilson?"

She looked up at his soft smile, uncertain whether to be grateful or annoyed.

"I thought barbecue would be nice," he said, sheepish.

"Surprise!" exclaimed a voice behind her. She turned to find Trudy, balancing a plate of slathered ribs and potato salad. Her short curls bounced atop her head as her friend bobbed up and down on her toes.

Elise jabbed a finger at her friend. "You! You knew about this?"

She waved a ruddy-colored meaty rib bone toward the gathered crowd, muttering as a tiny splat of red sauce landed on her plaid button-down shirt. She swiped at the stain, licking the sauce off her finger. "Well, you aren't hiding anymore, and you need to meet your townies. Right?" A raised eye brow held a challenge, and Tru's apparent nonchalant attitude set her teeth on edge.

This was her best friend throwing down the gauntlet. Fine. Two could play that game.

Elise cleared her throat and slapped a wide grin on her face. "This is fantastic, Jimmy! Thank you!" She stood on tiptoes to peck him on the cheek.

Matthew rolled his eyes, and surveyed the crowd. "Mind if I go over there? I see someone I met at school yesterday."

She shooed him away, but her eyes didn't stray far from his back.

"Relax," Jimmy whispered into her ear. The warmth of his breath tingled her neck.

"Right. Relax. Okay. Well, let's meet some people and beg for food. I'm famished."

He watched Elise like an overprotective mother hen, all the while doing his best to appear at ease and in control. While he guided her from family to family, he made conversation, pigged out on delicious catering from Dixie's side business, and kept a wary eye out for any potential informant.

Jimmy had to excuse himself once, when he received a comm message. He needn't fear leaving Elise alone, though, as her watchdog, Trudy Blue, appeared to have her personal security under control. Funny, that. The woman, who worked for the government finance office, certainly held herself as though she *were* security. Alert, squared shoulders, head on a swivel. Trudy reminded him more of law enforcement than a number cruncher. But at least Elise was safe, he thought, as he wandered to the vacant stand of trees near the far corner of The Square.

"Sheriff Wilson, go ahead."

Pete patched him through to the caller, and Jimmy found himself conferenced into a statewide alert meeting. All border counties of the Republic were officially on high alert status, as the rise of Dissenters in Socialist America created chaos at the borders. It seemed as though a considerable number of people claiming allegiance to the rebel faction had become distraught and were apparently storming select entry stations along the Texas border. But there were a lot of miles of unpatrolled river shoreline, where would-be immigrants might find their way across the nation's boundary.

All sheriffs were cautioned to train their deputies in the correct procedure for handling any illegal immigrants found in the Republic.

Jimmy ended his side of the call with a heavy heart. With this news, added to the knowledge that the El Lobo Ring was holed up somewhere in the Arkansas or Oklahoma mountains, the threat of the mouthy reporter looming, and identifying the mole in his department, he could almost feel a jagged noose tightening around his neck.

He sought out Elise in the crowd, and she waved when their eyes connected. The smile on her face tamped down the moodiness the call had inflicted.

She was the sunshine breaking through his cloudy day. He rolled his neck to ease the tension, waved back at his woman, and walked through ankle-high grass across The Square.

Chapter 23

When Elise arrived at Doc Tucker's house Thursday morning, she hurriedly dragged a sweat-soaked Windy to the stable behind the cottage, unsaddled the sorrel mare as though it were a timed event, and ran across the grassy yard as the first chubby raindrops began to pound the metal roof of the double duty home and clinic. The five miles from her tiny cabin to Cora's place had seemed an eternity. Now that the rain fell, the heavy gunmetal clouds lost their looming threat, transforming instead into soft, lazy sheets of gray. By the time she plunked her boots on the tray next to the front door, the shower had transformed into a deluge roaring on the tin roof overhead.

"In the nick of time, it seems," Cora pointed out as Elise entered. The very gravid physician pushed aside a white lace curtain with a grimace on her face, and waved a dismissing hand in the direction of the shower outside. "They say it will do this all day."

Elise noticed the way Cora one-handedly massaged her lower back, and wondered if the far off look on her face was directed at the gray weather, or more of the inward look a woman gets during labor.

"You sure you have a couple weeks to go?" Elise nodded at her belly, which was at the moment undergoing a rather interesting squiggling shift.

Her own womb clutched at the memory of Matthew pushing and shoving in utero.

Cora laughed. "I'm sure. He's just having a go at my kidneys. We might have a boxer on our hands."

"Good. Not sure I'm qualified to deliver a baby just yet," Elise noted with a wry grin. "Although I have learned quite a bit. What does the schedule look like today?"

Elise doubted many would keep their schedules. Nearly all of Doc Tucker's patients traveled by horse, either in the saddle or in a horse-drawn buggy of some sort. Having lived in larger cities, she was slowly becoming adjusted to the placid way of life in the more rural areas of the country. It was akin to the weeks directly after being granted asylum in Texas, going from the nomadic tent life to bustling cities filled with solar-electric automobiles and electronic technology.

"I only have two appointments booked. Normally I don't schedule Thursdays, but I do treat a handful of drop-ins." Cora shrugged with a small smile, a resigned gesture. "I can't say no. But the weather will probably deter those, today. Could be just you and me. If no one shows by noon, you can go home."

Elise grinned as Cora waddled – for there was no other word to describe it – toward the hall leading to the clinic. It wouldn't be too long before a newborn's cries filled the house.

She wondered aloud, "Where's Kitty? Surely she's not sleeping."

"That child? She's part rooster, I swear," the physician snorted. "Up at first light, and goes strong all day long. No, Ben took her to visit his sister early this morning. The rain puts a damper on his tracking contracts, and he likes to give me a break on Thursdays, when he's not working."

The next half hour passed with idle conversation, tool sterilization, and inventorying the apothecary cabinet in Cora's office. Elise hadn't lied when she told Cora she had learned quite a bit in the short time she had been employed. The fiery redhead was a deep well of knowledge, and an accomplished teacher as well. Who knew so many healing plants existed? Neatly labeled amber vials stood side by side behind glass-paned cabinet doors, naturopathic sentinels at parade rest, waiting to be snatched up and used. Comfrey, lavender, peppermint, garlic, and on and on. The simple act of opening the cabinet doors led to an assault on her olfactory system. The mingled fragrances of dozens of herbaceous medicinal tinctures and solutions created an indescribable cloud of wafting earthiness. Cora grew most of the plants in the expansive garden on the south side of the cottage, but a few special orders came in through Wainwright's Pharmacy.

While they worked, Elise daydreamed, fleshing out an idea she had been brainstorming for the last several days. She knew the proposal had merit, but would her employer go for it?

"Out with it," Cora announced into the silent air, and Elise jumped, jolted out of her mental debate. She carefully replaced the squat jar of eczema cream on the shelf, and closed the cabinet.

"What?"

Cora snorted. "You're thinking loud enough to rattle the windows, not that they're not rattling enough as it is."

The storm had indeed picked up, now being a symphony of rolling thunder and flickering light.

"Well, I, um, just had an idea."

"And?"

Elise explained her proposal before her nerve vanished. Cora listened, obviously intrigued and nodding along. At the end of the impromptu presentation, the doc clapped her hands, delight written on her face.

"Jimmy said you liked to bake, but I had no idea it was a calling."

"So you'd be okay with it? It wouldn't interfere with my duties as your assistant, I promise."

"I think it's a fabulous idea! Not that I need more cinnamon rolls or muffins attaching themselves to my hips, but I'll never say no to them."

While the flood continued, and the thunder faded to the east, they planned out a way for the idea of a fledgling bakery to grow and prosper. Elise would bake at home, and bring in an assortment of her goods to be displayed for sale in the dining room. On her days off, Elise planned a home delivery order service to augment the productivity.

"I have the perfect rack for it, too, out in the barn. It's an old buffet and hutch I picked up at an auction a couple months ago. Needs scrubbing and painting, but it will fit right along that wall."

In addition to bringing her tasty bounty from home, Cora gave her permission to use her kitchen during slow times, and on Thursdays when the patient load was light. By the end of their discussion, what had started as a seed had several blossoming ideas.

"So when should I start?" Elise posed the question bouncing on her toes. Cora laughed, and rubbed a slow hand over her baby bump.

"I have a mad craving for banana bread, and we have an empty schedule and a handful of overripe bananas. No time like the present!"

The Nomad Bakery was born.

***

No matter how many ways he worked it, or from whichever angle he attacked it, the county jail's summer vacation schedule refused to let go of its wrinkles. Jimmy ground his teeth, and tried another variation of employee assignment; when the door opened he growled, but left his eyes on the dilemma in front of him.

The sudden thud of a heavy file landing on his desk jerked his head up in surprise, his heart a thwumping kick drum.

"What the – Oh. Hello, Miss Miles."

"Katherine. Remember?" Her smile was a frigid slash across a slightly bemused face.

"Hmph." Jimmy nodded to the file stamped *Confidential* in front of him. "What's that?"

"I'm here to brief you on Operation Blackbird."

The kick drum kicked up the rhythm in his chest, and the tiny hairs on the back of his neck rose in anticipation. She didn't mean ...?

"Your mystery lady is a national security interest, Sheriff," Katherine Miles confirmed.

She pulled a chair forward from its place against the wall, sliding it toward his desk. He fuzzily registered the fact that the federal attorney wore plain clothes, not a business suit. Her chestnut hair hung long over one shoulder, not in the severe bun of her business attire.

But his eyes kept sliding back to the file in front of him. He wondered how much of his involvement with Elise the prosecutor knew about, if anything. He yanked his fractured thoughts together, lassoing them and pulling them toward his center of concentration. Jimmy cleared his throat, and eyed the woman across from him.

"Does this mean I've been cleared to be a part of the, what, investigation?"

She waved a manicured hand is dismissal. "It's not so much an investigation as it is a continual surveillance. The woman you know as Elise Gomez is the key witness in criminal charges against the man commonly known as El Lobo. The Wolf. No one knows the man's true identity, though. Except this woman. We call her Blackbird."

Jimmy thumbed through the file as Katherine briefed him, listening with half an ear, while the other half of his attention remained focused on the images of the woman he loved. Photo after candid photo filled the manila folder; images of Elise laughing at the park, pushing her toddler-age son on a swing, some of her working in various jobs, wearing assorted uniforms over the years. Everyday life of a woman who thought she was hiding. There were other documents in the portfolio. Deposition transcripts, handwritten statements, a list of assumed names and identities Elise had used over the last thirteen-plus years. Reports on sightings of the El Lobo Syndicate, missing persons records for dozens of young girls and boys near the borders who had disappeared, feared dead by their families, but suspected of captivity.

And Elise was the key to destroying the organization, from the inside out. She knew El Lobo's face.

"Does she know? About ... this?" Jimmy's voice remained distant, calm, in complete opposition to the tornadic swarm of emotion raging through his psyche.

He glanced up, found a wistful smile on Katherine's face. "We don't think she knows about the surveillance, no. She believes The Wolf sends agents to find her, and honestly, he may very well be doing it. But every indication is that she becomes alerted somehow to the presence of one of our guys, and then picks up and moves again. Not too worried about it, though. We know where she is, most of the time."

Those hairs on his neck stood on end this time. "Most of the time? How?"

The struggle to appear nonchalant began to take a toll on his body. Sweat trickled down the narrow canyon between his shoulder blades, and he felt moisture ringing outward from his armpits.

"You don't have clearance for that part, I'm afraid." The shark in women's clothing smiled, cunning. "How many times have you seen her, *Sheriff?*"

Jimmy caught the emphasis on his title, and ignored the unsaid threat.

He shrugged. "Like I said, I saw her in Austin at your brother's wedding. She bolted in the middle of dinner, and I haven't seen her since."

As soon as the words were said, Jimmy sealed his commitment to Elise. He had perjured himself to the federal prosecutor, on the record. For better or worse, he was in neck-deep.

She eyed him, if a cold stone could be said to stare. Katherine tapped a well-groomed fingernail on the open file in front of him. "Are you in, Jimmy? I need to know if you want to be a part of this investigation. Because if you do, you will be monitored, make no mistake about it."

He was under no illusion about what would happen if his relationship with Elise was discovered. The loss of his job, possible jail time. Those were viable consequences. But the one that felt like snakes writhing in his belly was losing her. If being part of this case could help him protect her, then so be it. Jimmy filled his lungs, exhaled slowly, and then locked stares with the President's daughter.

"I'm in."

Chapter 24

What did he pray for?

Jimmy warmed the seat, the black leather office chair swiveling lazily underneath him in repeated half circles, and bored holes into the plain white wall behind his desk. For the last hour, he had gazed at the blank wall. His thoughts blazed within, and not for the first time he wished he could simply project them out of his mind and onto the wall. Maybe then he could rearrange the pieces, the facts, into a semblance of order. Instead, he writhed in the mental chaos left in the wake of Katherine Miles' visit.

That wasn't fair, though. The moment he decided to pursue his relationship with Elise, his fate was sealed. Katherine only confirmed it for him.

Fate? Did it exist? He had made a choice, picked one option out of a multitude and said, *yes, this is it. I choose her.* Was it fated to happen, or had his thoughts and actions determined the path? And if it were all planned out, and he was a puppet dancing on heavenly strings, then what?

He growled and stood, the abrupt motion shoving his chair into the desk with a clatter. The open file with its pages shuffled and strewn mocked him. One crucial piece of new information lurked in the forefront of his mind, and he desperately wanted the peace of mind that came from prayer.

But the quiet refused to come. Prayer normally calmed him, centered him in an unseen place, where he pictured himself sitting on a park bench next to Jesus, with tall pines surrounding them both. He couldn't help it, really. The day he accepted Jesus as his Savior he sat on a weathered, splintery park bench with his dad. He remembered Dad's solid legs under his own small ones as he sat on his father's lap, the tears running down his rounded cheeks, tiny droplets striking the bench with a splat, and soaking into aged fissured wood. Now, as an adult, he returned to a place in his mind which resembled the special place, sitting next to his Father instead.

But the peace and serenity of prayer eluded him. Instead, his muttered thoughts were confused, angry, skittering to and fro in the way jagged lightning branches in dozens of fiery fingers as it strikes the ground. Outside his office window, the sudden thunderstorm echoed his thoughts. Rain sheeted from a steel gray sky. His mood mirrored the storm.

Right and wrong, black and white. Jimmy swore to uphold the law, and despite his oath, every minute he failed to report his relationship with Elise he betrayed his promise. But on the other hand, he made a commitment to Elise to protect her, and there was no other way he could see to hold himself accountable for her safety.

The reporter was missing. Tandy Newman, the one who claimed to know the identity of the key to the El Lobo case, had not shown up for work for the last two days. Her coworkers labeled her a shark, and a shark did not abandon a juicy meal mid-bite. While it had been a hastily scrawled note in the prosecutor's neat hand, the information was more than an innocuous tidbit.

Too irritated with himself, he strode from his office, careful to mask his feelings beneath a façade of firm professionalism.

Desks were butted nose to nose and columned in the wide open room. Two deputies hunkered at their workstations, pecking their reports into the system. On the far wall, a dated task screen listed active investigations, county and nationwide bulletins, officer locations, and the like. No alerts flashed, so he ambled over to Deputy Wallace's desk, positioning himself to be seen.

The seasoned deputy glanced up, catching Jimmy's questioning look. "Hey, Boss. Just finishing that domestic call from this morning. You'd think people would give it a rest at six in the morning." Wallace chuckled, rubbing closed eyes with a groan. "First time I've ever listed coffee pot as a weapon."

Jimmy flicked his chin toward the task screen. "Any word on the missing reporter?"

"Naw. She's probably off with a man, down at the Gulf vacationing or something. And cursing the rain, at that. Pete's tracking her comm records, though."

He recalled how naked ambition had oozed from Tandy Newman's pores, eyes greedy for fame, and silently disagreed with Wallace's casual theory. Jimmy grunted a noncommittal response, and clipped over to the task screen. He had lost touch with the beat, under the strain of supervising, scheduling, and administrative work.

Tapping Newman's name, he pored over the list of report headings. Most were statements from friends or acquaintances. One from a coworker stated that Newman's company-assigned work tablet was missing, but that the reporter often took it home with her. He closed the statement with a swipe, and opened another. There. One William Remington, also a reporter with the news station, stated he believed something dire had happened to Tandy, because she lived and breathed reporting. If she wasn't at work, then something was keeping her away. Clearly, this reporter saw the predator in the missing woman, just as Jimmy had. The statement included a contact number, and he was tapping the last number when an alert flashed on the task screen.

MISSING PERSON ALERT: The personal vehicle registered to missing person Tandy Ruth Newman has been identified, located approximately two miles south of the Texarkana Border Crossing Station. The Bowie County Sheriff's Office is instructed to cooperate with Texas Bureau of Investigation and Texas Border Patrol officials, in reviewing video surveillance evidence to identify said missing person.

The alert punched him in the stomach. Not a coincidence. It couldn't be. Newman poking around, asking questions about El Lobo, and now her abandoned vehicle had been located near the border crossing with the American district identified as a potential current location of the syndicate.

He didn't know Wallace stood behind him until the deputy said, "Well, I'll be. Didn't see that one coming."

"I wish I could say the same."

Jimmy stalked to his office, shutting the door quietly, but firmly. He tapped the glass twice, which transitioned to frosted panes in an instant; the signal to his guys in the bullpen that he required privacy. Outside his window overlooking downtown, though, the rain had eased into a lazy shower. He left the shades up, looking down on the slick, wet streets below. Umbrellas bobbed in a rainbow of colors amidst the gray; here and there, bareheaded people darted into shops, their clothing drenched and clingy.

He should warn Elise, of course. Anything to do with the slave syndicate pertained to her safety and well-being. Guilt niggled at the edges of consciousness, though. The nasty little voice in his head crowed, *Well, at least now Newman can't expose Elise.* Slapping a mental hand across his inner smartaleck's mouth, he plunked himself in his chair, bracing his elbows on the desk and resting his head, eyes downward, in his roughened hands.

Tandy Newman had most likely followed one lead too many, and was either captured and sold, or dead. How many others were in captivity? Jimmy knew for a fact the number was nowhere near solid. How many missing persons in either Texas or America were, in fact, abducted and sold into slavery? The investigation into El Lobo stretched back years, and yet the horrid monster eluded agency after agency. The Wolf most likely had insiders, paid to derail and distract. Once more he was struck by disbelief and amazement that Elise escaped and lived to tell about it, saving not only her life but that of her unborn son.

His head was still down when the door opened. What did Wallace want now? Or was it Pete, back from lunch?

He sighed and was prepared to give his privacy speech, but when he looked up it wasn't one of his deputies darkening the doorway.

Trudy Blue quirked an eyebrow, a sad smirk dimpling her chin.

"Bad day, Sheriff?"

Jimmy lifted a shoulder. "It is for Tandy Newman, I'm afraid."

Trudy's slender face remained the same, showing neither question nor surprise. He considered her business attire, her squared posture, the direct look in his eyes. She reached inside a smallish purse, and flung something onto his desk.

The badge gleamed, the cast silver emblem of the Texas Bureau of Investigation shining against the black leather badge wallet. It was like the last brick fitted snug in a wall. Now it made sense.

Trudy said, "Looks like we need to have a talk."

He was, quite frankly, tired of talking to women today.

Chapter 25

Her feet throbbed despite the supportive tennis shoes she wore, and her lower spine begged for mercy. Both forefingers and a thumb sported four new burns between them, bits of dried bread dough clung desperately to the cuticles of her nails, and her jeans were a lighter shade than they were this morning when she rode into work, thanks to the hundreds of times she had wiped floured hands on her thighs.

Elise was happier than she had been in weeks.

Though, she predicted Cora would need to buy more groceries tomorrow. They had depleted Doc's pantry of flour, sugar, butter, lard, and various fruits and berries. Banana bread led to muffins, and muffins segued into cupcakes. While the rain silenced birdsong and halted chirruping squirrels outside, inside Cora's cottage laughter and big band permeated the air as thickly as the scent of warm yeast bread.

Elise chuckled, recalling Ben's face as he walked in the door, toting Kitty on his monstrously tall hip. His eyes had bulged wide, and his thickish brows arched, drawing attention to his striking green eyes. The sweet, chubby redheaded miniature version of Cora had taken one look at the mound of edible delights covering the round dining table and squealed, "Puccake!" loud enough to wake the dead, then promptly wiggled and shimmied her way down her dad's side as he fought to not drop her.

Ten minutes later, Kitty peered through frosting coated bangs, and was covered eyebrows to dimpled chin in the sugary goodness. The three adults groaned in gluttonous pleasure. Elise laughed aloud as Ben mirrored Cora in rubbing circles over his full belly.

Now, standing in her own kitchen, she thought the likelihood of her eating supper in an hour was pretty much nil. With a glance at the wall clock, she wondered where Matthew was. Outside, the rain had subsided, but left a mucky driveway and pasture in its wake. Slogging through clay mud might have slowed him somewhat, but he should have been home fifteen minutes ago. Her heart stuttered, thinking about the incident a few weeks ago. No, he promised not to run off like that again, and her son had an unusual sense of honor. There had to be another reason for his tardiness.

Still, giddiness bubbled in her chest. Her dream of owning a bakery was one step closer to reality. Elise closed her eyes, and concentrated on the image of the mound of wrapped muffins and bread loaves, cookies and cupcakes, covering Cora's dining table. A beginning, that. A desire for something great, born of the most miserable of circumstances.

When she was about twelve years old – though the years blurred together in a heartrending haze – a new influx of children were brought into the nomadic slave camp. Half a dozen blank and staring faces, smudged with dirt and the far off look of the bewildered, traumatized, and drugged, replaced her and three others' places in the cleaning and laundry detail. She felt the remorse all over again, how she had gingerly rubbed her dried and bleeding cracked hands, the twin emotions of relief and guilt warring in her calloused heart.

Elise had been shuffled off to the cookhouse, after the new ones arrived, all those years ago. Yet, there she flourished. Her arms and shoulders grew strong from kneading dough. For the first time in years, Elise enjoyed the labor. Oven burns and beatings because of charred bread spurred her forward. She absorbed recipes and techniques like a hungry sponge. Her love of baking gasped its first hot breath in a sweltering canvas tent over the crudest of ovens, and for once, she found something worth living for. An odd sensation had sprouted roots, its intertwining branches wrapping around her heart, sort of like a second sheltering heartbeat. Looking back, Elise saw it for what it was. Hope.

A quivering ball of anguish settled in her gut. Those kids, and countless others, were still at the mercy of The Wolf, either manufacturing or delivering illicit drugs, or part of the Candy Store. Or they were dead, and better off. They wore the same mask, had the same face, peered at their new home with the same desolate gaze. Maybe one of them escaped. A handful had tried.

She knew, because she had buried them.

The suddenness of the panic attack obliterated her earlier bliss. It started with a heavy weight pressing inward on her chest, and extended toward her fingers, like fire ants biting their way to her fingertips. Her breath came in fits and starts, and Elise blinked away hot tears. Heart galloping, in a cold sweat, she yanked open the front door. A cool breeze shimmied through the screen door, caressing her face with the freshness of late spring, easing the flashback. She braced herself in the doorway, head down and eyes squeezed shut. Minutes passed where the only thing she knew to do was to breathe.

Inhale.

Exhale.

Repeat.

Soon, though, a sound other than her ragged breath registered. Splashing squelches, coming closer. Elise raised her head and spied her son nearing home, his shoulders slumped to mirror hers. He'd had a bad day, then.

She could not let him see the wrung-out exhaustion of the unexpected wave of anxiety; instead, Elise dwelled on the aroma of fresh baked bread, and the recent memory of laughter bouncing off kitchen walls of a clinic turned fledgling bakery. The Wolf and his bosses may have controlled her body for twelve years, but she would not allow him to control her mind. After all, she thought with a weary smile, her most beloved treasure trudged toward her this minute. If she had Matthew, all was well.

She took one look at his shoes, and instructed him to leave them next to her mud-caked boots, on the stoop. Wrapping an arm around his shoulders, she drew him in and kissed him on the forehead. Despite his melancholic posture, he grinned. Then he inhaled deeply, and his eyes rose.

"Do I smell cinnamon bread?"

Elise ruffled a hand through his dark chestnut hair, and rolled her eyes. Boys. Always thinking with their stomachs.

"Sure do. Go on, then. You look like you could use a couple of pieces."

After the second piece, his silence continued. Normally she would let him tell her in his own time.

"What's up, kiddo?" she asked, her chin braced in her hands, elbows docked on the island. She smiled conspiratorially to lighten the mood. "Is it a girl?"

"Mo-om! No." He exhaled in a huff, and shoved the last bite of gooey cinnamon bread in his mouth. After he swallowed, he shrugged. His well-worn t-shirt hugged his shoulder, and she noted once again how much her son was growing. He would need a new wardrobe soon.

"There was a meeting after school. That's why I was a little late."

She raised an eyebrow. "And?"

"It was a cross-country meeting," he blurted, suddenly defensive. "They start up in two weeks, and practice through the summer."

Ah. "And you want to join the team, but you're afraid I won't let you?"

He nodded, his mouth twisted to the side. "I understand. If you don't want me to, I mean. I know I scared you when I took off like that. I did promise not to do it again."

"Do you have the permission form?" Elise held her outstretched hand expectantly.

Matthew's forehead wrinkled in surprised delight. "Really?"

"Sure. You gave me your word, honey. I trust you."

In the way of teenagers, all was sunlight and sparkles once more. No longer in the depths of despair, Matthew allowed a full smile to stretch from ear to ear. "It's in my backpack. Hang on."

He rifled through the canvas bag, pulling out a wrinkled paper in triumph. She smoothed the crumpled page, filled in the required information, signed it, and he shoved it back into the disreputable mess within his bag. Buoyant, he barreled down the hallway, shouting over his shoulder that he was going to call someone named Kyle and let him know.

Two victories in one day.

One of the old jazz tunes that was on at Cora's played on a loop in her cluttered mind. She hummed happily as she pulled a skillet from the lower cabinet, and gathered ingredients for black bean burritos. Quick, easy, and the kid loved them. Trudy would eat anything, so she didn't worry about her preferences. She winced and sighed as she opened the canned beans. Normally, she would have soaked dry beans overnight, but a mom's gotta do what a mom's gotta do sometimes, including cooking with a can opener. She rinsed the purplish black beans, and tossed them into the skillet with a little water; then she chopped the onions and tossed them in, then seasoned it all with salt, pepper, garlic powder, and cumin.

Just as the sharp knife bit into the head of lettuce she intended for a shredded topping, her wristcom showed an incoming message: Trudy was working late and wouldn't be home for supper. Again. This was becoming a habit, and frankly it worried her. What did a government finance officer need to work on after hours?

"Mom, you all right?"

Matthew intruded on her ruminations, and she realized with a start that the chopping knife hovered in the air just above the halved lettuce.

"Hm? Oh – yes. I'm good. Aunt Trudy messaged me that she won't be home for supper, that's all."

"Gee, that's odd," her son snorted with a sarcastic roll of the eyes. "She's been doing that a lot lately."

Elise shrugged, then settled back to work.

As Elise knew he would, Matthew polished off three burritos, and half of a fourth before pushing back his bar stool. He belched, then covered his mouth in surprise.

"'scuse me," he chuckled. "All right if I play *Martial Law*?"

"Sure. After you feed and brush Windy, and rinse off your shoes. Oh, and do your homework. Use the outside spigot, not the sink!" she yelled at his swiftly departing backside.

Despite her earlier reservations, she had eaten supper after all. If she kept this up, she would need a new wardrobe. Would Jimmy still like her if she gained a few pounds? She grinned at the thought, and realized she had not spoken to him all day.

Maybe he could use a loaf of fresh baked bread. Oh, who was she kidding? She wanted to feel him beside her as they walked the hills, longed to accidentally-on-purpose bump into him while avoiding the horse chips fertilizing the ground. If she closed her eyes, the ghost of his calloused, gentle palm caressed hers. It jittered her stomach, set the butterflies aflutter.

On an impulse, she sent him a quick message. *I miss you.* Then she tapped the send icon before she lost her nerve. Goodness, she was acting like one of those teenagers in a coming-of-age drama. Well, and what of it? Her life had been devoid of such frivolities. Part of her stubborn refusal to run, to take a stand, included allowing herself to experience the giddiness of flirtation, of infatuation.

To experience love.

Love. It reminded her of a verse of the Bible she read last night before rolling over, switching off the nightstand lamp, and closing her eyes.

"For God so loved the world, that He gave His one and only Son, that whoever believed in Him should not perish, but have everlasting life."

This Jesus she had been reading about stirred her soul in an indescribable way. What had seemed like an intriguing and imaginative tale had begun to take on the guise of truth, of history rather than fiction. Could it be true? That God impregnated Mary, and had a Son? It boggled the rational part of her mind, but it held the ring of truth. Elise was incapable of explaining it, though, and she wished she could logically explain it.

Faith.

The word hung in the air, as though she could reach up and pluck it from a tree, its fruit ripe and ready. She had read about faith as well, and thought faith would be the *only* way to believe a story like what she was reading in the stolen Bible. Logic made little sense when applied to things like virgins giving birth, and a man raising himself from the dead.

Before she knew it, she sat on the edge of her bed, holding the bound book. Quietly, she said to the ceiling, "God, if you're there, show me a sign. I want to believe You are there. But I'm ... afraid."

Glancing at the bedside clock, she frowned. It would be over an hour before Jimmy arrived home from work. She opened the book to its bookmarked place, as the sun dropped below choppy gray clouds, and grasshoppers buzz-jumped in the field outside her open window.

Chapter 26

"Elise, honey, your best friend is a bald-faced liar."

His haggard reflection showed a disgusted visage, a mouth tightened with exasperation. Jimmy did not recognize the old man glaring at him from the silvered mirror. Lines flanked his eyes. He leaned in, squinting. Three new gray hairs. He tilted his head to the side, and grunted. Make that five traitorous strands. Fabulous.

He inhaled, his chest swelling, shoulders braced wide, and tried again. "Elise. Baby, Trudy is not who you think she is. She's a TBI agent assigned to dupe you into friendship and keep close tabs on you for tracking and evidence purposes."

The woman – no, the special agent – had sat in his office bold as day, and recounted her first few weeks observing and surveilling the scrawny kid who told an unbelievably fantastic tale to the immigration office in El Paso. At the mention of El Lobo, the TBI had been immediately notified, no matter how small or unverified the battered girl's claims had been. For weeks, Trudy – if that was her real name, which he doubted – tracked

Elise, keeping tabs on her movements to and from the refugee shelter that served as the girl's temporary home in a new country.

First contact with Elise had been made in San Antonio months later. Agent Blue's superiors felt the time was ripe for a more intimate relationship to be established. The lonely and obviously pregnant teenager, while hesitant and skittish in the beginning, warmed to Trudy faster than they expected.

Of course, Trudy claimed true affection for Elise by that time. She admitted to going so far as to falsify reports of their whereabouts and activities, even claiming to lie about his and Elise's blooming romance, thereby endangering her own badge. By this time in her tale, Trudy's eyes shined with unshed tears, and had dejectedly slumped in the chair across from his solid oak desk.

He hadn't known what to believe.

His knuckles whitened around the drinking glass which lived on the bathroom sink counter. How could Trudy do it, act the Judas for more than a decade?

With one last growl at the mirror, he released the glass, its bottom edge clinking dangerously on the stone beneath it. He raked a frustrated hand through his hair, then padded to the adjacent master bedroom, halting at the end of his bed. The khaki and brown sheriff's uniform lay where he hastily shucked it when he came home early. He couldn't get out of it quickly enough. Everything he stood for, upholding the law and protecting the people, seemed wrapped around the cotton fibers of the rumpled clothes tossed on the foot of his queen-sized bed. What right did he have to the uniform, to the badge? What ate at him, scourged his insides and clanged around in his mind, was the need to protect Elise at any cost;

but in the process, his sworn duties as sheriff were heaped onto the altar of sacrifice. He felt dirty, stained.

The still, quiet voice chirped once more. Throughout the day, Jimmy had managed to shove the soft presence into a corner, ignore the insistence, and grit his teeth in obstinate defiance.

Resign.

One word, but oh, the implications. And if he obeyed God, for he knew it was Him who spoke, how could he offer Elise protection? His occupation allowed access to inside information unknown to the public. Official status reports of the El Lobo Syndicate, new developments and evidence for the same. Without his law enforcement clearance, he was as useless to her as a toad on a log.

I will fight for you; you only need to be still. I will make a way.

He collapsed onto the edge of his bed, the quilt-covered mattress compressing beneath him with a springy squeal. His hand came to rest on his badge, threaded onto the belt loop of his discarded pants. Trailing a cool finger along the ridges of the gold-plated emblem of his office, the weight of God's truth sank into his weary bones.

"I know you fight for me, Father," he whispered into the silence. "But I swore to fight for her."

Be STILL.

Jimmy ceased fighting. An overwhelming peace stole into the room, bathing him in reassuring tranquility and washing away his weariness. The small vertical crease on his forehead vanished, and neck muscles taut with tension eased, like ice melting on a hot August day. It crested over him, cool water of God's protection and safety, from mussed hair to bare feet on the gritty wood floor.

He became hyperaware of his surroundings. Outside the window, the blue jays cawed, and a grasshopper smacked into the window with a hollow *thunk*. A gentle wind ruffled the simple beige linen curtains his grandmother had made as a newlywed. One panel billowed out to caress his ankle with a soft gliding touch. He inhaled the damp and fecund late spring air, filling his lungs to bursting, and exhaling slowly.

He listened, and God spoke.

I will fight for you, and for the soul of your beloved, because she is My beloved as well. Do what is right in the eyes of the law.

Fifteen years in the sheriff's department stretched before him. He closed his eyes, saw the faces of his friends and coworkers. As though he blinked, he witnessed himself raising his right hand and swearing to uphold the law and protect the citizens of his county. His heart clenched into a tight fist, and he accepted the hard facts. God was right. He needed to resign.

His eyes fluttered, and his breath stammered. Tomorrow, then.

Jimmy braced shaking hands on his knees, and rolled his head, easing the kinks. With a sigh, he peered at the nightstand. Nearly an hour until supper. Was she thinking of him, at this moment? Or was she enveloped in the daily routine of cooking and cleaning, homework and chores?

His wristcom buzzed, and he flinched.

"I miss you," the message read. Half a smile tugged his lips toward his left ear. Guess that answered his question. He left the message unanswered, though, planning to respond in person instead.

He rose and walked to the closet, the dusty floor coating his naked feet with a fine grit. Later. He would sweep later. He pawed through his hanging shirts, sliding one against another until he found a casual shirt in

189

decent shape with few wrinkles. Squinting in the diffused light of the late afternoon, he thought the shirt was light blue, maybe gray. He should really get around to changing the light bulb. He snatched a pair of well-worn denim jeans, and dressed in record time.

The realization happened as he wiped the grime from his left foot, the white cotton sock dangling limp is his other hand.

You won't be able to protect her with the law, but you can offer the protection of your body. Do not fear.

"For I am with you," Jimmy continued aloud, a wistful expression on his face. He hummed as he laced his boots by the front door. His hand gripped the doorknob, ready to turn it, but on impulse he trotted to his bedroom.

Where was it? The contents of the small upper drawer of the chest-high chiffonier jostled and clanked against one another as he shoved them around. He knelt down, the drawer at eye level, and spied his prize in the rear corner. Quick as a snake, he flicked out a hasty hand and clutched it to his chest.

"Lord, am I crazy?" Should anyone have seen him at that moment, they would think him talking to the ceiling fan. "Just give me a sign."

Foxlike, he set off along the worn path running between his house and the far cabin, as though a pack of hunters were on his trail. He smiled into the late afternoon sun, a blessing shining between slate darkened clouds.

All he needed was a sign.

Chapter 27

Halfway through the chapter she had begun, a rapid knocking on the door startled Elise out of the book of Acts. She jumped, and the leather-bound Bible slapped against the rustic wood planks with a *thwack!* Her heart had thump-clawed itself to the top of her esophagus, and the hastily flung hand covering her sternum was ineffective at calming it. She hustled to the door, and plastered her eye to the peephole. The eye widened, and she flung open the door.

"Jimmy!"

Her trembling prayer from just minutes before surfaced in her short-term memory: *Lord, give me a sign.* If this was not it, she didn't know what was.

He stumbled, and just before she laid her head on his chest in an attack hug, she saw the surprised whites of his eyes. His laugh rumbled in his chest beneath her ear.

"Well, hello to you too, darlin'," Jimmy laughed, shaking and trying to steady himself beneath her assault. She couldn't care less. He was here, and God provided the proof she needed.

With one last squeeze, she pulled back. He opened his mouth, but she laid a tan finger across his lips. Elise grabbed his hand, and pulled him into the yard and over to the A-framed wooden swing she had placed near the fenced kitchen garden. She ignored his chuckling protests, shoved him onto the seat, and on the backswing, she jumped on beside him.

Elise stuck out her lower lip and blew a hasty breath upward, flicking a dangling lock of black hair to the side and out of her eye. She clutched Jimmy's hand in hers, laid it on her knee. Gosh, she loved to look at the man. His kind brown eyes, ringed with laugh lines; he grinned, and she noticed for the first time how his left incisor sat slightly crooked, overlapping the front tooth a smidgen. He squeezed her hand.

"What's going on, honey?"

"You'll see. I promise. But, I need you to do something with me. Right *now*."

His mouth pulled to the side in a cheeky grin. "Yeah? What's that?"

"Pray with me."

The moist warmth of the day suffused her bones; a weighted sun lit her closed eyelids with a rosy glow. They swung to a slow stop, her feet tip-toed and stretched. As she spoke, a gusty breeze swept across the land.

"God," she began, her throat clutching at a knot of emotion. "Lord, I believe in You. I don't understand it. I can't explain it, God, but I know you are there. I have faith in what the Bible says about Jesus, Your Son, that He came to save me from all the wrongs in my life." Swallowing, she squeezed Jimmy's hand, a vise drawing strength from the man next to her. "Jesus, save me. Please. I ask your forgiveness. I want to be Yours."

Beside, Jimmy hoarsely ended with a whispered, "Amen."

Elise opened her eyes to radiant love, filling her body with bubbling joy. Then Jimmy tackled her.

She hardly noticed the swing's chain digging underneath her shoulder blade. Well, maybe a little. But she much preferred her man's arms muscling tight around her, feeling his hot breath in the hollow where sternum meets neck. Another breeze whipped through the open field, chilling tear tracks on her face, and those at the neck of her shirt, where Jimmy wept joyfully with her. Such love. Human imagination could barely interpret the overwhelming and confident affection, possession, and love that quivered beneath her skin, in every cell, each fibrous strand holding it all together.

But yes, the swing chain was really gouging her back, and she shifted her weight. Jimmy sat up hastily, but kept her hand hostage in his. He could have it. He swiped a sun-darkened hand beneath his eyes, wiping away the salty-wet evidence of emotion, but the broad smile dominated his features. She reached across, snagging a tear with a gentle sweep of a thumb.

"It's amazing!" Elise kicked the swing into motion, feeling like the kid she was *before*. In this moment, the heavy burden she had carried for a lifetime no longer crushed her soul. She was light, airy, as though the creaky old bench swing could launch her into the sky, and she would swoop and fly, dart and dive through the cloud-smudged canopy overhead.

Jimmy wrapped his arm around her shoulder, and nudged her head onto his. "I remember, even though I was only a kid when I was saved."

"Saved. That's a marvelous word for," she gestured wildly in a figure-eightish motion, "this. This feeling."

He released the captive hand, and ran his fingers through her short-cropped hair. "Mm-hmm."

Jimmy kept the swing in motion. Occasionally one of the chain links would thud in protest, its twang interrupting the comfortable stillness. The loud silence was the buzz-whir of grasshoppers in the pasture, the call of songbirds in the trees behind the house. It was the occasional sniffle from the remnants of a good cry, and the swish-flick of Windy's long tail as it scattered the amaranthine cloud of inquisitive flies.

Elise wished the silence could last forever.

He could hold her like this forever. Except for the fact that he was getting a cramp in his thigh from pushing the swing, and the arm encircling Elise had gone numb about five minutes ago.

Her hair smelled of lavender and mint, and oddly, yeasty bread. With a grin she couldn't see, he planted a chaste kiss on her silky head, and shifted his weight. Jimmy thought he heard her sigh.

She turned and blinded him with a radiant smile. "I asked God for a sign, you know." Her cheeks flushed with the admission. "And then you showed up. What?"

Startled, he had jerked. "Oh, nothing bad. I, uh, asked Him for a sign, too. Right before I came over here."

Raven manicured eyebrows arched in surprise. Pleased surprise, and question.

How did he begin, and how much did he reveal? The short jog over had been a mindless excursion. Jimmy winced, realizing a little planning would have gone a long way, in this case.

Trudy-if-that's-her-real-name had asked him as she had stood at his office door, her hand on the knob, as though it were an afterthought before she exited, "You won't tell Elise, right? It … it needs to come from me. And I will. Just not yet." She had left without a backward glance.

Jimmy halted the metronome action beneath him. His hands suddenly clammy, he swabbed them across denim-covered thighs. Turning to face Elise, he hitched his right knee up onto the seat of the bench swing. God provided the sign. Now Jimmy needed the courage. Elise watched him with a patient face, and she mimicked his posture, turning into him with a leg kneed up. She laid her head on the wooden plank on the swing-back, waiting. *Well, here goes nothing.*

"Do you know someone who Trudy doesn't know who can get you and Matthew fake identities?" he blurted rapid-fire, not pausing to take a breath.

She bolted upright, the earlier joy overshadowed by curious nervousness, swiveling her head and surveilling the yard. "Is he … ?"

He clasped both her hands in his. "No, honey. He's not here. I – " He cleared his throat, a harsh bark. "Do you have a contact like that? If not, I know a guy." It was the same man who had covertly placed the ad in the American papers that had drawn Cora Thomas Tucker to Cotton Springs. If he didn't have to use him, though, he preferred not to.

Elise nodded, a slow bob. "I, um. Yes, I do. And Trudy doesn't know about her. I don't *think* she does anyway. Why can't Trudy know about it?"

This was the sticky part. "I want to keep her out of this, as much as possible. Just between you, me, and Matthew."

"You're scaring me, Jimmy," she quietly admitted. "Please tell me what has happened."

"I can't, yet. I will, though. Promise. But I have a very important question to ask."

He stood, and the swing glided backward. She slowed it with a toe which barely scraped the mucky ground. Despite the grave tone of the conversation, it brought a grin to his face. His petite blackbird.

Jimmy slid a hand into a front pocket, and palmed the diminutive box. Elise peered at him through concerned eyes, her earlier jubilance gone. Despite the mud, he kneeled in front of her, the knee of his jeans sinking with a wet squelch.

"Elise Gomez, you stole my heart from the moment I first saw you."

Tears leaked from her widened eyes, and he continued around a lump in his throat.

"Then Matthew did the same. I love you, honey. All I want to do is provide for you, shelter you, love you."

Both of her slender hands covered her mouth, and she blinked rapidly.

"I offer my heart to you, the protection of my body, all that I own, all that I am, if you'll have me. Will you marry me?"

Chapter 28

"I – I ..." Elise stammered, her mouth as dry as the western desert. In direct opposition, her eyes flooded and left rivulets down her cheeks. She blinked in rapid succession, causing the welling tears to join their counterparts in their descent.

Oh, how she loved this man. But –

"I can't." It escaped as a choked whisper.

Confusion puckered his brows, and he lowered the hand holding the ring box. The ring blazed in the late sunlight, the sizeable garnet glowing as if lit from within. Her heart twinned the stone, pulsed and burned beneath her ribs. Her hands darted out, quite on their own, clutching his shaking ones in hers. She slid from the swing to land on her knees with a sodden squelch.

Searching his eyes, she found hurt laced with embarrassment. With an outstretched palm, she cupped his left cheek and he pressed his face firmly into her hand.

"I *want* to, Jimmy. More than anything. But, I can't. Not until I know what you are not telling me." She refused to hide the anguish washing through her at the decision, but Elise would not begin a marriage with lies. She said as much, and his distress mirrored hers.

He groaned, falling backward. The mother part of her winced at how hard it would be to get the clay stains out of his jeans, but she squashed the thought. Jimmy sat knees up, his elbows resting on them, and his head cupped in his hands. He raised forlorn eyes, met her gaze, and then lowered his brow once more.

What was he concealing? He normally withheld nothing from her, and her stomach churned imagining what hid in that brain of his. Elise glanced at the brown, watery stain spreading around her knee, and resigned herself to half an hour of stain scrubbing. She collapsed next to him, and laid her head onto his shoulder.

He said something, but all she heard was a mumbled, "rock and a hard place."

"I have to resign from my position as Sheriff," he said. He tilted his head, peering from behind mussed hair, a sad, wry half-grin pulling his lips up into his cheek.

"What? Why?"

"Because I can't keep lying! I told Katherine Miles I would turn you in the minute I saw you. Instead, I'm defying her every second of every day. Elise," he groaned, "it's eating me. Inside and out."

Abruptly, he rose, the mud sucking in protest, and he slipped, windmilling his arms. Elise held up a hand and he grabbed hold, steadying himself and side-stepping to a patch of grass for traction. Without breaking contact, he pulled her to standing. They stood in the mewling evening, dripping brownish-red clay water, each miserable in their own fashion. She would not marry him – but, oh! How she desired to! - as long as he kept her out of the loop, and he would not reveal the source of his distress, which she felt must be rooted in covering up his connection to her. But his resignation? It might be a part, but it wasn't the whole.

Jimmy opened his mouth, then closed it, reminding her of the tragic guppy Matthew won at a carnival years ago.

She tugged gently on their tenuous connection, and he drifted in. Wrapping her arms around his broad chest, she snuggled her cheek against the soft cotton. The thump of his beating heart muffled the frog chorus coming from the pond. Elise grinned when she felt his bony chin settle atop her head. Maybe, just maybe, all was not lost. Reassuring warmth formed a pocket of stillness in the space of heartbeats. In its center, she knew she was home.

"I want to be your wife, Jimmy," she told his chest. He laughed, the rumble bumping her face, but it was a bitter sort of laugh that tightened her stomach in fear.

He cupped her face, pulling her away, and staring deep into her soul. "You sure have a funny way of going about it."

Then he stepped away, turned his back on her, and the warmth she knew seconds before dissipated, like low-lying fog struck by the sun's rays. Elise shivered. How could she make him understand? She lingered near the swing. He scuffled in lazy, wide circles, ranging away then coming toward her, but with his head downcast and not meeting her searching gaze. Space to think, to breathe. It was one gift she could give, and did. Though it fairly shredded her soul to do it.

The sun flared behind him as it slid behind the pine curtain surrounding the cleared pasture, silhouetting his dejected pacing and highlighting his flyaway hair. Elise swallowed the knot of worry, and returned to the swing to wait for him. A glint of red sparkled near the A-frame bracing, and she scooped up the tiny hinged box.

A deep maroon, the oval garnet cabochon was nestled in a humble silver setting. The stone itself was roughly the size and shape of her pinky fingernail, and the band itself was slender, elegant. Hesitant to remove it from its velvet home, she turned the box to and fro, examining the ring from different angles. Simple, beautiful.

His shadow swept over the ring, darkening the cardinal glow for a split second. Jimmy settled on the swing next to her, exhaled heavily. He remained silent.

Cautiously, she laid a slender hand on his knee. He leaned forward and reached to pluck the box from her other hand.

"This was my grandmother's wedding ring. My grandfather had it made for her from a stone he found during a dig in Alaska. He and some friends traveled there hoping to mine some gold during a revived gold rush. They were only dating, but serious, at the time."

She settled against the swing back. Her pulse slowed as he wrapped an arm around her shoulders. A breeze chilled her damp pants, and Jimmy tightened his grip, fending off the shiver.

"He thought it was a sign, you see," he explained quietly. He turned the stone so that it caught the sun in its depths. "Grannie's birthday was in January."

Tall grass bowed in the wind, and she shivered again. With the sun on its way to slumber, the air cooled.

"Can't you trust me, Elise?" The anguished plea fissured her resolve.

"I do. Jimmy, I do. I only want to know what it is you're not telling me. My whole life has been one betrayal after another. I finally found a home of sorts with Trudy. We tell each other everything. I don't want to begin a marriage with lies and secrets. I refuse to."

She had become too strong to compromise.

"But I tell you what," Elise said quietly. She nimbly opened his fingers, peeling the ring box out of his clutched hand. Laying the box in the valley between her knees, she bowed her head and unfastened the necklace clasp from around her neck. Reverently, she pulled the ring from its black velvet home, and threaded it onto the chain. It nestled alongside a petite gold hummingbird pendant.

"Trudy gave me this necklace for our one-year Friendaversary, as she called it."

Jimmy flinched, and she glanced at him, her brows puckered in question. "What?"

"Nothing." He cleared his throat. "Horsefly."

"Oh. It's gone? Good. Well, she gave me this on the one-year anniversary of our meeting. The only time I take it off is at night, to sleep." She inhaled, filling her lungs with his earthy male scent, spiked with wet red clay and pasture. It smelled like home. "I will make you a promise."

Elise held the two ends of the necklace out, and he took them wordlessly. He fastened it around her neck, and she contemplated her next words.

"I will marry you, Jimmy," she promised, squarely facing him. "I will wear your ring around my neck, close to my heart, until the day you feel you can tell me everything. I love with no holds barred. I expect the same in return. When that day comes, I will marry you on the spot."

His Adam's apple bobbed as he swallowed, but a shy smile stretched from the corners of his mouth to the lined edges of his eyes. But his shoulders carried a disappointed slump, and she felt his hurt keenly.

"I promise to be the man you deserve." He closed his eyes, as though praying, and an infant fire sprang to life beneath her sternum. She felt the same, the light of – what? – new life, a hope not there before. "I *will* be your husband, Elise Gomez. Find your contact, get the new identity documentation. No, don't argue."

She closed her mouth, pinched her lips together.

"It has to be this way. There has to be no chance of you showing up on someone's radar, honey. And Elise? I want you to tell Matthew, obviously. Talk it over with him. But –"

His lips grazed hers with a lingering kiss. The spark inside grew to a bonfire as she lost herself in his touch. Day's end whiskers sanded her chin, an afterthought only. She no longer noticed the cool evening air, and was breathless by the time he retreated. His cheeks were flushed, but the happiness on his face was replaced by the sudden pucker of his eyebrows into worry.

"But?" she asked, a hand caressing his stubbled cheek.

"Please, don't tell Trudy. Not yet."

Don't tell Trudy. Long after his shadowed form disappeared from sight over a hillock, more than an hour after she and her nestled secret returned to the quiet cabin, his words echoed. Elise debated on telling Matthew tonight, but found she wanted to huddle with the hidden knowledge of her promised engagement, and keep it to herself. Just for one night. She had to dodge Matthew's questions about why she was smiling so much, but eventually he shrugged and stopped asking, no doubt more intent on the last few minutes of screen time he was allowed before bed.

Outside her bedroom window, a cricket chirped, its high-pitched violin song calling to his fellows and they responding with enthusiastic chirruping replies. The basket of laundry on her bed was not going to fold itself, so she sat and began the monotonous, never ending task. Her mind drifted while she folded, and scattered thoughts turned to prayer. She found herself asking God why Jimmy wanted to keep Trudy in the dark about their engagement. It niggled at her, made her uneasy.

Her finger brushed against a straggled, dangling thread. Elise *tsked,* reaching for the sharp nail scissors she kept in the nightstand drawer. She brought the pair of underwear into the light, the better to see the snag. As she traced the thread to its root, her finger brushed against something oblong and hard, but miniscule, stuck in the raveling seam. What was that? A seed, a stone?

Grumbling about getting older, she reached once more into the drawer. With her reading glasses firmly in place, she held the garment closer to the bulb. Like pressing a splinter out of the skin, she pressed downward, and squeezed. *Something* shot out, skidding across the tabletop with barely a clink in its wake. With nimble fingers, she pinched it between two fingers.

Smaller than a sunflower kernel, but similar in shape, it had a glasslike casing around a silvery center. It looked electronic.

Nanotech. The word blossomed in her brain.

Don't tell Trudy.

"No," she said aloud to the still, lace curtains. "Please, no."

Chapter 29

Near the Texas border of Unified Socialist America

The coarse woolen hood was ripped away, and with it, clumps of hair still attached to the scalp, taking skin as well. It burned. But amidst the sharp fiery stabs of pain spread over her body, she hardly cared. They shoved her onto a stool, and unbalanced, she crashed heavily onto her side on the frigid concrete floor. Her captor cursed, and his boot thudded into her stomach, knocking the breath from her in a blinding explosion. His vulgar rant subsided, fading from the room. At least he had left her alone. For now.

How long had it been, she wondered, since she had been taken by the smiling woman in the clean khaki pants and collared shirt? Pink. The shirt had been pink, with a little embroidered animal on the chest, just above where her heart would have been. A howling wolf. It was the symbol she had been instructed to seek out and follow in the dated, but clean, roadside café near the border north of Texarkana.

Leave your vehicle at the recharging station called The Last Stop, *two miles south of the border station. Walk half a mile north to the café on the right side of the road. Your contact will be wearing a wolf on her shirt.*

The anonymous email. She had been so desperate for the story. Ambition had clouded her judgment, fogged her thinking. Who sent the email and why?

She shivered and huddled in a comma-shaped mound of scrapes, cuts, and bruises, eyes still cemented shut from edema, caked blood, and fear. Tandy thought with a rueful laugh that they had not needed to cover her head when they brought her here. The beatings blinded her effectively enough.

She did not realize she had laughed aloud until his steel toe boot connected with her kidney. Another burst of red-hot pain shot down her back and hamstrings, all the way to her toes, and she groaned. Nausea rose and crested, threatening to erupt.

"Something funny, little mole," he growled, his voice like gravel under tires. "If I had known you enjoyed it, I could have given you more, sweetheart."

Tandy whimpered, her head bunched and touching her knees, crying silently. He had raped her first, before the beatings began. And after. During. Three days? Four?

Absolute determination had its price. What did they want with her?

When would they kill her?

The woman in pink, with her oily smile, had placed her in the back seat of a nondescript sedan. She motioned to the driver, and they pulled onto the deserted highway. Excited, nervous, and anxious, she turned her upper body and prepared to ask her escort a question; but as she opened her mouth, the woman in pink slammed a needle into her thigh, and the world faded to a prick of light, then vanished altogether.

They had called her by name. She remembered that, shaking in the fetal position in the brightly lit room. Light. Her eyelids glowed, and she twitched. In the beginning, they questioned her; when she refused to answer, the beatings began. By the end of the first hour she had spilled all the information she had on the petite black-haired woman and the sheriff. Everything she knew, and whatever she suspected. Hours, days pulsed and faded until her captors were sure she held no more information.

Rough viselike hands clamped onto both arms, and hauled her upright. She complied, knowing the price of disobedience. Tandy was ready for the stool this time, and braced her wobbly legs to hold her onto the round, cold seat.

"Now that's a good girl," Gravel Voice crooned. "You behave, and I'll be nice to you later." She shivered, and it had nothing to do with temperature.

A few minutes later, shuffling feet announced another person in the room. Haltingly, she attempted to open her eyes. Only the right one cooperated, opening the barest of slits. She saw what looked like stage lighting, and a stunted man bending over a piece of equipment. A camera?

They wanted to send a message. The moment of clarity in her pain-corrupted brain blazed, a ray of hope. Maybe they were ransoming her? She wasn't big time yet, but her last piece on El Lobo had made the national news.

Shorty finished his preparation and turned, making a face of disgust as he looked at her, spitting off to the side. He probably thought she could not see him beneath the swollen, blackened twin orbs on her face.

Advancing on her, he swiped a dingy hand across his mouth, and cocked his head to the side, evaluating.

"You see outta that face, mole?"

Rather than answer, she clenched her jaw, instantly regretting the action. She had more than a few loose teeth, and several lacerations in her mouth. Mimicking his earlier behavior, she spat off to the side, her spittle thick with blood. A curt nod answered his question.

The disgusting little man withdrew a rolled and flattened sheet of paper from his back pocket, and thrust it at her. After one last hateful glance in his direction, she peered at the paper he gave her.

Her stomach sank, and her heart throttled her chest.

Not ransom. Tandy Newman was bait.

Chapter 30

The glowing numbers on the alarm clock taunted her. For the four-hundred and thirty-seventh time, she flopped over onto her other side, flipping her pillow as well. Tomorrow – no, today, she realized grimly – was Friday, the last day of the week, but one of the busiest for Doc Cora as far as patients were concerned. Hours on her feet, the hustle up and down the hallway, washing soiled linens and folding the clean ones, sterilizing the Doc's tools. All on less than three hours' sleep, if she were to fall asleep this second.

Which would not happen, because all she could think about were the more than four dozen seed-sized tech bits she had found hidden and sewn into her clothing, and even her shoes. Elise had resisted the urge to raid Matthew's chest of drawers and pull out the sum total of his clothing to inspect them as well, but only barely. The small voice of logic whispered into the still night air, *You know they are there, so leave them until tomorrow and go to sleep.*

Elise rolled onto her back, stared through the grit of sleeplessness at the hazy grayish-green shadow of the lamp on the ceiling, and contemplated betrayal. For no other person had the access to her wardrobe besides Trudy. Every single undergarment concealed one, some two.

Tracking devices, she was certain. Her troubled, exhausted brain fumbled with tying the devices and Trudy together, yet she knew the woman she called sister was responsible. Which led to the question: who did she work for?

A yawning void filled the part of Elise that was simply *her* in the most basic sense of the word; the deep well of her true being, like a secret name known only to her, and now God. Her soul bore a mottled bruise where trust once lived. It threatened to implode, drawing her in as a black hole funnels matter into the nowhere somewhere on the other side. She blinked, and it hurt, like moist sandpaper scraping her eyelids from the inside. The result of crying until the tears no longer flowed, and sheer weariness from the absence of slumber.

Her hand drifted to the chain around her neck, to the golden bird and its new companion, the garnet cabochon. Had it only been a few hours since she promised herself to Jimmy? A lifetime had passed between sunset and the wee hours of the morning. She held the promise ring, worrying it like others counted rosaries. The cold figure of the bird rested on her chest. Disgusted, Elise bolted upright and switched on the lamp, no longer wanting anything Trudy had gifted her to touch her skin. Fatigue-clumsy fingers fiddled with the clasp until it released, and yanked the golden bird from the chain and tossed it into the nightstand drawer.

"Probably another tracking device anyway," she mumbled to the walls.

Elise's legs dangled off the side of the bed, her feet hovering inches off the floor. Too early to do anything without waking Matthew, and too late to try to get some sleep. The glowing numbers read 3:47. A fly buzzed and bumped into the window, bouncing back and forth like a ping pong ball between the curtain and the glass. She sympathized with a fly for once in her life.

As she rolled the kinks from her neck and upper back, she decided a shower was her best option. Then maybe she could catch up on her reading. She pulled clean – and debugged – clothes from the lumpy pile at the end of the bed, and then padded down the hallway barefoot. Trudy's door remained open, and as she saw when she peeked inside the bedroom, the bed unoccupied and still neatly made. Where was the coward? Bitterness burned in her throat, and she whirled and dashed across the hall to the bathroom.

Twenty steamy minutes later, hair towel-mussed and fully dressed, Elise unfurled a crocheted afghan and snuggled onto the couch with a mystery novel set in 18th-century England. The lamp cast its warm, yellow light across her shoulders and onto the page, and she was transported to slick cobblestone streets smelling of filth and greasy meat pies, and skulking devils hiding in plain sight.

A chapter and a half into the story, the book tipped and tumbled into her lap, oblivious to the soft snore of the woman who once held it.

Jimmy watched the sun rise from the old rocking chair on the front porch, sipping on coffee too hot to gulp. The nippy air raised goosebumps on his bare forearms. A tardy bat swooped low, its shrill call echoing off elderly trees and guiding the winged creature, then darted off with a haphazard flap of tissue-thin wings. Crows cawed at one another overhead. In the distance, mockingbirds mimicked them. As the sun climbed, rays glinted off the dew, millions of diamonds adorning the long blades of grass.

A normal beginning to an anything-but-ordinary day.

With a regretful sigh, he stood. The screen door thwacked shut behind him. He found himself staring at the dining table.

Fifteen years of service lay on the beeswax-buffed wood, folded and stacked in a neat brown and khaki square, with his sidearm and badge topping it. It had taken five minutes to sum up more than half his life.

Judge Waters was an early bird, often in her wood-paneled office by seven o'clock. He planned to march into her domain, shoulders square and nerves beaten into submission, lay the stack of county property on her desk, and hand in his written resignation. If possible, exit without speaking, maybe add a respectful nod on the way out the door. He thought it would work. Possibly. Like a swift and deadly airstrike.

At which point, he would transition to life as a civilian, about to covertly marry a federally-wanted person of interest who happened to be the key to obliterating one of the largest human trafficking organizations in history, while avoiding arrest for obstruction of justice, and maintaining secrecy about an undercover TBI agent who happened to be the lying Judas of a best friend to his affianced.

He snorted. No problem.

But first, he needed to get out of his faded purple SFA Lumberjacks t-shirt and plaid boxers, shower, and dress for the day.

A fierce knocking ensued as his hand turned the hot water knob. He rolled his eyes, gritted his molars, and crawled into his ratty old robe as he trotted down the hall. Hastily tying the frayed belt, he rounded the corner where the hall met the foyer, and stopped cold when he saw Elise framed by the screen door.

"What is it? Is Matthew okay?" He shoved open the door, and she rushed to him. She smelled of honeysuckle, and oddly, wool. "Baby, what's wrong? You're trembling."

She held him for minute longer, squeezed tight, and pulled away.

"Open your hand," she commanded, her voice shaking as she unscrewed the lid of a glass Mason jar. "Cup it. Yes, like that."

Dozens of beads tickled the soft part of his inner palm.

"Look closely," Elise said to his questioning glance.

He edged closer to the window. Sunlight glinted off bits of oval glass. But inside, they looked silver. Metal. His eyes flew open.

"Nanotrackers?"

A grim slash of her lips was the only answer she gave. There were easily three dozen, close to four. "Where did you get these?"

She explained how the chore of folding laundry turned into a frantic examination of every stitch of clothing she owned, and that she was sure there were more hiding in her son's closet and dresser. Elise paced as she related the sleepless night, and being jolted from couch slumber when Matthew awoke, banging and slamming through cabinets in search of breakfast.

"He's wearing them, on his body, at this moment. I – I couldn't tell him. That we had been monitored for who knows how long, and that his Aunt – Aunt ..."

Jimmy pulled Elise in close, the clenched hand holding the trackers supporting her back, and smoothed his hand over the nape of her neck, gentling her. He whispered into her hair, his breath a warm rebound on his lips. "I wanted to tell you. I only found out yesterday. Trudy came to the sheriff's station yesterday."

He felt her temper flare under his hold a second before she flung herself out of his arms. "That my so-called *best friend* has been working for El Lobo this whole time!"

Startled, he shook his head. "No. No, honey, she's Texas Bureau of Investigation."

Elise froze, her lips parted a fraction of an inch. She made as though to speak again, and clamped her mouth shut. Then in a voice that would shatter the hardest heart. "I don't know who she is. She is a stranger to me."

Dust motes sparkled in the slanted swipe of morning sunlight through the screen door, dancing around her heedless of the heavy emotion weighing down the room. Her head hung, dejected, black hair falling in choppy locks to conceal her face. His palms sweated around the slippery mound of the nanotrackers he held.

He thought this type of device only traced and plotted geographic positioning; he dimly recalled at his last annual training that the ones capable of recording audio and visual events were larger, but no bigger than a fingernail. Jimmy imagined there were a few of those discreetly hidden around whatever house was home for them, every time they fled a city or town. The a/v nanotech employed a stealth casing, modeled after stealth fighter jets, and standard bug sweepers missed them nearly a hundred percent of the time.

His mind leapfrogged ahead along the thought-train tracks in his brain. Bugs. Info-mining. Undetectable. A reporter who knew more than she should.

"She didn't!" he exclaimed, and Elise jumped, hugging her arms against her stomach.

In a miserable croak, she agreed with him, but he shook his head. "No, not Trudy. I mean Tandy Newman, that reporter."

"The missing one?"

He clamped his thumb and forefinger around one of the trackers, holding it in the air. "I think you're not the only one who was under surveillance."

Chapter 31

The first comm message came through ten minutes after the glass doors of the county courthouse and Judge Waters' office closed behind him with a soft click. Half a dozen calls later, he resigned himself to letting voicemail fend off the masses. He would screen them later. News in small towns traveled faster than a shotgun wedding happened after prom night, and though he had expected it, the explaining did not get easier with the telling. Too many secrets, not enough reasons. As Cotton Springs came into view, he slowed the cruiser. His assistant – no, former assistant – planned to drive out with another deputy to retrieve the official vehicle at the end of the business day. First, the guys not out on patrol would be going over the office building, his former office in particular, with a fine-toothed comb. His gut knew they would find some type of recording device.

Just as Cora's place came into view on the right, he made the snap decision to stop for a visit, see how Elise was holding up after a night with no sleep. The tires bit into the gravelly drive, the crunch of rocks overpowering the sound of the electric engine. Ben Tucker, his back to the drive and brushing his monstrosity of a horse, turned as Jimmy pulled up and saluted a greeting with the curry comb. An idea sprung to life, full of hope and anticipation. Why hadn't he thought of it before?

The Mountain ambled toward him, and so did his Beast, until Ben shook his head and grabbed the lead rope. He looped it over the hitching post and dumped a can of feed on the ground with a sharp, "Stay, Goliath." He gently slapped the horse on the rump, and got a tail-flick to the face for his troubles.

"Don't know why I put up with the monster," Ben mumbled as he took Jimmy's hand.

"Because he's the only horse on the planet that could hold you?"

With a snort, Ben smiled. "Funny guy." He flicked his chin toward the cottage. "You here to see mine or yours?"

"Hmm. Mine, but you first."

It took a good-sized blow to stun Ben Tucker. Learning about the resignation from the sheriff's office seemed to have the effect of a sledgehammer to the face. Dumbstruck, the bounty hunter's eyes glinted like fiery emeralds in a sea of diamonds.

"You ...*resigned?* Are you flippin' insane, man?" His voice rose an octave with every word. "You put in too many years to give up like that."

Jimmy raked tanned fingers down his face, and shrugged. "Don't think I did this lightly. But I told Katherine Miles, I swore to her that I would turn Elise in, if and when I should make contact with her. *After* we had already started dating again. It wasn't right, Ben. I could not keep lying, wondering when someone would see us together, and report it. I could still be brought up on charges, for Pete's sake! Obstruction, at the very least."

Beside him, Ben kicked a dirt clod down the puddled drive, where it landed in a rusty, sludgy pool of brackish rain.

"Yeah, well, I suppose I can see your way to it. Just a shame, that's all. So, what? You looking for a job?" Ben threw his head and laughed at the sky.

"Actually, um," he mumbled, a twist to his mouth. "I do. Want a job. Ready to take on an assistant? Someone you've known almost your whole life? Excellent job set and good references." For the moment, at least.

"Are you kidding me?"

"I wish, but no. I'm not."

Ben rubbed the bristle coming up along his chin. "Tell you what. Let's go see the women, and I'll figure something out."

Elise looked up from the mound of white cotton sheets she was folding when he walked into the home clinic. Her dark eyes were shadowed, ringed with blue-black exhaustion, but her smile was a bright sun burning through the fatigue cloud. The promise ring sparked just below the shallow scoop at her collarbone, nearly the color of the scarlet scrubs she wore, and his heart tightened in pleasure at the sight. She *would* be his.

Ben brushed past with a thump on the shoulder, heading down the hall to Cora's clinic room.

No patients waited, and when asked about others, Elise shook her head.

"Light day, and thank goodness for it. Not just for myself," she added, massaging the small of her back. She angled a quick nod down the hallway leading to the treatment room. "Doc's been contracting a lot today, but she won't say anything about it. A mother knows, though."

Jimmy moved to stand just behind Elise, and used his thumbs to knead the base of her neck. Nearly purring in relief, her head hung loose upon her shoulders. An enthusiastic raspberry sound, quickly trailed by hilarious giggles, came from the clinic. He couldn't help but smile. Ben was a good father, and little Kitty had him wrapped around her chubby finger.

Matthew was too old for tickling and tummy raspberries, but still young enough to need a father. Jimmy felt, with God's guidance, that he was up to the job. Matthew would be coming to the age of flirtation and infatuation, hormones, and the Big Questions about life. With sudden clarity, Jimmy realized Elise's son must think of himself as the man of the house; would the boy accept him, be able to relinquish the assumed role? He hoped so. It was no burden for a teenager to bear.

Elise peeled herself away from his thumbs, and turned to face him. "You're thinking so hard I can hear you."

He chuckled. "Sorry. It's been a strange day, as you well know. You are, by far, the best part of it."

She swiveled her head, taking in the empty room, and leaned in to whisper, "Is it done? You resigned?"

Jimmy nodded and planted a kiss on her forehead. She leaned into him with a sigh. "Everything is arranged. For that matter we spoke of last night."

The new identity and papers for her and Matthew.

Laughter echoed and bounced from the clinic, down the hallway, and it reminded him of his conversation with Ben in the yard. He told her his idea for new employment. Elise tapped a thoughtful finger on her bottom lip.

She grinned. "Actually, I think that's an excellent idea. You have the knowledge necessary for the investigations, and having worked closely with Ben and other trackers, you know the laws. What would you need to do?"

"Take the certification test and become licensed," Jimmy replied with a shrug. "Shouldn't be too hard. How long before you hear back from your contact?"

A couple of days, the woman had said. Elise looked wistfully at the round dining table. He hadn't noticed the baskets, filled to overflowing, displayed strategically to grab the attention of Cora's patients. It thrilled him to see Elise's baked goods up for sale.

"Took a good bit of the rest of my emergency fund to get the ... items ... on such short notice, though. I'll have to work here at the clinic for a while longer before I can realistically go forward with the bakery." He frowned, but she waved a hand in dismissal. "It's okay, Jimmy. Truly. We are worth it."

But it was not acceptable to him. He had money set aside, more than he needed. Speculation turned the brainstorming cogs, and an idea took shape.

His thoughts were interrupted by a shout from the clinic.

"Y'all get back here and look at this!" Ben boomed.

With a startled shared glance, Jimmy and Elise rushed through the hallway and into the treatment room. Cora stared at the viewscreen, one hand supporting her very round pregnant belly, the other covering a gaping mouth. Ben, behind her to the right, rested an enormous hand on her shoulder while holding Kitty on the opposite hip. The doc turned her rounded eyes on him.

"Jimmy, that slave ring has the reporter, the one from the East Texas News." She pointed unnecessarily at the screen.

"Can you replay it from the beginning?" he asked, but she was already sliding the icon to the left.

Hardly recognizable as a human, much less as the attractive young journalist, Tandy Newman teetered on a battered stool, facing the camera. Her eyes were swollen shut, so that only a slit opened on one eye. Purplish black and blue, crusted with rust-colored dried blood, Tandy's face had been pulverized. Behind her, rugged bare concrete block walls served as the background. It could have been any location, above ground or below. He thought below, though, because of water stains trailing along the junctures of the gray blocks.

Newman held a paper, and began to read from it. Her speech was slurred, and no wonder. Her lips were split and bloody, inflamed and swollen. The words she spoke chilled the blood coursing through his veins.

"I caught a Mole in my back yard.

It doesn't pay to dig too hard."

The lacerations on the poor girl's lips fissured, leaking blood trails down her chin. Pity washed over him, hearing her monotone rasp on-screen. Tandy lifted her head and stared into the camera boldly. So, a fighter then. That explained the extensive physical damage. The hands holding the wrinkled paper in her lap were swollen and bruised, cracked and coated with dried blood; but amazingly, she straightened her shoulders a fraction of an inch and continued with a hint of defiance.

"Blackbird, Blackbird, once you flew,

But it's time to come home again.

Your life for the Mole,

And the chick makes me whole,
Your son flies on the wind."

The blood drained from Jimmy's face, and a shiver shuttered through his body, a jolt of white lightening, fierce and brilliant. Elise gripped his forearm, leaving divots where crescent-shaped nails dug into the skin.

Frantically, Elise tapped the face of the wristcom. Her eyes were black caverns in a face whitened with fear. The call connected and she swallowed, then rasped, "This is Elise Gomez. Can you please ask Matthew to come to the office. I will be picking him up in five minutes."

"I, uh – hold one minute, Mrs. Gomez," the secretary replied, her voice hesitant and questioning.

Beside them, Kitty babbled in Ben's arms, heedless of the gravity of the situation. The silence spoke, in the hushed sounds of deep breaths, shifting feet, and the soft whish-click of the front door opening on the other side of the house.

Cora turned toward the door, saying, "Probably my next patient." Ben, however, urged her with a light squeeze to stay. She gazed up, and after a brief wordless consult, stood in place.

Classical music flitted around while the call was held. Though the live streaming report had been muted, images of the continuing American riots played across the screen. Shaken fists, burning flags, angry faces yelling at the camera. Then the hold music ceased, and a male voice spoke.

"Mrs. Gomez, this is the principal, Roger Sykes. I, um, I am afraid I don't understand. Matthew was picked up an hour ago by your brother. We have a note with your signature authorizing it."

Elise whispered, "I do not have a brother." She wavered, and Cora darted over, steadying her and leading Elise to the examination table.

Jimmy unsnapped the wristcom from Elise's arm, and spoke in concise terms, explaining the situation. He ended the call with shaking hands, and racing heart.

"Where is he?" Elise wailed at the ceiling. "Oh, my boy! How could she? That stupid reporter!" She sobbed into his chest, and Jimmy rocked her, his heart shattering with every tear soaking into his shirt. "How did she find El Lobo?"

"I can answer that," Trudy Blue said from the open doorway.

Chapter 32

One hour.

The fictitious uncle and Matthew were one hour ahead of them, and gaining, with each passing minute of deliberation. Jimmy and Ben huddled in the corner behind Cora's desk, both keeping one eye on the news while developing a strategy to find her son and bring him home before they reached the border. She, meanwhile, chewed her nails and silently prayed.

Oh, mijo. My baby. God, let him be safe.

Elise winced at a sharp stab of pain, and clenched her burning fingertip into a fist. It had been years since she had bitten her nails. The ring finger stung and throbbed, its nail chewed to the quick. Outside, Trudy passed in front of the window, gesticulating wildly, and disappeared once more around the corner of the house. She had been on her communicator nearly non-stop since she tried, futilely, to explain her betrayal. Sickened, Elise had turned her back on the only sister she had known, and told her to get out of her sight.

The utter depth of duplicity stunned Elise. Trudy had tried, through sheeting tears, to reassure her that her relationship with Jimmy remained confidential, that the undercover agent had stopped reporting as frequently over the years and only checked in when necessary; the latest was the move to Nacogdoches. As far as the Bureau knew, according to Trudy, Elise and Matthew were still there. She claimed to have inactivated the trackers, only having turned them on once in the last month; that had been the day Matthew had disappeared on his run.

The trackers. But ...yes! She had not gotten around to removing them from Matthew's clothing! Elise hopped off the table, and Jimmy's eyes flew to hers.

"What? What is it, honey?"

"Matthew! He might be wearing a tracker!"

Trudy looked horrid. Red-rimmed eyes swelled, and splotches marred her face. Elise found it difficult to feel sorry for her, but a tiny part of her did. She loved the woman, but the love was trampled and bruised, encapsulated in raw hurt, disappointment, and distrust. Elise forced herself to forget the unfaithfulness, and direct her concentration to finding her son.

"Elise?" Trudy asked, unsure, worried eyebrows raised. She realized the woman had called her name before, but she had not heard.

"Yes, Agent Blue."

Trudy closed her eyes, swallowed, then repeated herself. "You haven't told Matthew? About ... who I am?"

"No," Elise replied curtly. "As far as he's concerned, you're Aunt Trudy."

The woman exhaled in a gust. "Well, that's something."

"A lie, is what it is."

"Elise, please – "

"No." She held up a hand, forestalling the argument. "We find Matthew. That is all I need you to do at the moment."

Jimmy's arm tightened around her collarbone. His arms encircled her from behind, acting as rigid support. She drew strength from him, and coldly eyed Trudy Blue.

Another quieter exhalation, and the agent nodded. "He has one active tracker, but an old one. Kids are hard on their clothing, and ..." She trailed off, shrugging. "The signal is weak, but there."

She pointed to a blue dot fading in and out on Cora's viewscreen. "They're heading north, not quite to Marshall. It would coincide with the intel we have on Newman's border crossing."

Another pained looked skittered across Trudy's face, and no wonder. She confessed to sending the reporter the anonymous email. Everything had gone horribly wrong, though. The intel was outdated, it seemed, and the incorrect key word Trudy provided had alerted the El Lobo thugs that something was off. Surveillance at the border had proved to be a dead end, as the video recording equipment had been offline for maintenance. A fact Trudy admitted to be too convenient not to be suspicious.

"I've been in contact with my supervisor, and agents are en-route to intercept Matthew at the border." Trudy tried to reach out to console Elise, but she turned aside the gesture, and the agent's hand fell to her side. "As long as the signal holds, we'll get him back, Elise. I love him, too, you know."

Trudy sobbed the last word, and stumbled from the room. The bathroom door clicked, and the muffled sound of a blown nose seeped through the walls.

Jimmy took her by the shoulders, spinning her to face him, and smothered her in an embrace. His scent, woodsy and earthy, drifted lazily, relaxing her. As much as she could, under the circumstances.

"Let's take a walk."

She followed, numb, out of the rear kitchen door. Cora and Ben's yard was in full bloom, a riotous rainbow of colors and blooms. Bees and butterflies busied themselves among the petals. A calming breeze fluttered limbs and leaves in the shadows of aging oaks and tall pines which surrounded the landscaped garden. Cultivated pathways allowed for easy harvesting. A cedar bench beckoned in the shade, but Elise needed to move. She would go insane sitting still. Waiting, helpless, for news from the woman who betrayed her to the Texas government.

A white moth soared and dipped on the air currents. She followed its trek to land on a grassy explosion with purplish bottlebrush heads. One day she would learn all the plants in the Doc's garden. Oh, to be able to fly like the birds. Overhead, a crow called; agitated, it darted to the ground to harry a fat, ruddy squirrel. Probably guarding a nest of eggs.

As though reading her thoughts, Jimmy spoke into the busy quietude. "They call you Blackbird."

Her brows rose in surprise. "Who?"

"The Bureau." His kiss to the top of her hair shivered from hairline to toes. "It's your codename. Blackbird."

Absently, she ghosted a hand over her short, raven black hair. Then, reality crashed over her in waves. Her son, her Matthew, the one she braved death to protect, was at the mercy of his captors. A life on the run, of hiding at the first sign of trouble, all for nothing. All a lie, since the government had eyes on her from almost the beginning. Lies and deceit, cloaked in the guise of sisterhood.

The tremor began in her shoulders, and spread like an earthquake to the tips of fingers and toes. She collapsed on the cobblestone path, shaking and sobbing. Jimmy rocked her like he did the day she told him about her past.

"It's like I'm his slave again," she said brokenly, words forced from a throat tight with hopelessness. "The Wolf has my baby. And I can do nothing about it. Nothing!" Another wracking sob shook her, and she collapsed further into her man's arms. Minutes passed within the sun-dappled shade of the garden, where her only link to the real world were Jimmy's arms and his hushed reassurances that they would find her son.

"No matter what," he whispered, laying a gentle kiss on her temple. He swiped a thumb under her eye to clear away the wetness.

Elise stared, through a sheet of salty tears, at the red cotton of her scrubs, and thought of blood. The blood she shed escaping from The Wolf, and the blood of birth, when her son came into the world. Unable to countenance harm done to Matthew, she shook her head violently, as though to scatter the chaotic images her mind was producing. Jimmy hugged her closer.

It was some time before she understood his words, spoken softly into a world still alive, still vibrant with lush beauty around them. He prayed. Nothing stiff or formal. Heart-rending pleas on her and Matthew's behalf, and prayers for Tandy Newman. She focused on his words, and imagined herself prostrate before the feet of Jesus, begging for the life of her son; and grudgingly, that of the reporter.

Ever so slowly, the peace of God's presence covered her. Her body calmed, and her soul sighed in relief. Whatever happened, she knew God loved her.

A fat, black carpenter ant scuttled across the back of her hand, tickling its way to the other side. Birdsong flitted from shrub to tree as she wiped away the last of the tears. She and Jimmy huddled together, listening to nature surround them with the humming assurance that God provides for even the smallest of creatures.

"He will bring Matthew home," she said.

"Yes," he affirmed. He traced a finger along the chain around her neck, and pulled the ring from its warm home near her heart. "I promise."

Unexpectedly bold, she stole a kiss. This man grounded her, tethered her to hope, and anchored her in the knowledge of love. She craved him. But as he deepened the kiss, the screen door of the kitchen squawked open, then slammed shut with a *crack!*

Ben filled the doorway, shading his eyes. His gaze lit upon them, and he bounded down the stairs.

"School security pulled the image of the vehicle from the parking lot cameras. We have a plate. Sheriff's office has signed off on the contract. We're clear to go."

Jimmy sought her face with a questioning stare. She nodded, and stood, brushed off the ground debris from her scrubs.

"I'm ready. Let's go get my boy."

Beside her, Jimmy clutched her hand, and made as if to angle around the house, but Ben stopped them.

He ran a hand through his tousled hair. "I know how you feel, Elise. I do, trust me. But," he said, a cringe wrinkling his mouth and eyes, "can you stay with Cora? She's been holding her belly all day, and I am afraid to leave her alone. I know it's a lot to ask – "

Elise inhaled, and at Jimmy's hairsbreadth nod, laid a hand on Ben's forearm. "Of course. Just, bring Matthew home. Please. He is my world."

Ben nodded, and as he and Jimmy angled around the house, Ben turned his head and yelled with a sad grin, "I'll take care of your world, and you watch over mine."

Chapter 33

Cora retreated to the house, telling Elise she needed to put the rugrat down for a nap. The crunch of tires over gravel had long since faded, and Elise found herself circling the cobbled pathway through the doc's extensive garden once more. She wandered through mottled shadows and blazes of sunlight, yesterday's rain a soggy memory discovered in low-lying shady pools and puddles.

Fear had stolen her heart, as though the integral, essential organ were removed and cast far away. Hollow, and expectant. Worry scampered through her thoughts, and dread crouched in the dark recesses, waiting for an opportunity to pounce and dominate. Her hands itched, her mind galloped restlessly. The need to *do something* warred with the inability to do anything at all. While Ben and Jimmy raced to find Matthew, she was left here to watch over Cora.

She snagged a palm-sized rock from beside the pathway and hurled it into the woods. It *thunked* hollowly against a tree trunk, and the lower limbs exploded with the startled, flapping wings of doves. Useless! Elise hadn't grown a backbone only to sit around being a babysitter to a hugely pregnant woman!

Guilt nudged worry out of the way, and she regretted the thought an instant after it formed. The doc had given her employment with no questions asked, and was helping get her bakery off the ground. No, she would not resent her assignment. If only there was something she could do to help bring her son home.

Elise lifted the oiled latch, and closed the gate behind her. She paced around the exterior of the house, kicking downed limbs and scattering gravel while she chewed over the ineffectiveness of her situation. What she wanted to do was punch something, and she eyed the solid wood siding of the cottage with speculation. Disgusted with herself, she rolled her eyes, and lengthened her stride as she turned the corner to the front of the cottage.

Trudy slumped on the white porch swing. Its chains groaned under the slow undulation, masking the sound of Elise's steps. Elise turned, prepared to retreat to the back door; then she squared her shoulders, and refused to run. She would face her betrayer.

The words floated in waves over her subconscious: *Forgive her.* Shaking her head in refusal, she marched around the end of the porch, the swing protesting above her. The swing halted in mid-squeak when Trudy noticed Elise's footfalls on the wooden steps.

Tears streaked Trudy's face, her mascara running in fine rivulets, only to be swept away with the back of a hand. Elise did not know how to even think of the woman in front of her. Once called sister, friend, companion, she found it difficult to assign an identity. Anger thrived in the place of sisterhood, and treason superseded trust.

231

Elise positioned herself squarely in front of Trudy, standing with shoulders straight and confident, though she felt anything but.

"How could you?"

Trudy's face threatened to crumple in on itself. She sniffled, wiping her nose with a wet sleeve. "It was my job," she answered brokenly. "At first, anyway." She met Elise's glare without flinching. "I love you, Elise. You're the only sister I have ever known."

"Sister?" Elise's voice rose shrill. "I trusted you with my life, with Matthew's life. I loved you as a sister, too. But you know what? I'm done. How could I ever trust you again?"

Trudy lowered her head. Tears dropped onto her knees, making darkened wet circles where they soaked into the linen of her suit pants. Elise despised the venom dripping from her own mouth, but deception was bitter to the taste.

Still gazing at the worn porch boards, Trudy said, "I have been reassigned." Her clutched hands writhed slowly in her lap, grappling each other. "To Austin, the main office. I – I need to go home and pack." Her voice broke on the word *home*, and Elise's chest tightened. "After today, you don't have to see me again."

Forgive, came the still voice of command.

NO! she raged silently. But aloud, she bit off the words, "Don't let me hold you up."

Elise's hand gripped the screen door's knob, when Trudy sobbed behind her, "Will you write to me? About Matthew, at least? Please?"

With a frigid glare, she turned once more to face her former friend. "Go away, Agent Blue. Your work here is done."

She slammed the door with the force of cold finality, and collapsed against it on the other side. Sobs wracked her, shaking her shoulders, and she covered her mess of a face with both hands.

***

"It could be worse," Ben claimed with a twisted half-grin, glancing at Jimmy for a moment before turning his attention back to the road. "We could be on horseback."

Jimmy snorted, acknowledging the truth of the tracker's statement. "This makes no sense," he said, pointing to the truck's on-board display. "There is nothing out here besides trees and chiggers. And the Sabine river, but there are border patrols out in full force, with all the American riots going on."

They were nearing the border between Texas and the Louisiana District. Not only was there no easily accessible crossing, but the trajectory of the surveillance device was taking them nowhere near where the reporter's vehicle had been found near the Arkansas District. Currently, the blue dot representing Matthew lazily blinked itself east along Hwy 43. Ben had the pedal floored on the long, deserted stretches of highway. His vehicle was registered with the state as an official bounty hunter and tracker transport, so any patrolmen they encountered who scanned them as they flew by would see the wireless transmission on their readouts indicating he was in pursuit of a criminal. Being a member of Ben's team in an official capacity seemed more appealing as the trees blurred outside the window. But he remained baffled at the roundabout way the kidnapper was trying to smuggle Matthew across the border.

Ben glanced over at the palm-sized screen. "Still on 43?"

"Yeah." Jimmy shook his head. "I don't get it. That leads right into the Army Ammunition Plant."

"And Caddo Lake."

"And Caddo Lake. They must have a boat on standby, but heck if I know how the Army hasn't noticed it."

They drove in silence for the next twenty minutes, the cheerful cloud-splotched sky making light of his heavy heart. Carthage gleamed dully in the side-view mirror. In the wake of their accelerated dash through the center of town, horses reared and danced at the end of their reins; their owners pumped fists in the air, gesticulating wildly. It was almost comic. Almost.

Jimmy studied the palm screen once more, then blinked when he realized the change. "It stopped. Ben, they're at the lake."

The tracker mumbled words which blushed Jimmy's cheeks, then muttered an apology. Jimmy echoed the sentiment, although mutely.

They drove, and he stared, until the blue dot was his world, narrowed into one tiny focused pinpoint. The tracking device never wavered after it halted.

"Are you sure it's not on the water?"

"For the twelfth time, Ben, no. It's still at the edge. Drive faster, will ya?"

"I'm going as fast as the truck can go."

Jimmy fidgeted in his seat, tapping the window ledge rapidly. He looked at Ben, and found his friend's jaw knotted and the pulse in his neck throbbing rapidly. They were both on edge.

"You called it in?" Ben asked again.

"You heard me do it," Jimmy gritted through clenched teeth. He forced himself to relax. It wasn't as if he had not asked himself the question in his head, replayed the conversation a hundred times already. "They were sending two teams to the location ahead of us."

Another grueling five minutes passed with no word, only the whir of tires on pavement and the green smudge of tall pines skating by outside. When the call sounded, he jumped as though stung by a bee.

"Wilson here. Go ahead."

"Nothing," the voice on the other end spat. "There is nothing here. Why are you wasting my time, tracker?"

They glanced at each other in confusion. Jimmy spoke frantically. "What do you mean there's nothing there? Did you check the woods?"

"I know how to do my job, civilian. We swept the area. Your man is not here."

As the soldier signed off, Jimmy stared at the blinking blue light, frozen in place at the edge of Caddo Lake. "He has to be there," he said to himself. Ben answered.

"Something isn't right."

"Nothing about this is right."

Chapter 34

With the forewarning in place, entering the Longhorn Army Ammunition Plant happened expeditiously and without incident. Meaning, it only took ten frustrating minutes for the gate guard to verify Ben's credentials and interrogate them on the nature of Jimmy's involvement. The national database already listed him as a civilian, rather than law enforcement. It sliced at his ego, the fresh wound still raw, but he shoved it aside. He would deal with his own situation later. Right now, they needed to find Matthew. Though both he and Ben were beginning to doubt the boy was here, in this remote and unlikely area.

They exited the truck, slamming the doors. Caddo Lake sparkled blue in the distance, and brown at the shore. The tracking device continued to blink, but the soldiers were right. All he saw were the lake, plenty of trees, a pebbly beach, and miles of briars and brambles ringing the good-sized body of water. A sailboat darted in the distance, past the boundary of the military base.

Footsteps crunched behind him.

"If you're looking for the Invisible Man, you might have the right place," their grizzled escort said, spitting into the bushes. "Maybe your tech is faulty."

The sergeant had made his disgust with his assignment quite clear, noting vociferously that he was no babysitter for a cut-rate bounty hunter and his tag-along. Ben rolled his eyes, sizing up the short, squat man with the crew cut and salty camouflage fatigues. Jimmy smiled as the man craned his neck to stare up into Ben's face, and nearly laughed as the escort shrunk under the giant's peaceful stare. Sergeant Teague, as his name tapes indicated, cursed and grumbled, and wandered off to stand beneath the shade of a gnarled oak.

"Jimmy! Over here!"

Ben hunched over an area a few feet from where his truck waited. When Jimmy's shadow fell on him, Ben pointed to the ground.

"See that? Those tire tracks are fresh. They haven't been here long."

They carefully paced along the grooves, present where the sand was most prevalent, and fading along the grassy parts of what served as a dirt road to the boat landing a hundred feet away.

Jimmy watched as Ben worked. The tracker slow-stepped, studying the ground, then leaned over to touch a single branch on one of a thousand bushes surrounding the shoreline. He veered into the briars, heedless of their stinging tugs and biting thorns. Jimmy stayed behind, careful to observe his technique and not disturb the scene. Dappled light fell on the tracker's back and shoulders, transitioning to enveloping shade as the big man eased into the tree line.

The scent of burning tobacco curled itself into his nostrils. His nose wrinkled in reflex. He glanced over his shoulder to find the terminal sergeant propped against Ben's pickup, flicking an ash to the ground. He raised the cigarette to his lips and drew a lungful of smoke.

"A century of research into the risks of smoking isn't enough?" Jimmy asked, flippant.

Sergeant Smileypants grunted, and blew a thick stream of smoke in Jimmy's direction. "We all gotta die sometime," he shrugged, flicking another ash. "What's your boss doing anyway? We swept those woods. Wasn't nothing out there except bird crap and pine straw."

"Your guys are obviously not pros, since you missed the fresh tire tracks."

With a twisted set to his mouth, the soldier shrugged again. "Tire tracks aren't boys. In case you haven't noticed, this is a boat ramp. Lots of people put in here."

Jimmy opened his mouth to give the annoying soldier a piece of his mind, but a shout erupted from the dark of the woods. He took off at a run, his hands snagging through briars. He hissed, and sucked at the deep, burning scratches, and kept jogging. A whistle sounded off to his right, and he found Ben standing beneath a pecan tree. He held a cloth rag high enough for Jimmy to see it over the brush. When he reached the tracker, he extended a hand to examine the cotton fabric.

Not a rag. A blue t-shirt. Matthew's shirt.

"Found it buried under straw and a pile of pecans," Ben explained, pointing to a disturbed bed foliage nearby.

"But why ..." Jimmy trailed off, swiveling his head to take in the woods around them.

"I'll tell you why," Ben growled, slamming his fist into the rugged trunk. "As a decoy. We've been had."

Crap. They had been played like a piano on Sunday morning. The two men shuffled under the limbs of the pecan tree, each quietly puzzling out just why El Lobo would lead them on a wild goose chase. The chances of his knowing about the tracking devices Trudy had sewn into Matthew and Elise's clothing were slim, and they were undetectable to wand sweeps. As he chewed on possibilities, Ben stilled, whispering, "No. Please not that."

"What?"

Ben punched his wristcom. "Who knew about the nanotech?" he asked, echoing Jimmy's earlier thoughts.

"Trudy, her superiors."

The dial tone sounded in the expectant air. "Exactly."

His stomach burned, churning dread. "They wouldn't."

But he knew the government would do anything to bring Elise in. She was the key to unlocking the entire El Lobo Syndicate.

***

Cora's wrist vibrated, stirring her awake from the nap she had not intended to take. She groaned as she sat up, rubbing her lower spine with one hand. Goodness, how her back ached today! When she read the caller identification, her senses jolted into alertness, flooding her system with adrenaline.

"Please tell me you found him, Ben."

"No, we didn't. We found his shirt, though."

239

She screwed up her face in confusion. "But that doesn't make sense. Why would they toss his shirt at the border? If they knew about the tracking device, they would have tossed it long ago to cover their tracks."

Ben explained to her that the signal led them to the ammo plant, and not the border crossing in Texarkana.

A harsh, hurried knock sounded at the front door, and she groaned again. Elise yelled from the clinic, asking Cora if she wanted her to get the door. Cora covered the wristcom, so as not to deafen her husband. "No! I've got it."

On the wristcom, Ben asked, "Got what?"

Cora opened the door. "Just someone at the door, babe. Hang on."

"No!" Ben shouted through the wristcom, even as a smartly dressed man yanked open the screen door.

"Can I help you?" Cora asked the man, suddenly nervous.

"Cora, get out of there!" Ben's urgent bellow caused the suited man to reach out and snatch hold of Cora's wrist.

"Hey! What do you think you're doing?" she yelled, trying to pull her wrist out of the stranger's grasp.

Ben's voice was cut short as the man tapped the wristcom with his free hand. Cora struck out with her right hand, but the man gripped her wrist before the blow could land. She struggled, even as he forced her backward into the house.

"You can't do this!" she screamed, loud enough to alert Elise to the intruder. "Get out of my house, or I'll call the police."

The man barked a laugh, a hideous sneer streaking across his pasty, pockmarked face. "Sugar, I am the police. Now where is your little friend, the Blackbird? We need to have a conversation."

Cora fought, but in her condition, with her belly throwing off her balance, and her back screaming in protest, it wasn't enough. The Suit reached behind him, and with an obviously practiced motion, slapped handcuffs on Cora's wrist. The cold metal bit into her wrists. She shrieked in protest, but he ignored her.

The agent – if the jerk was telling the truth – snarled, boring into her head with a cruel stare. "You tell me where the woman is, or I'll arrest you for obstruction of justice and harboring a fugitive. You will lose your daughter, Dr. Tucker. Think about it."

Defiant, she raised her voice, praying Elise heard everything happening in the living room. "Elise is not here! How many times do I have to tell you?"

Please let her escape, she silently, fitfully prayed on a loop.

"Little lady, you do not want to mess with me. *Where is she?*"

"I know my rights, Agent Whoever-You-Are. I request to speak to your supervisor."

The agent's face underwent a transformation, from agitated to calm in an instant. A far-off look briefly clouded his eyes, and then a wicked smile slashed across his face. He knowingly tapped the side of his head, grinning. A concealed earpiece, then.

Feet stomped and shuffled on the front porch, and the screen door screeched open. Another agent, dressed in a somber navy blue suit, poked his head inside the house.

"We've got her, sir. Tried to escape through the window at the end of the house."

"No!" Cora cried. "Elise!"

From down the hallway, Kitty began to cry, waking up from her nap in noisy chaos.

Agent Jerk released Cora's hands, and she rubbed the indentions in her skin where the cuffs had clamped down. "Go get your daughter, Doc. And forget Elise Gomez. She's only a ghost, now."

He strode without a backward glance through the front door, and she flew to the window. Elise's head was a hazy silhouette in the rear window of the nondescript, black government sedan. The three vehicles trailed in a line down her driveway, and onto the narrow highway.

Tears zig-zagged down her cheeks as she stumbled into Kitty's room. She collapsed heavily on her daughter's bed, and pulled Kitty shrimplike onto her shrinking lap. As she stroked Kitty's sweaty mussed red hair, she called Ben.

Chapter 35

The restraints furrowed into her wrists, and she stumbled, blindfolded, through what felt like a house; but she wasn't sure. Elise was not sure of anything these days. El Lobo had kidnapped her son. Men in suits with shiny badges swarmed Cora's house, and abducted her. How had her life turned upside down in such a short amount of time? And, dear Lord, where was her son?

Her knee bashed into a corner, and she cried out. Then hands rudely shoved her, and she fell to the carpeted floor, unable to break her fall with her hands secured behind her. Elise crashed with a muffled thud. Behind her, the door closed with a click, and the lock bolt slid home. But it was the sound of Matthew's voice which brought her upright despite her awkward balance.

"Mama!" he yelled, and the blindfold was tugged upward, over her head. Through her tears, her son wavered, smiling. She rolled to the side, sitting with her knees tucked up, and Matthew's arms wrapped and trembling around her.

"Where are we, *mijo*?" she asked her son. "And where is your shirt?"

He sniffled, and wiped a bare arm across his nose. "No clue. A house of some kind. I've been here for hours. They took my shirt off after they shoved me into the car. Mom, I promise. I didn't do anything wrong. They just showed up at the school. I got called to the principal's office, and then there was a man, smiling all fake-like. He pulled his pistol out of his pocket just enough so I could see it, but since he was on the other side of the counter the secretary could not. Then he leaned down and whispered that if I didn't go along with what he said, that they were going to hurt you. And it would be all my fault."

He recounted it all in a rush, his words running frantically together. She wanted to put her arms around him, comfort him, but the restraints prevented it. When he grew quiet, she gave him what she hoped was a comforting smile.

"It will all be okay, Matthew. Can you help me up?"

"Oh!" he exclaimed, smacking himself on the head. "Hang on. They said I could use this *later*, but I didn't understand."

He fished a small, white plastic tool out of his pocket, then moved behind her. Elise's arms fell forward, the tension of the restraints suddenly gone. She rolled her shoulders, and flexed her fingers.

"Thank you, baby." With a raised brow, she asked, "Where did you learn that?"

He shrugged. "Screen."

Matthew stood, reaching downward. He tugged, and she rose. She planted a hasty kiss on his nose, laughed at his protesting groan, and then began a visual sweep of the room. Every one of her survival instincts was in high gear, her senses alert and focused. The windows were blackened, and upon closer examination, she found not glass but steel sheets in place of the window panes. The sashes refused to budge. She moved onto the walls, searching for cameras and hidden recording devices. The ones she located she yanked from their homes in potted plants and tchotchkes, tossing them on the squat, square coffee table. A love seat and sofa, both done in beige, cotton upholstery, paralleled one another with the coffee table lengthwise in between. The entire room reminded her of the generic motel rooms she and Matthew would hole-up in while searching for a new place to live. Except the mirror on the wall above the sofa was more than likely two-way glass, and no motel she knew of had multiple deadbolt locks on the outside of the door, rather than on the inside.

She faced the pseudo-mirror and announced, "Well, kid. I guess we'll just make ourselves at home. Until these cowards come in and talk to us."

She sank onto the couch. Its cushions were firm, unused to human occupation. Matthew tossed her an apple, but she only held it. While the cool mottled red and green flesh of the fruit warmed to her palm, the animal inside of her stormed against its confines. A cage was a cage, no matter the decor. The animal snarled and spat, throwing itself against the confines holding it. So many years since she felt imprisoned, trapped. Slowly, she brought her mind under control, subduing the fretful creature until it quivered in a dark corner. Her hand felt wet. Elise glanced at the crescent nail marks in the fruit, and the juice leaking from its flesh onto her palm. It went uneaten as her head fell backwards onto the stony cushion-top.

The minutes ticked by audibly; the second hand on the noisy clock above the faux fireplace mantle grated her nerves. Matthew settled against her, laying his dark head in her lap. She ran her fingers through his roasted chestnut hair, the feel of his silky mop a soothing balm to her frayed emotions. Whatever came at her, she had her son. Matthew was safe.

From behind, a lock bolt clicked. Then another. She refused to acknowledge the intrusion, not moving from her steady contemplation of the plaster swirl patterns on the ceiling. The cowards could come to her.

A soft sigh escaped the love seat as whoever it was sat across from her. She could guess who it was, judging by the light perfume wafting through the small room.

"Elise. It's good to see you."

"You know what, Katherine?" Elise said lazily, still running her hand through Matthew's hair and staring upward. "It's really not."

Matthew breathed heavily on her thigh. He was asleep. Poor kid had been through a lot in one day. Her anger rose, searing, at the danger the woman across from her had put her son in. Elise tilted her head forward, staring down the federal prosecutor. "Let us go. Now."

The woman was a good actress. By all appearances, this debacle saddened and frustrated her. She had chosen casual dress, a sky blue button-down shirt and denim jeans, rather than the official-looking suits of the thugs who abducted her. Another day, another coercion tactic.

"Elise, please. You know by now that we have protected you all these years, let you live a normal life, to give a normal upbringing to your son. Trudy protected you."

Elise's voice rose an octave, and Matthew stirred. "You think my best friend turning out to be a traitor and moving time after time was *normal?*"

Katherine pinched her lips shut, shaking her head slowly. "No, I guess not. But you were free."

" *Were* being the key word."

"Look," the attorney grated, agitated. "You are only here for your protection. The Wolf has a hit out on your son. If it wasn't for us, Matthew would be in the Arkansas District mountains, in the clutches of that monster."

"What are you talking about?"

Miles threw up her hands, and they landed with a slap on her lap. "We have an inside guy. It took years to get him into the syndicate. We lost three agents before him, trying to get a man on the inside. He contacted us as soon as he got word that The Wolf planned to take Matthew. By the time the reporter's message aired, we already had a plan in place to keep your son safe."

Breathing heavily through her nose, Elise gritted her teeth. "Go on."

"We intercepted the syndicate agent outside the school. He is in custody, but not before he was given a cocktail that insures honesty. We discovered his key word for reporting in, for when he had taken Matthew. El Lobo thinks *his* guy has Matthew, and is on his way to the border as we speak."

"But why lead Ben on a false trail? You knew we would go looking for him."

"We counted on it. You threw us for a loop, though, staying behind with the good doctor. It was easy to follow Ben with his vehicle's wireless law enforcement identification. The original plan was to house you and Matthew at the Army depot, but this safe house works just as well. Good thing we had a contingency plan in place."

Elise snorted, rolling her eyes. "I don't get it, though. Why go through all this," she stammered, waving a hand in the air, "charade? It is not only to protect Matthew. I don't buy that."

"You are correct, of course. We have a deal for you."

She bit off the smart retort on her lips, instead saying, "I'm listening."

"Your freedom. Yours, and Matthew's. In exchange for rescuing the reporter, and bringing down El Lobo and his syndicate."

The clock above the mantle ticked, and Matthew snored softly. Elise laughed, a soft halted undertone.

"Oh, is that all?"

Chapter 36

Kitty's non-stop chatter filled his ear and the cozy living room with warmth and activity, despite the thick tension in the room. Cora reclined on the plush sofa, her feet in the lap of her massage-capable husband. Every once in a while, she sighed in pleasure, only to grunt occasionally with a hand on her rounded belly.

The chubby weight on Jimmy's back wiggled and fidgeted, and he readjusted her before she tumbled to the floor. Kitty, however, was undaunted and resumed bouncing up and down in his hands.

"Giddy up, Unca Dimmy!"

With a snort, he made another loop around the room, weaving around furniture with the ecstatic munchkin trying her best to put him into a gallop. Jimmy halted near the fireplace, jostling and settling Kitty with one arm, and picking up the framed wedding photo from its home on the mantle.

A scene from their wedding, frozen in time. Ben, dressed in a classic black tuxedo, held a slender Cora aloft under her arms. Her infectious grin mirrored his, their noses touching tip to tip; the white train of her elegant dress dangled, mimicking her flowing bright red locks trailing down her back. Their wedding day had shut down the entire town of Cotton Springs, with every able-bodied citizen in attendance. He smiled, though dimly, as he compared that day to this one.

His fiancée – for he thought of Elise as such even though his ring lay nestled around her neck rather than on her finger – was missing, taken by government officials and whisked off to an unknown location. He felt helpless, and it didn't sit well with him at all.

Kitty decided to scalp him, and he nearly dropped the framed photograph.

"Ouch!"

"Soddy, Unca Dimmy. I get down now."

Before he could replace the photo on the mantle, the imp scampered down his back and legs, like a monkey shimmying down a tree trunk, leaving a trail of drool from his neck to his belt line. She toddled over to her basket of building blocks, shoved a bright yellow one into her mouth, and began building with the others. With an amused shake of his head, he wondered how she could still jabber with a mouth full of toy block.

It was foolish to wish for the carefree innocence of a three-year old, but he did all the same.

He paused his pacing at a lace-curtained window. Outside, the world went on living, oblivious to the turmoil racing through his veins. The setting sun lit the clouds from below, creating pink and purple cotton candy in the sky. Birds flitted from shadowed bush to silhouetted tree, and bats swooped to snatch unwary prey. Squirrels sprinted and froze with a flick of bushy tails. Life breathed, inhaling with the setting sun and exhaling the promise of a new day ahead. At least out there, beyond the glass separating them, life was normal. In here, in Jimmy's mind? Not so much.

"We'll find them," Cora said. Her voice was soft, confident. The tone she used with patients in need of reassuring.

"But will it be in time?"

A heavy hand gripped his shoulder. "Absolutely," Ben barked. For such a large man, he moved pretty darn stealthily.

Jimmy turned from the window with its serene promise of tomorrow, and examined his best friends. Ben, a big ole trustworthy bear of man, who had overcome the violent loss of his parents and found peace in salvation. Cora, fiery-tempered and fiercely loyal, who also emerged from her vicious encounter with Gordon Wilkes with scars fortified by forgiveness. Could he be like them? The fear, the doubt, and yes, the fury, raging through his body made his fists clench, tightened his jaw, and urged his feet to get on with it already, and go find his family.

Family.

Yes, Elise and Matthew had nestled themselves in his soul alongside Ben and Cora. He would do what it took to have them safe. Sometimes, it meant admitting he could not do it alone.

Cora shifted on the sofa, dropping her feet to the floor and pushing her shoulders straight. She rubbed her lower back with a groan. When Jimmy stepped in her direction, Ben did likewise; she waved the them off with an impatient flick of the hand.

"Come on, Kitty Cat. Let's get a bath, shall we?"

"Baff time!" She sprung to her feet, and ran ahead, Cora waddling after her with a tight smile. Over her shoulder she said, "I'll get the munchkin bathed and in bed, then we can come up with a plan."

She disappeared around the corner, and seconds later, the rush of water and giggles sounded from the bathroom. Ben pointed to the plush arm chair, and plopped down on the sofa. "Might as well stop pacing and make yourself comfortable."

"Not likely." But he sat, nonetheless. What else could he do?

He stared at the ceiling, the cushioned headrest pillowing tense neck muscles. Where had they taken her? He had checked all the known safehouses in the area. Nothing. No sign of her or Matthew, not a whisper or a peep. Jimmy slammed the butt of his fist into the armrest. The plumped fabric muffled the punch, which was not satisfying in the least.

"When Wilkes took Cora," Ben said to the frustrated quiet, "I was angry. Raging, really. We had fought, and I left, took a contract and was on the outskirts of Houston when you called me."

Jimmy sighed. "I remember."

"When she needed me most, I was on the road. God dealt with me then and there, showed me that I needed His help."

With a tiny wisp of a smile, Jimmy nodded. "I also recall you asking me to pray with you before we went into the woods. Surprised the heck out of me. What's your point?"

"I think we need some help of the human kind, this time."

He knew what Ben was thinking. "You want me to call Cullen, use his contacts to find Elise and Matthew behind his sister's back." He had been mulling over the same idea.

Ben nodded. "Help comes in all forms, even that of the President's son."

It made sense, but putting Cullen in the crosshairs rankled. The man was a newlywed, the son of the President of the Republic, and a respected businessman in his own right.

"It seems – "

"Dishonest," Ben finished. "I know. But Elise is out there, and you can bet Katherine Miles is maneuvering her like a chess pawn without a second thought. The woman is a barracuda."

Or a school of piranhas. Jimmy leaned forward, elbows on knees, and locked eyes with his long-time friend. "Do you think we'll find her before they move her? Honestly?"

Ben scooted to the edge of the couch, grabbed Jimmy's hand. "Yes. I do. But for good measure, we'll pray on it."

They went to their Father in prayer, with the sounds of splashing and laughter in the background, and the mantle clock ticking away. Gradually, Ben's deep bass conversation with God soothed him, washed over him in waves of peaceful reassurance, and Jimmy knew his Maker held them in the tiny living room.

Just as Ben said, "Amen," a very wet and extremely naked three-year old redhead bounded into the room, with Cora on her heels.

"Come back here, you wee heathen!"

"Unca Dimmy take baff?" Kitty asked, her bluish green eyes shining behind long, pale lashes. She grabbed his hand, and tried to pull him toward the bathroom.

He kneeled in front of her. "Unca Dimmy already had one, sweetie pie. You go with your mama and get dressed for bed, okay?"

Kitty shoved a plump thumb in her mouth and nodded. When she spun around, Cora wrapped a bath sheet around her shoulders, pinning the little imp in place. Kitty giggled, then yawned around the thumb.

"Let's go night, night, Little Bit. Lots of time to play with Unca Dimmy tomorrow." Cora grinned up at him, ushering her daughter around the corner and down the hallway.

"She hates it when I say she waddles," Ben said with a grin, "but she does. I love her like this, you know. All big, pregnant, hormones and everything."

"Wonders never cease."

Jimmy took the punch in the bicep in stride, with only a small grunt. Ben's love taps tended to hurt.

"So we're agreed? Call Cullen, ask him to work his SatNet magic and find out where Katherine Miles is holding Elise and Matthew?"

He rolled his neck, wincing at the loud pops, but eventually nodded. "I don't see a way around it. I'll do what I need to do."

Ben disappeared down the hallway as well. While he retrieved Cullen's number from the office, Jimmy resumed pacing. He had the man's contact information in his wristcom, and could have called him then and there. But he took advantage of the lull, however short, to compose his thoughts and formulate a way of asking in a way in which he didn't seem like a good old boy calling in a favor.

But that is exactly what he was doing, no way around it.

Ben returned, passed him a slip of torn paper with a scribbled number written on it.

"Do we wait for Cora?"

"Naw," Ben said, "I told her what was going on when I went in to kiss Kitty good night."

The call went better than expected. Cullen answered promptly, listened quietly, and seemed definite in his decision to help them. Jimmy exhaled at the end of the call, and unclenched his fists. His head throbbed from all the jaw clenching.

Cora rounded the corner, belly first. "He'll help?"

Jimmy nodded. "Said give him ten, fifteen minutes. He'll send a comm of the address."

With a thoughtful expression, she asked, "What happens when we have the address? Go in guns blazing?"

Ben rolled his eyes. "We'll ask them politely to hand her and Matthew over to us. If they don't comply, I suppose it might escalate."

Cora raised a reddish brow. "Escalate?"

Jimmy caught the warning tone. "I won't jeopardize our safety, and I won't get us arrested." *I hope not,* he thought; but he kept it to himself.

"Stake out the place and follow them when they move, most likely," Ben said in a reassuring tone. "No stupid testosterone stuff. Scouts' honor."

The doc snorted, then her eyes grew wide. Her hands flew to embrace a belly that tightened like a drum. Fluid splashed around her feet, wetting the material of her shorts, and trailing in rivulets down her legs.

"OH! Oh, crap! Whoa. No, no, no, not NOW!" Cora gritted her teeth, the muscles of her jaw line standing out as she leaned one-handed against the wall with a moan.

Ben's mouth hung open as he stared at the puddle around Cora's feet. His mouth gaped and closed, but no words came out.

When she could breathe normally again, Cora held one arm under her pregnant belly, and swiped at the fluid on her leg with the other. "You have got to be kidding me. Ben? BEN!"

"Huh?" His vacant stare would be amusing at any other time than this.

"Get the bag, babe. Looks like it's time for your son to arrive."

Another contraction seized her, and she double over with a stifled wail. Jimmy's training kicked into overdrive, and he put in the call to emergency services.

"Get an ambulance out to Doc Tucker's place. She's having the baby. Yes, now. No, her water broke, she needs a bus to the hospital. Contractions are about three minutes apart."

Cora dragged agonized breaths in through her nose and pushed them out her mouth. Ben, finally in motion, rushed to their bedroom to retrieve a bag obviously packed in advance. In Ben's absence, Jimmy reached out a hand to her. The vise-like clamp crushed his bones.

"You need. To take. Ben. With you," she managed around breaths.

"No way. I'll take care of my end. You go ... take care of your end?"

She barked a laugh. "Would you get me a towel? I'll be okay. It's easing off now. Guess this explains ... my back ache ... today."

The ambulance arrived two bone-crushing contractions later. As they loaded her into the ambulance, Ben opened his mouth to apologize again.

"No more saying you're sorry, man. This is your wife and son. Go, take care of them. I'm not exactly a rookie, you know. Kitty's asleep and Mae is here to babysit. Go."

Ben nodded, and waved to Mae Crockett, who stood on the porch behind him. The older woman waved as the ambulance trundled down the dirt driveway and headed toward Lufkin.

She pulled Jimmy into a tight hug. "I don't know what you're into, young man. Not sure I want to know. No," she flapped a hand, "for Pete's sake, don't tell me! Just go, do your thing. I'll watch Kitty."

Jimmy squeezed once more, and released her.

He was on his own. Resigned, he sat on the weathered porch and waited for Cullen Miles' call. A dove cried in the darkened, inky tree line. The night sky twinkled, a blue the color of deep ocean trenches, fading into the near-black of a moon-lit darkness. She was out there. His woman. Waiting for him. And all around him, life breathed in and out, waiting for the dawn of a new morning and all its promise.

Chapter 37

Elise slipped in and out of sleep, fitfully grasping at slumber on the full-size bed, but not able to hold on. Coarse linens scratched against her chin and cheeks, and her hip ached from the rock-hard firmness of the new mattress. Matthew slept curled like a shrimp in front of her, spooned in to the only safety she could provide – that of her body. She had shielded him in the womb from his horrible sire, and would continue to protect him from the monster for as long as she had breath in her lungs.

Lightly, she ran a gentle hand over his arm. A mother's mind was an interesting, unique place. She could study her child in sleep, and see the infant who preceded him and the man he would become. She could hear the distinctive wail of his cry, and the deepening timbre of his maturing, fluctuating voice. Those images strung together into the story of his life. Elise cherished these quiet moments, but wished for the thousandth time for a different circumstance in which to treasure them.

Now fully awake, her brain processed the tingly numb right arm pillowing Matthew's head. She eased the heavy limb from beneath him, careful not to jostle him. As though it would make a difference. A marching army of trumpeting elephants could parade across the room and not wake the boy. With her left hand, she brushed a tousled lock of deep chestnut hair out of his eyes.

The clock on the nightstand glowed 2:50 am. Weary, she rolled onto her back and counted ceiling tiles. Again. Too many thoughts, too many what-ifs and maybes trudged across her troubled, exhausted mind. Could she truly end it? The fear, the uncertainty of knowing The Wolf was out there, always searching over her shoulder, constantly surveying the future out of nightmares from the past. But the bigger question was this: was she ready to potentially give her life to secure a panic-free life for her son?

In a heartbeat.

She traced the silver necklace around her neck until she found the garnet cabochon. Jimmy would raise Matthew as his son, if she did not return from Katherine Miles' imposed mission to bring down the syndicate. Her child would not be haunted by the soulless eyes of the camp slaves like she was; nor ever see the shallow graves, the bruised faces, the shivering mounds of pathetic human existence huddled together on thin sleeping mats. If she succeeded in bringing down El Lobo, hundreds of children would be spared from hell on Earth.

Elise assumed the stifled thump she heard was a door slamming next door, but the next *whump-thump* came from inside the safehouse. The short hairs on her neck stood on end, and goosebumps rose on her arms. More clatter interrupted the night silence, and she bolted into action.

"Matthew!" she whispered fiercely, shaking him by the shoulders. "Matthew, wake up! Something is happening!"

He blinked and smacked his mouth, and she straddled him. She reached under his arms and hauled him to sitting. "Wake UP!"

Matthew scratched his head, then his eyes widened. "What's going on?"

"Shhh! Someone is in the house. You need to hide. Now."

He shook his head. "You too, Mom."

"No," Elise said, pulling him off the bed and onto the floor. She pointed to the narrow space between the mattress frame and the carpet. "Scoot. Now. Whatever you hear, do *not* come into the hallway. You stay here until you see me again, or it is quiet out there for an hour. You hear me?"

His bottom lip quivered, and he shook his head again. "No, you ..."

"Don't you dare disobey me, son. Move!"

As he shimmied under the bed, she smoothed out one pillow case, and tossed the bed to look as though only one person had slept in it. In the dark, on hands and knees she found his tossed, crumpled clothing and shoes, and shoved them under with him. More banging came from outside the room, less muffled and more frantic. Then the room shook with an impact that sounded like a body meeting a wall at full force. Her heart jittered in her throat and she glanced over the dark room once more, hoping she had erased evidence of her son's presence. If they didn't know he was there, they would not know to look for him.

The door knob rattled, and muffled cursing followed. She scrambled to the floor next to the bed, flattened herself on the stiff carpet, and reached a hand under to grip Matthew's arm.

"Whatever happens, stay quiet. Please. If it is who I think it is, they do not know you are here. Stay put, and when you're sure they have gone, run. Find a safe place, hide, and call Jimmy. Here," she whispered, glancing over her shoulder into the darkness. "Take my wristcom. Do you understand?"

"Mama, I'm scared," Matthew cried in a hushed and jagged voice.

"I know," Elise said around tears. "You will see me again. I promise. Whatever you do, don't make a sound. No matter what."

The knob rattled once more, and she gasped. "I love you!"

Elise scampered across the room, as far from Matthew's hiding place as possible, and huddled, shaking, in the corner next to the closet. The door burst open, and a hooded figure in black clothing stood silhouetted by intense light from the hallway. Sudden light blazed, blinding her, and she whimpered as she covered her eyes. She peered through splayed fingers and watched the figure rush to her corner. He yanked her to standing and dragged her into the hallway. Elise fought, but not so much that he couldn't pull her from the bedroom quickly, and away from her hidden son.

Carnage littered the safehouse. Through tears, she saw two of the agents sprawled on the floor. Blood poured from the neck of one, and the other's head rested at an unnatural angle. Debris from broken glass and furniture lay scattered around the room. The agents had put up a fight, then.

One of the abductors raised his black, woven face mask enough to reveal his chin. He cursed, dabbing at a split in his lip. It bled profusely, but he quickly dropped the balaclava over the lower half of his face. Like a stalking lion, he walked toward her. When he spoke, blood outlined his teeth, making his grimace even more menacing.

"Hello, darlin'. The Wolf has a few things to ... say ... to you."

As they hauled her out of the house, she prayed she could fulfill her promise to Matthew.

*****

The borrowed truck pulled to a halt in front of the modest home in one of the older neighborhoods of Nacogdoches. With the addition of the horse trailer in tow, the rig stopped a foot shy of jutting into the deserted road. Jimmy flew from the vehicle, stumbling when his foot landed in a mole hole. The ankle rolled, and he stifled a cry. No time for pain, no time for himself. Clarence kicked the trailer's metal door. The percussion echoed from house to house, like an old-fashioned gunshot in the night.

Light spilled from the open doorway. No door should be gaping wide in the middle of the night. He limped around an azalea bush, and flattened himself to the brick wall of the small front porch. Pulling his sidearm, he lowered himself to a crouch and entered the open door slowly. He scanned the living room for movement, and found nothing but broken possessions and bodies. Two men lay unmoving amidst the evidence of their struggle. His boots crunched on glass shattered from the middle of the coffee table. Briefly, he checked the pulse of both agents, and found them dead. Jimmy's head swiveled, his body tense, as he cleared each room of the house. His instinct told him the house was empty.

He found the bedroom Elise had slept in. No visible blood stains reassured him that, at least for now, she was unharmed. The bed appeared to have only had a single occupant. However, Cullen had been certain both Elise and Matthew were being sheltered here. Curious, he moved closer to the bed, examining the evidence. There. Two longer strands of nearly black hair, longer than Elise's close-cropped style, were on the smooth pillowcase. So she had hidden Matthew. Good girl. But had they found him?

Half an hour later, Jimmy had called in the homicides to the Bureaue and combed over the house looking for further evidence of Elise or Matthew. He used a flashlight found in the glovebox of Ben's truck, and swept the front yard. Near the road, a swath of yard had withered to mostly dirt and a few straggling blades of yellow St. Augustine grass. Jimmy found two separate sets of tracks there. But the yard was large, and the footprints could belong to anyone. He slammed a fist into his thigh.

Two federal agents conversed with their heads together, their words an undecipherable buzz in the background. Another guarded the rear door. All were sleep weary and carried insulated thermoses of coffee. The crime scene investigation team was in route, and Jimmy had hit a dead end on his own assessment. It was a clean entry and extraction, plain and simple.

The truck he borrowed from Ben was blocked by the two black sedans parallel parked at the end of the driveway. He rolled his head to work the kinks from his neck, and reluctantly hobbled toward the agents stationed at the front door.

"Y'all need anything else from me? I need to continue my search for this bounty."

The one who introduced herself as Agent Paulson shrugged. "Got your statement, and think that's it for now. We have your contact information?"

Jimmy nodded, extending a hand. "Thanks. Do you mind moving your vehicles so I can back out?"

The other, the opposite to Agent Paulson's youthful professionalism, grumbled under his breath. Agent Stone resembled his name, a grizzled gray rock of a man who had more years on the job than Jimmy had life. Despite his less than sunny demeanor, he efficiently moved both sedans to the roadside curb.

"Don't get lost," the man advised. "We're going to talk to you again, Mr. Wilson."

"I would expect nothing less. Mornin'," he drawled in departure.

Jimmy reversed the rig, and was two houses down when the crime scene van met him oncoming. Though it was dark, and they weren't likely to notice it, he flipped a hand up off the steering wheel in the universal hello of drivers.

He said a prayer of thanks for getting him out of there before Katherine Miles showed up. The front-door agents had been discussing her imminent arrival when he had stepped over to ask them to move their cars. He'd be willing to bet she was in one of the hotels in town, rather than in Austin. Elise Gomez was too high profile to be left inaccessible. But now that he was free and clear of the so-called safehouse, where did he go from here?

In the early morning darkness, the streets were desolate. He pulled into an electrifill station, its bright light a beacon. Jimmy chewed his lip, tapped the steering wheel.

His wristcom vibrated, and he checked the readout. Wonderful. Katherine Miles. The need to answer the official call warred with the desire to be on the road, tracking down Elise and whoever took her. With his jaw clenched, he tapped the ignore function. Then he dialed Ben.

He answered, and from the background came a hair-raising, guttural yell so primal and fierce that it jolted him wide awake.

"Jimmy. You find them?"

Another throat-ripping wail penetrated the call, and he hurriedly explained the situation.

"Run a trace on her phone," Ben said, rushed. "Yes, baby. I'm here, keep pushing. That's it! Jimmy, I've gotta go. Check in once you run the trace."

The call went dead, and his head thumped against the steering wheel. Ben was not on his game, or he would have remembered Elise's wristcom was untraceable. Unless ... Trudy. Would she be able to locate it?

Every second of hesitation was a second Elise's kidnappers gained ahead of him.

Just as he was about to call Trudy Blue, the face of the wristcom glowed, buzzing against his skin. He flinched. Thinking it to be the federal prosecutor once more, his finger darted to the Ignore button. The name *Elise* flashed on-screen, and his heart leapt into his throat.

"Elise," he croaked. "Honey, where are you?"

Sobs answered him. "Mr. Jimmy, is that you?"

Not Elise. "Matthew? Son, where are you? Is your mom with you?"

"They took her. They took her," he managed, crying. "Can you come get me?"

"Stay with me, Matthew. Where?"

"The stadium."

"I'll be there in ten minutes."

Chapter 38

No more negotiations. His razor-sharp declaration sliced through the comm line. "Matthew stays with me. End of story."

Jimmy had driven to the northern outskirts of Nacogdoches, and pulled off the main highway onto a blacktop road winding through a sparsely populated area of farm and ranch land. He backed into the short gravel drive leading to the side fence of an expanse of pasture, no small feat with the horses in tow. Scattered trees were murky, fingered hands reaching to clutch the deep purplish black of the early morning hour. The sky would lighten soon; the stars would disappear. He hoped to feel the asphalt rolling beneath his tires by then.

"I can have you arrested, James Wilson." The federal prosecutor's threat rang hollow in the predawn air.

"Not likely."

Silence met his bluff. She could, in fact, arrest him. But she would not. He had called Katherine Miles for preventative measures' sake, as well as to respond to her earlier call. Truth was, he needed on an official contract to continue his search legally for Elise. When he had laid out the situation, spilled the beans on his continued relationship with her, Miles had launched into a coarse, foul-mouthed tirade the Marines could be proud of.

"Your hands are tied, Katherine," he reasoned, attempting to change his tone to a more diplomatic one. "With the border riots in western Louisiana District, and those farther north near the Texarkana area, the TBI agents are spread thin enough as it is. Have they deployed guard units, yet?"

"Yes," she barked. "We have Marines on the ground near the Toledo Bend incidents, an army company to the north. Look, I know you want to keep Matthew with you. But you cannot keep him safe if you are tracking Elise."

He glanced at the kid slumped in the passenger seat. Matthew's eyes, dark and shadowed, were trained on him as Jimmy discussed Matthew's immediate future with the woman who wanted to use him in a court of law to prosecute the monster who, unfortunately, shared half his genetic makeup. The idea of calling El Lobo his biological father turned Jimmy's stomach. But as much as he hated to admit it, Katherine had a valid point. He could not protect Matthew, and track Elise at the same time.

The prosecutor continued. "Do you know how much you have compromised the investigation, Jimmy? By continuing a relationship, not informing me earlier, you have broken countless laws."

"Why do you think I resigned as sheriff?" The retort stung his ego. "I made a choice to protect her instead. I love her, Katherine."

She sighed. "I know. It still doesn't justify your actions, and you know it."

He swiveled his gaze, sweeping across the placid pre-dawn pasture outside the truck windows. Beside him, Matthew sprung to attention, searching the fields around him as well. Jimmy rested a hand on the kid's knee, shook his head.

He whispered, "It's okay, Matthew. We're safe, for now."

Because of Elise's case, the prosecutor was tied hand and foot to the Bureau of Investigation, who was not only dealing with Elise's kidnapping, but also the explosive situation along the length of the eastern Texas/America border. Hundreds of protestors rallied violently, and dozens more had been captured while attempting to cross the Sabine River or Toledo Bend Reservoir in the name of political asylum. Border patrol was stretched thin, so the military had been deployed to those regions.

Jimmy wondered aloud to Miles about a possibility. "Do you think El Lobo is still near Texarkana?"

Next to him, Matthew flinched at the name. The reality of his mother's past and his own parentage seemed to be an open, festering wound for the young man.

"Our intelligence says his camp is still hidden in the southeast Ouachata Mountain foothills."

"How current is your intel?"

"Current enough!" she barked. "Matthew Gomez is a key part of this investigation and prosecution, Mr. Wilson."

"I agree, which is why I want him with me. Look, ma'am. You're scrambling. You need me out there looking for her. Can I have the contract? An official one? We're wasting time!"

She growled. "I must be losing my ever-lovin' mind. Yes, you have it. But I'm listing Ben Tucker as the primary."

"Fine by me, as long as my name is on it."

"How did you get your certification so quickly?"

She could not see him squirm in his seat. Her brother, Cullen, had worked a little more magic while searching out the safehouse location. "Better you don't know that."

Katherine grunted. "You're not getting off scott-free, though. I'm assigning an agent to you to guard Matthew."

"Now, listen – "

"No, you listen. You are in deep, and a TBI agent *will* accompany Matthew."

Beside him, Matthew shrugged, then turned to study the fading stars. The barest hint of morning lightened the inky sky to bruised blue. "Whatever it takes to find my mom."

Whatever it took.

"Fine."

"Come to the Fredonia to pick up the agent and the contract."

He pressed the ignition button. "I'll be there in fifteen."

***

Shoulders, spine, and thighs screaming in agony, Elise squirmed in an attempt to ease the pain of being hogtied in the rear seat of a sedan thumping down a potholed country road leading to who knew where. The gag biting into the corners of her lips was saturated with saliva. She grunted, and the abductor in the passenger seat turned. His face, once covered by the black balaclava, was cross-hatched with scars and deep wrinkles. A worn patch covered his left eye, and a scar jagged from the lower edge like a lightning bolt searing his cheek. The thug smiled, a grim slash devoid of mirth. She tried to convey with limited body language, squeaks, and groans that she needed to use the bathroom, but he was having none of it.

"Shut up. We have orders not to put a mark on you, but I don't have to make you comfortable."

In the beginning, after they shoved her onto her stomach in the back of a beat-up four-door sedan, she feared they would rape her. Elise fought like a cornered badger. They quickly subdued her, though, pinching pressure points in her collarbone and hands, then lacing her wrists behind her back, running a line to her feet, and tying them together with her knees bent. The two gagged her as she flung her head to and fro. The car rocked under their weight as they made themselves comfortable in the front seat. Around them, the neighborhood slept on, oblivious to the violent wreckage the two enforcers left in the house behind her.

Over an hour later, her tense muscles burned, an ache so deep it penetrated her bones. The garnet ring strung around her neck dug into her collarbone. Jimmy's ring. A promise to love and protect her. Would he have the chance to do that?

Would she see him again?

Matthew. Did he escape and call Jimmy like she instructed?

For the sake of seeing them both again, Elise chose to survive. To fight.

The night outside the windows relented to the coming morning. She swallowed the thick wad of emotion, and sniffled.

Then she prayed.

***

Jimmy guided the pickup and trailer under the awning of The Fredonia, and left the motor idling. Various vehicles half-filled the lot, but it was empty of individuals this early in the morning. Silhouetted, blurred people stood on the interior side of the revolving hotel door; their features were hazy and bright, but the bustle of motion told him these were not early-rising vacationers up for the breakfast buffet.

"Lock the doors after I get out," he instructed Matthew. Then he pointed to the passenger side floorboard. "Curl up, stay out of sight."

Matthew chewed his bottom lip, his eyes lowered with worry glazed across them, but he obeyed. He slid into a knot, and kept his hand on the door lock. But no sooner had Jimmy opened the driver door than a woman pushed through the opaque entrance and into the dim light of dawn.

He ran a hand through his hair, wishing he could tug it all out. "Not her."

Trudy Blue strode toward him with a sense of purpose. She was dressed casually, in jeans and a tee, but a pistol perched on her right hip; her badge was clipped to the other. A quick glance at her right ankle showed a slight bulge where her reserve sidearm hid. The woman before him was all federal agent. None of the best-friend-in-disguise remained. The set of her shoulders conveyed the impression that she had accepted her relationship with Elise and Matthew was at an end, and all that remained was the job at hand.

Jimmy opened his mouth, but Trudy forestalled him with a halting gesture.

271

"I know. You don't want me around, Mr. Wilson. But finding Elise and keeping Matthew safe is all I have left, and you will not keep me from doing it."

He sighed, shifting on his feet, and hooking a thumb onto his worn pocket. "He's been through a lot. Elise never got the chance to tell him. About you."

Trudy's lips compressed in a grim slash, but she nodded, resigned. "I'll explain it the best way I can."

She gestured to the passenger door, and nodded again. Jimmy opened it. Matthew's wide eyes saddened and angered him. No child should have to go through what this young man had been through in the last few hours.

"It's okay, bud. You can sit up." Jimmy grasped the boy's shoulder, gave it a quick squeeze. "Just ... give her a chance, okay?"

"Who?" Matthew scrambled into the seat, unfolding his lanky legs and twisting into position. "Aunt Trudy!"

He leapt out of the truck and flew in to her arms. Trudy pulled him close, and Jimmy watched as the agent battled the brimming tears.

Then Matthew retreated, and with a puzzled stare asked, "Why are you carrying a gun?" He looked at Jimmy, then back to Trudy. "What's going on?"

Jimmy tried to quell the rising anxiety in Matthew. "Easy, man. Hop in. Your Aunt Trudy will explain on the way."

"Good call, bringing the horses. Head east," Trudy called as Jimmy rounded the front of the truck.

"Intel says north," he countered, sliding into the driver's seat.

"Old intel."

Matthew, quiet but still confused, stared at Trudy as she buckled her seat belt. "Why are you wearing a badge, Aunt Trudy?"

She sighed, a hitch pulling it up short. "I'll explain everything, Matthew." To Jimmy she said, "She's still wearing the necklace. The signal is faint. Going in and out, but I can find her."

He threw the truck into gear. *Hang on, baby. I'm coming.*

Chapter 39

"The American riots continue to beleaguer border patrol forces on both sides of the Sabine River, and around the Toledo Bend Reservoir area. President Miles has confirmed Congressional authorization of the Texas Armed Forces to augment border security in light of numerous illegal attempts by desperate Americans to enter the country. The Dissenters, *an organized group of protestors calling for a return to the democratic government of the former United States, claim responsibility for the numerous uprisings across the socialist nation.*

"A spokesman for The Dissenters, *whose name has been withheld, issued this statement: 'There comes a time when humanity must throw off the chains of oppression, and rise up against the ruling powers. It is time to reclaim our country.' When asked about the number of illicit attempts to cross the border between the two countries, the spokesman replied, 'I can only assume these citizens feel like our cause may take longer than they are prepared to commit to, and I respect that. The Republic of Texas still holds dear the democratic values we seek to reestablish in America.'*

"*An anonymous source within the border patrol also reports that several individuals have, in fact, eluded capture and escaped into the deep thickets and forests of east Texas.*

"*In other news, the Texas Bureau of Investigation continues to monitor the hostage situation of an East Texas News reporter, Tandy Newman. No new demands have been made, and she remains in the clutches of the notorious El Lobo syndicate. The TBI has no comment on the efforts, if any, that are in motion to facilitate her rescue.*

"*The body of an unidentified male, approximately thirty years old, was found early this morning, near the Texarkana border crossing. Authorities have not confirmed if the man was involved in the investigation or rescue attempts of the abducted journalist. Morgan Mitchell, the Chief Agent of the Northeast Region Border Patrol, issued this statement: 'We can confirm that the human remains of a Texas resident were found inside the Republic's boundary. At this time, the nature of the active investigation into his death does not allow me to comment on the details of the situation.'*"

Chapter 40

The soft ball of cloth thudded into her midsection. She caught the bundle One Eye threw at her. Elise was just happy to stand upright, and not be restrained hands to feet.

"Strip."

Elise blinked, uncertain. "What?"

"Take. Off. Your. Clothes." Behind One Eye, the other one sneered.

She took in her surroundings. Sure, it was a deserted backroad. What used to be a well-maintained highway had deteriorated into a pockmarked and potholed asphalt ribbon through the forest. Weeds flourished alongside the gravel shoulder. A narrow game trail paralleled the so-called road, a foot-wide red dirt path choked with clover and thistles.

"You want me to undress here? Why?"

"Look, lady," One Eye growled. "I'm following orders. Boss says bring you here, make you change into that." He pointed to the dull gray wad clutched to her belly. "So change."

The two goons stared at her. She licked her lips, nervous, searching the surrounding area for a place to change. A wicked grin from One Eye, and an amused gravelly laugh from the other, told her they weren't the slightest bit uncomfortable watching her undress.

"Come on, darlin'," One Eye drawled. "Ain't like you never been naked in front of a man before." Her skin crawled under his cruel leer.

She knew better than to argue with them. Humiliated, she laid the bundle of clothing down and undressed down to her underwear. She stood beneath the morning sun, its rays exposing the silvered stretchmarks on her lower belly. Nerves shook her slim body; she cradled her arms beneath her breastbone. With a half-formed prayer that was more of an unintelligible plea, Elise lifted her chin in defiance.

One Eye slowly shook his head, and looked at his buddy. The buddy grinned, and hooked a finger downward.

"All of it, sugar." His voiced scratched the air. Elise shivered.

She obeyed, with furtive glances along the roadside. Overhead a buzzard circled and departed, but there was no other sign of life. Gravel bit into the soles of her bare feet, and the sun beat down on her naked skin.

"This too," One Eye said, walking forward. He hooked a finger beneath the silver chain around her neck. Jimmy's ring glinted blood red. "I just might have to keep this for myself. Look, Joey."

Joey spat into the tall grass. "I'll take the chain."

"Naw, it's not worth nothing. It's not heavy enough to be real silver. Fake."

One Eye grasped the necklace in his fist and yanked, breaking the chain at the clasp. The garnet cabochon fell to the cracked asphalt. He bent over to pick it up, but on his way to standing he ran a finger lightly along Elise's naked outer thigh.

"I can see why he wants you back, girl," he whispered, eyes roving. "Maybe we can be friends before I deliver you to the Boss."

Anger seared, and in a blinding sudden rage, Elise slapped the disgusting man with as much strength as she could muster. "Don't you touch me!" she yelled, startling a wren to flight.

One Eye's right hand flew claw-like to her neck. He squeezed, choking her. "Sweetheart, I'd hate for an accident to happen to you." The pressure increased, and she began to panic. "Do we understand one another?"

At the imperceptible jerk of her head, he pursed his lips and nodded. "Good. Get dressed."

One Eye sauntered over to Joey near the rear of the vehicle. While the thugs examined her ring, speculating about melting it down and splitting the profit, she poured herself into the drab clothing they provided. It was the uniform of the camp laborers. Pants and short-sleeved top were the color of gray putty, and so threadbare that the once coarse cloth had softened. Anguish, fear, and desperation felt woven into the thin fabric. She remained barefoot, as no shoes were provided and hers were left behind in the carnage of the safehouse.

Joey examined his wristcom. He glanced at the sky, then walked another twenty yards or so along the road in the direction the beat-up sedan faced. He motioned One Eye over, who growled at her to stay put and reminded her he was watching. They seemed to be trying to locate coordinates.

Her broken chain lay a few feet away, half obscured by weeds, rocks, and dirt. Gravel gauged the soft pads of her feet, and she shifted from one foot to another as she divided her attention between her captors and the discarded necklace. Elise chewed her bottom lip in thought. One Eye glanced at her, narrowing his eyes, but he stayed where he was, speaking to Joey in hushed tones. She inched her way onto the road's shoulder scrub until her toes touched the silver chain.

Elise adopted a defeated stance, angling her back to the two men. She clutched her arms to her ribcage, while inching her toes over the silvery rope. If she could somehow place it nearer to the road, the glint of it in the sunlight may draw Jimmy's attention if he were on the right track.

If he followed.

Before she could grasp the chain between her toes, however, the men stalked over to her. One Eye grabbed her by the bicep, and muscled her into the brush between the dilapidated road and the thicketed forest fifty feet away.

"Where are you taking me?" Fear seeped into the question, and she hated how her voice shook. She needed to remain strong if she was going to take down the man who ruined her life.

"I have my orders. They say to take you through there," he grunted with a nod toward the trees.

Felled branches stabbed the underside of her feet, and briars snatched at her, snagging skin and clothing alike, as they entered the shadow of the forest. Behind her, an explosive *whoosh* filled the air. She halted and turned, like the story of Lot's wife she had read just a few days ago. The sedan pulsed and bloomed with rolling flames, silhouetting Joey as he joined them in the tree line. A yank on her arm stumbled her forward.

"Let's go."

Joey slapped her on the rump as he walked by, laughing in despicable glee. "He's waiting for you, sugar. We don't keep the boss waiting."

Elise hobbled, bare feet scraped and bleeding, into the lush forest. Thoughts of her son flowed through her mind like a slide show. If she had to do this to save him, she would.

But Lord, she prayed, *let me see Matthew again. Please. And help Jimmy find me.*

With One Eye in the lead and Joey following, Elise trudged through the understory. Tall pines towered overhead, forbidding the sunlight to enter.

Stay alert. Stay alive.

The mantra dictated her cadence, and she disappeared into the forest in the company of devils.

Chapter 41

Trudy shot a look at him, which straddled the line between exasperated and annoyed.

"Yes. I am sure. For the ninth time," she pointed out. "The signal stopped, and hasn't moved in almost an hour."

Jimmy slammed a palm on the steering wheel. Matthew turned wide eyes on him at the outburst. He swallowed the knotted guilt, and forced a smile.

"It's okay, son. Really. We're going to find your mom."

He increased his speed, but after only a minute, reluctantly slowed. The last turnoff had brought them to a road no longer on the general map. Trying to barrel over the pitiful excuse for a road would either land him in a crater, or break an axle. Not to mention overturn the horse trailer he pulled.

"The signal died," Trudy growled. "Make this heap go faster."

Jimmy ground his molars. "If I do, we'll be hiking the rest of the way, and dealing with broken legs on the horses. We may still need them, if they took Elise overland."

Tediously, they picked their way over the derelict pile of asphalt that was once a main road leading beach-goers and anglers alike to Toledo Bend

Reservoir. Over the years since the Second War of Secession, cities and towns migrated, leaving once well-traveled roadways to fall into disrepair. This close to the boundary between the countries, it stood to reason that this road also suffered some artillery damage as well. Whatever the cause, the pitted and chunky boulders laying catawampus in the semblance of a narrow highway made it more difficult than simply traveling off-road.

"I have an idea."

Jimmy engaged the four-wheel drive, angling the truck and trailer over weedy shoulder and onto the wide swath of earth between the jumbled road and the forest. The ride became smoother, but not much faster. He exhaled and rolled the knotted muscles of his neck. After a tedious hour of weaving between the unpaved easements and the more in-tact parts of the roadway, Trudy gave a warning.

"Three hundred yards ahead."

They rounded a curve, and Jimmy's heart jumped into his chest.

"No," he croaked.

Ahead, a sinuous ribbon of black smoke snaked into the sky. The charred shell of a sedan angled half-off the jumbled blacktop, facing the trees on the opposite side of the road. He parked and jumped from the truck in one fluid motion, yelling, "Stay here!" at Matthew as he tumbled toward the burnt remains. Trudy nipped at his heels.

Coughing, he shielded his nose and mouth with the neckline of his shirt. His eyes watered and drained from the thin veil of acidic smoke. The fire had eaten its fill, leaving the metal skeleton of the car behind. Through the haze, Trudy shook her head on the opposite side. He did not see any evidence of human remains either. The knot in his chest eased, but not by much. All he knew now was where Elise was not.

Jimmy hacked more, spitting out mucus thickened by smoke, and trudged to the truck where Matthew hovered, his face plastered to the driver's side window. He opened the door, and the boy fell out running; Jimmy restrained him by the shoulders.

"She's not there," he reassured. "Look at me. Matthew? She is not in the car. No one is."

Trudy laid a hand on Matthew's shoulder. "They burned the vehicle to get rid of the evidence."

Matthew glared at her, flinging his shoulder out of her grasp. He turned his back on the woman he had called Aunt, and said, "She's alive, Jimmy. I know she is."

Jimmy knelt, sweeping the young man into a hug. He held him as Matthew shook. Then he whispered, "Give Trudy a chance. She wants to help."

Matthew swiped a hand under his eyes, and shook his head. "I don't know her anymore." He sounded so much like his mother, like a knife to the heart.

Clarence and Dolly stomped the trailer floor, neighing and snorting at the remnants of the fire. Matthew kicked chunks of rock and concrete, occasionally throwing one down the abandoned road. By unspoken agreement, Jimmy and Trudy split up. The TBI agent followed her GPS system to find the last known coordinates of Elise's necklace. Jimmy examined the area around the burned sedan, finding what appeared to be three sets of footprints.

One of them was barefoot.

Elise.

Trudy shouted and waved him over. He trotted over, Matthew quick on his heels. The agent held out a hand, indicating a need to preserve the space, but pointed to the ground. There, in the leggy weeds, lay the silver necklace Elise wore without fail.

"It's just the chain," he pointed out. "Her ring, my ring, it's not there. Neither is the golden bird you gave her. If the bird's not there, then how is the tracker not still active somewhere out there?" He jabbed a finger in the direction of the trees.

Trudy shook her head, kneeling to scrutinize the ground surrounding the chain. "The tracking device is in the clasp of the chain," she explained. "It's powered through a thin, kinetic energy strand woven into the metal of the chain itself. Without Elise to power it with motion, eventually the nanotech stopped working."

The dust held a loose impression of a foot track, but it was smudged, pulled as though the foot were dragged. A heel mark lingered a pace away, leading into the brushy edge bordering the thicket of woods. He followed the scant signs as well as he could. Broken branches and bent grasses told the tale of passersby. The leafy canopy overhead provided shade, cooling his shoulders and neck. He nearly missed the droplet of blood. The only reason he saw it was because he turned at the sound of crunching natural debris. Trudy reached behind her to offer Matthew her hand. The boy shook his head and glared. Trudy swiped at a tear as she resumed their trek, and Jimmy glanced at the ground with the intention of affording a small amount of privacy in which to grieve. It was then he saw the blood, glinting on a blade of grass.

Elise was barefoot, the tracks testified. With the sharp rocks, jagged deadfall, and spiky shed sweet-gum balls, he wondered why he hadn't seen blood sooner. Her feet must be shredded by now. Jimmy clenched his fists, his jawline a taut rope.

The agent and Matthew caught up to him. He raised a hand, halting their progression.

"We need the horses." He indicated the blood trail. "I can follow this."

"Matthew and I can ride together," Trudy announced with a jut of her chin. She forestalled him with a glare. "We will not stay behind. You need the backup, and Matthew can jump off and hide if need be. Look around you. Not exactly desert terrain here."

She was right in that aspect. The vegetation grew intensely thick in parts. Under the pines, burnt orange pine straw covered the forest floor; but briars, bushes, and shorter deciduous trees flourished in large clumps here and there.

Jimmy weighed the pros and cons. Time won the argument. Every moment second-guessing and debating was another minute Elise distanced herself from him.

"Fine. Under the condition that you do what I say, when I say. No arguments."

Trudy nodded her assent, and the three backtracked to where the horse trailer waited alongside the broken road.

***

Through a narrow fissure in the green ahead, the sparkle of light-speckled water beckoned. It spurred her forward, pushed her through the agony of each step. Maybe they would allow her to soak her raw, lacerated feet in the lake. Clinging to the hope of relief, she stumbled forward.

Elise had no idea how many miles they had walked since the sedan went up in flames. Sweat ran in rivulets, trekking southward down her chest and back, soaking dark patches into the thin material of the gray pants and shirt. The thick, humid air felt solid, as though she breathed boggy water with every ragged inhale. When she lagged, One Eye or Joey took turns slapping or hauling her into motion. They were careful, however, not to mark her. Their apparent fear of El Lobo was justified.

She clung to the hope that Jimmy followed; the blood seeping from her wounds to the earth would leave a trail for him. Would he have asked Ben and Cora to watch Matthew? Most likely. The couple were as trustworthy as they came. To keep her sanity, Elise imagined the face of her son, tracing a finger in her mind's eye around his visage. The ground sloped downward, and lost in her thoughts, she stumbled, crashing to her knees with a muffled cry.

"Up!" One Eye barked, painfully gripping her elbow. "We're almost there, girl."

He yanked upward. She had no choice but to follow, or have her shoulder ripped from its socket. Her right knee, bloody and skinned, peeked through the torn and stained fabric of the thin pants. Elise shoved the fiery pain into a quivering lump in the corner of her brain, the place where fear and suffering lived. She would deal with it later. For now, she placed one sore foot in front of the other, dragging them slightly to leave evidence of her passage. When her captors turned their attention elsewhere, she made sure to snap branches and make as much of a natural-looking disturbance to the surrounding area as possible.

They topped the next rise, to find Toledo Bend Reservoir fingering out to the horizon. The lake shone sapphire blue in the sun; but as they neared the calm shore, the illusion bled into the murky brown typical of Texas lakes.

Elise waded in ankle-deep and collapsed onto the warm, pebbly sand, heedless of the tiny rocks burrowing into her skin. The tepid water lapped onto her feet, stinging with a thousand bites all at once, and upward to soak the seat of her cotton pants. After the initial shock, the cool liquid was a balm to her abused body.

One Eye and Joey conversed two paces away, their heads together, but she only understood the occasional muffled word. Joey pulled a silver disk-like object from his pocket. It disappeared into his palm. His body mostly shielded the activity. From across the lake, bright light flickered. She realized Joey was using a mirror to signal someone on the far shore.

A canteen landed in the sand next to her, thumping into her outer thigh. The impulse to ignore the gesture was overruled by sheer thirst. She sipped the warm water, instead of gulping it. The last thing she wanted was to add vomiting to the mix. Elise stared across the gentle waves nudged by the wind, swallowing the metallic liquid. It tasted of steel and sweat. With her thirst slaked, she tossed the canteen to land on One Eye's toe. He didn't notice.

Instead, he continued to monitor the dot on the lake's horizon, which swelled in size as the minutes passed. Soon, Elise made out the shape of a small, narrow boat. It was almost the color of the lake, blending in so well as to hardly be seen at all. If it were not for the shock of white hair shining against the dark silhouette of the tree line, she would not know anyone was on the water. She thought the craft must be painted with reflective camouflaging paint, the same the syndicate used on the tents to blend in with their surroundings; and in realizing this, her heart began to beat wildly. Not a splotch of white. A shock of silver hair.

El Lobo.

She tried to crab walk backward, desperate to get away, but One Eye had positioned himself behind her while she had been distracted. Joey shouldered their packs, an evil, jagged grin slicing his face. Elise whimpered, ashamed of the sheer terror suffocating her, and unable to do anything about it. Panic rose from her stomach, into her esophagus. She turned and vomited onto the pebbled sand. One Eyed cursed, thwacking her on the head, just as the boat beached onto the shore.

Elise tucked her head to her knees, shaking and rocking to and fro. The man of her nightmares stood before her. He called her name.

"Hello, Liza. I've missed you."

Her prayers fractured into a thousand unintelligible pieces, a jigsaw puzzle of peace heaved to the floor and scattered in the wind. She heard his footsteps, muffled crunching on the sand. A hand applied pressure to the top of her head, forcing her to face him. If his smile was meant to soothe, it failed miserably.

The Wolf knelt beside her. She met his gaze; her lower lip trembled. Her gorge rose again, but she mentally shoved away the urge to vomit. He did not like his pets to be messy. Elise remembered.

"I was beginning to think I would never see you again," he began, as though conversing with a long-lost friend. "I have to admire your skill in evading my pack members."

The jaw muscles beneath her ears ached with tension. "What are you going to do to me?" she whispered.

"Do to you?" he laughed, looking at One Eye and Joey with mirth. "Honey, I'm here to bring you home. We have a lot to ... catch up on."

Dread was a lead fist in her stomach. She licked her lips, careful not to look away, and meet his stare eye to eye.

"Is your camp far from here?" If she could gather some intelligence, maybe she could leave a clue in the bushes near the forest. Surely they would allow her some privacy to take care of bodily business.

The Wolf shook a finger at her, as if she were a naughty student. "You know the rules, Liza. No questions."

She lowered her head in submission. It was the only way to survive. Elise struggled to stand, to make her way to the boat; but his large hand pushed her to the ground.

"Not quite so fast, my dear," he soothed. "Though I *am* happy to see you go so willingly. I see that you haven't forgotten everything I taught you. No, we're waiting for someone to meet us."

She looked the question, rather than voicing it.

His brows raised in surprisef, he answered. "We're waiting on our son. Matthew. He should be here within the hour. Then we will all go home. One happy family. Isn't that right, Liza?"

Her vision narrowed, gray fuzz darkening into a tunnel swallowing the light. She greeted the darkness as an old friend.

Chapter 42

For a thousand-pound animal, Clarence made surprisingly little sound as the horse picked his way over the russet pine needles carpeting the ground. Most of the noise on their trek through the woods came from the grunts and sharp complaints uttered when a briar snatched at Jimmy's arms, or when a low-hanging branch whacked him in the forehead before he could duck. The beastly animal had a proclivity for clotheslining him. Jimmy colored a time or two at the words he bit off, casting surreptitious glances behind him to see if Matthew or Trudy heard. Once, Matthew grinned over Trudy's shoulder, and Jimmy cringed. Busted.

Aside from the weighty desperation to find Elise and bring her home, their journey through the thick forest could almost be described as pleasurable. A cool, May breeze chilled the light sheen of sweat along his arms and on the back of his neck. Though the humidity flirted with miserable levels, the mild morning warmth in the dappled shadows kept them comfortable. The air smelled of pine, rich earth, and leather; each rocking step creaked the saddle seats, and the swish of long, coarse tails held the nosy flies at bay. They rode without speaking to each other, lost in their thoughts and concerns for Elise.

The blood trail and broken vegetation had intersected a deer trail about a mile back, and it appeared Elise and her abductors had preferred it to breaking through the overgrown understory. The narrow track widened, opening to a clearing of sorts. Overhead, pine needles intertwined with broadleaf oaks to create a canopy. Ferns flourished in the shade, and for once, the prickly briars that had menaced them were absent. Dolly snorted from the region of Clarence's rump, and Clarence tossed his head in her direction. Trudy reigned to a halt alongside him, with Matthew grim once more. Jimmy's heart ached for the young man.

"The lake is just ahead, maybe a quarter of a mile," Jimmy noted as he swung from the saddle to thud softly to the ground.

Elise's trail was not difficult to follow. Judging from the condition of it, he surmised she was near exhaustion, dragging both wounded feet. He followed for another dozen paces, finding an area which could have been where a person had fallen and struggled to rise. The ground was disturbed, more branches snapped and some left dangling. Dried, rusty blood coated a patch of desiccated pine straw. He knelt, narrowing his eyes. A scrap of torn gray linen, smaller than his thumbnail, laid amongst the needles.

He turned and found Trudy still in the saddle, studying her wristcom. "I am almost certain they are bound for the reservoir."

She nodded absently, squinting at the leaf-hidden sky, then again at her wrist. "Mm-hmm." Her free hand stroked the contoured grip of her stun pistol at her waist, while Dolly's tail twitched away flies.

A niggling suspicion chewed at him. The agent was up to something.

"I think we need to hide Matthew soon. We're catching up to them."

She looked up at his clipped tone. "Yes, I think so too." Trudy flicked her eyes skyward once more, then nodded. "Yes, about a tenth of a mile away from the lake should be enough."

Jimmy battled the urge to ask her what she was up to. He doubted she would tell him anyway.

He visually traced the clues leading northeast as he stood, leaning and twisting to dislodge the kinks. No time for him to concentrate on his own aches. Not when Elise remained in danger. Jimmy hitched his left foot in the stirrup, and swung up into the saddle. Clarence bobbed his head, stamping his foot twice. He patted the sweaty sorrel on the shoulder, whispering reassurances of a break soon to come.

For a time, the way widened so that both horses could walk side by side. Matthew rode stiff-necked behind Trudy, and the agent had slid into a bad habit of watching her wristcom and not the path. When Dolly nudged into them a third time, pinning all three of their legs between the horses, Jimmy finally spoke up.

"Spill it."

Trudy flinched, tightening her thighs and causing Dolly to skip a few paces ahead. She skillfully reined Dolly, allowing Jimmy to catch up. The federal agent sighed, a dramatic exhale.

"I can't give details," she hedged, "but I can say there is a federal operation in play."

He knew it! "If *any* of this puts Elise or Matthew in danger – "

"She's already in danger, James Wilson!"

"Don't you dare lecture me on her welfare, Special Agent Blue," he hissed, careful to not allow his voice to carry.

With a grim stare and a tightened jaw, she curtly held one hand aloft. "This is bigger than Elise, as much as I hate to say it."

"Maybe to you, but not to me, and certainly not to Matthew."

At the mention of his name, the boy flung a leg over Dolly's rump and slid to the earthen floor. "If you don't want to rescue Mama, I will!"

Matthew took off at a trot. A shot of adrenaline spurred Jimmy out of the saddle once more. He caught up to the distressed young man, jumping in front of him to halt his forward progress. A squirrel chirruped brazenly, annoyed by the sudden commotion, and it darted up a tree with a huff of its fluffy tail.

Jimmy met Matthew's tearful, worried gaze. He wrapped the boy in a tight embrace, and refused to let go when he tried to pull away. He placed a hand on the side of Matthew's tousled head, holding his future son to his chest.

He remembered his own father holding him like this. The steady, sure beat of his dad's heart had soothed his soul, once upon a time. He imagined the look on his father's face when he could finally tell him he was going to be a grandpa. Jimmy smiled, a rueful curve, despite the sadness of the young man he held.

A minute trudged by, then another. Matthew's shoulders quaked and Jimmy felt the cotton of his shirt grow wet with shed tears. When he was sure Matthew would stay and not flee, he released his hold a fraction. The boy picked up on the body language, hiding his face as he wiped a dusty hand over his face.

Placing his hands on Matthew's shoulders, Jimmy said, "I will find your mother. You need to trust me."

"I trusted *her*," he cried, jabbing a finger toward the woman he had called aunt. "Look where it got us!"

He heard Trudy gasp in the background, but focused on Matthew.

"Nothing means more to me than you and your mother. Do you understand? I will do what it takes."

The kid nodded, a jerky bob of the head, and Jimmy hugged him once more. "Good. We're nearly there. Let's find a place for you to hide."

"But I don't wanna hide!" he protested.

"I promised your mother I would keep you safe, too, son. I meant it."

Jimmy surveyed his surroundings. The tall pines which previously kept the understory from growing too thick had given way to a variety of deciduous trees, from middling oaks to smooth and narrow crepe myrtles. The result was waist-high bushes and thickets to battle, and overbearing limbs snagging at their heads.

"There," he said, pointing. He took Matthew's hand, leading him around a clump of briars and over a fallen log. A natural depression hunkered beneath a dead oak; where the roots were rotten, the ground fell inward, creating a cup of sorts. Between the hole, the fallen log, and the surrounding brush, Matthew would be nearly invisible.

He tilted his chin toward the hidey-hole. "In you go."

Matthew grumbled, but he obeyed. Jimmy gathered deadfall and leaves, scattering them over the tangle of vines and decaying roots to further conceal the boy. After retreating a dozen feet, he scrutinized his work. If Matthew remained still and quiet, no one would know he was there. He exhaled the nervous breath he didn't realize he had been holding.

With another admonishment for Matthew to stay in position, Jimmy hiked over to where the horses and Trudy waited. His ankle twinged from torqueing it earlier, but it was bearable.

"We'll walk the horses ahead a little, tether them, and then go the rest of the way on foot."

With a grim expression and red-rimmed eyes, Trudy glanced once more at her wristcom. He reflexively clenched his jaw, understanding Matthew's reticence in trusting the woman. Jimmy trusted her as far as he could toss her.

His future was torn in two directions. One half of his heart lay hidden in the brambles behind him, and the other somewhere over the next rise in the hands of madmen. He rolled his neck, and squared his shoulders, checking the stun pistol at his side.

With a hunter's practice step, he glided through the forest. He didn't look back.

***

A steely, gravid cloud slid in front of the sun at its zenith. Shadows of its heavy companions rippled along the surface of the lake. The underbellies of the nearby oak leaves gleamed silver, shivering on their limbs, and the air smelled of rain. A storm was coming.

The Wolf stood with his men beside the boat a dozen paces away, but he made sure to make eye contact with Elise often. He divided his attention between her and the thugs he employed. One Eye jabbed a finger at the sky, gesturing wildly with the other hand. El Lobo shook his head firmly, once. Then he aimed a glare at the tree line. He tilted his head to the side, halting One Eye's tirade with a flick of a finger. Judging by the stillness, El Lobo was listening to a communication only he could hear.

Her fingertips bled now, all the nails gnawed to the skin. A twisted knot of dread writhed sickeningly in her stomach. Surely Matthew was safe in Cotton Springs. The Wolf had to be wrong. As much as she would treasure seeing her son's face once more, it could not be like this.

The earlier terror of El Lobo's presence had faded. When she regained consciousness, she found herself dragged from the shoreline to where the sand mingled with tall grasses. Elise sat up, unsteady, and found him looming over her. For the first few minutes it was as if she were sixteen and at his mercy. Even though he stood a scant two inches taller, his reputation and demeanor increased his size. Larger men had fallen to his boundless wrath. Evil grew strong as it devoured fear; despite the man's deceivingly placid countenance, his soul banqueted on the horror permeating his camp. With a barked order to not move, he had taken up position out of earshot.

Oddly enough, her own dread had begun to recede with his departure. Whether it was being so far removed from his influence, or the steadfastness of her new faith, Elise found strength buried within. It flickered, a stuttering candle in the darkest cave. She fed it prayers, and the confident flame blossomed.

While the three men conversed in the distance, she assumed a broken posture. Lowered eyes searched the area under the guise of submissiveness. The sky strobed in the distance, and thunder echoed its call, rolling overhead through the darkening clouds. She pulled her knees to her chest, all the while examining potential escape routes. There were two breaks in the tree line behind her, but they were too obvious. Another brilliant flash of light electrified a towering thunderhead to the west, and ten seconds later, thunder boomed. Her gaze fell back to the place where pebbled sand met the encroaching green foliage, and her breath hitched in her throat.

Two eyes peered at her from no more than thirty feet away. Two slow blinks, and then a finger emerged to cover revealed lips. She would know those eyes anywhere.

Jimmy!

Chapter 43

"Where is my son?" The Wolf demanded, startling Elise. In the bushes, Jimmy shook his head a fraction; and she turned her attention to the men down the beach. They aggressively faced someone else, stun pistols leveled at a woman with hands held high.

Trudy.

Despite her friend's betrayal, Elise swallowed a knot of grief and apprehension. What was Trudy doing?

With a curt gesture from their boss, One-Eye and Joey patted Trudy down. They removed two sidearms, one from her shoulder harness, the other from her ankle. They each took a weapon, stashing it in the waistline in the small of their backs.

El Lobo turned to Elise and barked in her direction. "Liza! Get over here. *Now.*"

Elise once again assumed her defeated posture, scrambling across the sand and kneeling, face down, at her captor's feet. She hoped he could not see the fire blazing in her eyes, or the ropy muscles of her clenched jawline.

"Special Agent Blue," he growled, and Elise flinched. How did he know Trudy's name? He continued, "I've been looking forward to meeting you in person. After all, you've done so much for me already."

Before Elise could stop herself, her head whipped upward, riveted on the closest thing to a sister she would ever have. Her mouth gaped, and her unblinking gaze alternated between Trudy and the monster looming over her. El Lobo patted her head, as if to calm an anxious dog.

"Oh, yes, Liza. Your Trudy has been quite helpful. Why don't you explain, Agent Blue?"

A stone expressed more than Trudy's visage. "You lie. I have done nothing but protect Elise since the beginning."

The Wolf waggled a finger at her, like a metronome. "Mmm. Not always. You and your TBI counterparts became greedy, tried to plant a mole in my fruitful garden."

Elise saw confirmation in Trudy's eyes, and a piece fell into place. "The reporter. Tandy Newman. *You* are responsible for that?" Her eyebrows arched together high on her forehead, disgusted disbelief dripping from the accusation. "How could you?"

Trudy turned her attention from The Wolf to where Elise hunched at his feet. "The nosy little reporter was going to expose you. I couldn't have that. I fed her what intel we had at the time. The choice, ultimately, was up to Newman. Her ambition landed her in his camp."

Elise tried to rise, but The Wolf's viselike grip on her shoulder prevented it. "Tandy Newman may have been ambitious, but she was practically a kid."

Trudy flinched, and then once more assumed the mask of indifference. "I will do anything for my family."

"Family? He says," Elise gestured with a hooked thumb, "you have been working for him."

"He's a liar."

The Wolf grinned at them, clearly enjoying the emotional showdown. "Oh, but I am not. When you and your little friends in the Bureau planted your undercover agent in my camp, we had a bit of fun. He fed you passcodes, yes. But those codes piggybacked a gift. A GPS logger was embedded into the software of your wristcom. We have tracked you ever since."

Elise studied Trudy throughout The Wolf's explanation. Though her friend's face showed controlled surprise, there was something else concealed behind it. She knew her friend. Rather, she once did. Betrayal had a way of casting a long shadow over certainty. And yet, she had witnessed true surprise in her friend in the years spent with her. The feigned shock at El Lobo's revelation crept across her friend's face, but never quite reached her eyes. Interesting.

The wind gusted, and gloom dimmed the intermittent sunlight with thickening cloud cover. Lightning flickered in the distance, and the air grumbled its reply.

"Enough," The Wolf announced with the slash of his hand. "Where is my son? I know you have him."

Trudy exhaled a snort of laughter. "If you think I'd bring Matthew here, you are out of your mind."

Faster than lightning forking overhead, El Lobo backhanded Trudy across the face, dropping her to her knees. "Don't play with me. You will bring him to me, immediately, or suffer the consequences."

He seized a handful of Elise's hair, and she grunted, unwanted tears springing to life. El Lobo yanked, forcing her to meet his gaze. With a wicked smile, he caressed Elise's cheek with the other hand. "Bring Matthew to me, or Elise will pay. Your choice, Agent Blue."

"No!" Trudy shrieked, flinging a hand toward Elise. "Don't hurt her. Please."

"Don't you *dare* give him my son," she growled. Elise flung her head to the side and felt a chunk of scalp tear loose. She whimpered, but glared at Trudy once more. "I do not care about me. Keep Matthew safe."

Before she could blink, her cheek rammed into the jagged beach, and The Wolf's knee sank into her spine, pinning her to the rocky sand. She spat out a mouthful of grit. He fisted her hair once more and yanked. She grunted, closing her eyes against the searing pain.

"Tut tut. I will not have insubordination from you, pet."

The scuffle kicked up dirt and dust; despite hastily scrunched eyelids, ragged grains scratched her corneas. She blinked, hoping the tears would wash away the sand. It didn't help. In the brief window of time between blinks, all she could see was his right boot tip, blurred because of gritty tears and close proximity, and the rocks and weeds dotting the beach. Trudy's pleas hung in the air, and Elise wondered if Jimmy was close.

"Let her go!"

"Time's a-wasting, Agent Blue. Take me to my son, and Liza will live. I hope you cooperate, because the two of us have a lot of catching up to do."

"Okay! I'll show you where we have him, just let her go."

"No!" Elise yelled, getting another mouthful of sand for her efforts.

"Good girl. Now," he said, roughly pulling Elise to her feet. The Wolf gripped her right bicep, his fingertips digging to the bone. "Lead the way."

Her tormentor spoke to the two goons. "Joey, stay with the boat. Calvin, with me."

With a glance over her shoulder, Trudy hesitated. Then she walked toward the trees, and Elise's heart plummeted. Jimmy hid in there, concealed by the vegetation. But instead of going into the forest, Trudy skirted the edge, walking northward around the lake's edge. She picked her way carefully, glancing to the rear often. Elise stumbled on her wounded feet, grateful for Trudy's slow pace. The agent consulted her wristcom during one stop, looking around as if getting her bearings.

At her shoulder, El Lobo growled. "What?"

"I had to look at my GPS. He's here, just around this bend and into the woods a bit. Be careful," she advised, slow and deliberate. She locked stares with Elise. "There are some rocks ahead, and you don't want to fall and hurt yourself."

Something in her inflection alerted Elise. She haltingly limped alongside The Wolf, but tipped her chin a fraction to let Trudy know she understood. A candle flame of promise sparked to life once more. Each lurch was agony, but she pressed on, hopeful beneath the pain.

She allowed her gaze to wander. Overhead, ripe clouds were ready to burst, crowding together in gray lumps, each seeming to force the other downward. Off to her right, white-capped waves vied for attention across the lake. The wind vacillated between gusty and breezy, fickle and unpredictable. One Eye – no, Calvin – shoved her. She hissed when her foot landed on a broken limb, and Calvin earned a sharp look from The Wolf. With a few guttural words, and a pointed finger, El Lobo directed

Calvin's attention to Trudy. The guard relented, picking his way ahead with the promise of revenge written all over his face. He shadowed Trudy, who continued the slow pace.

Elise hobbled, focusing on the trees to her left. The leaves shimmied and fluttered on their branches, and pine limbs bobbed in the wind. Thunder rolled once more as the trail left the water's edge and turned into the forest. Ahead, a jumbled pile of stones and small boulders stood in stark contrast to the green and brown of the wooded shadows.

She barely registered the smudge of tan, black, and blue as it flew from the forest with a roar. A man-shaped projectile launched himself, torpedoing into Calvin and knocking him into the rocks. Calvin's head bashed into a sharp boulder with a sickening *thunk*. Blood oozed down the face of the rock. Calvin lay still, unconscious or dead.

Men suited head-to-toe in self-camouflaging body armor rose from the rocks, encircling them. They seemed to waver, like a desert mirage, the cloth of their clothes mimicking their surroundings. Every single one trained a rifle on The Wolf.

Jimmy crouched next to the downed thug, ready to spring and out of the line of fire of the professionals. "Let her go," he commanded. His jawline was knotted into ropy strands. "Now."

The Wolf threw back his head, laughing at the gathering storm. Jimmy's hand flashed to Calvin's waistband, retrieving the stun pistol and concealing it on the outside of his leg, all before her captor's moment of insane hilarity had passed. The Wolf dragged Elise to his chest, holding her as a quivering shield. The cool barrel of a pistol kissed her temple.

"Not so fast, lover boy," El Lobo chuckled. "If you want to have any hope of Liza's return, you will put down your weapon. And all of you," he addressed the other agents. "Lower your weapons, or I will have my drones open fire on you."

"You mean these?" Trudy asked. She knelt, then rose, tossing three dinner plate-sized twisted contraptions to the ground between them. One skidded to a halt a pace away from Elise's foot. "As you can see, they are no longer a threat. Neither are you. It's time to lay the weapon down, turn yourself in."

The Wolf stilled, but his grip remained firm. Elise kept her eyes trained on Jimmy, who had inched forward while Trudy played her game of distraction. He looked at her, then sharply dropped his chin, his gaze falling to the rocky ground.

"How?" El Lobo asked.

"That little piggy-backed present you gave me, the GPS logger? We expected it, and had a surprise package waiting for it to take back to your network."

He grunted, his chin brushing against Elise's hair as he swiveled his head. The heavens rumbled once more. This time, she felt the reverberation in her bones. If the storm broke, it would be mayhem. Anything could happen in the crossfire.

Another peal of thunder ripped across the sky; and closer, a giant clap exploded on the wings of a brilliant flash of purple-white light. Someone screamed in the distance.

Matthew.

He spoke her fear. "There he is." As the rain tumbled from the leaky clouds, El Lobo dragged her inch by inch, a dozen rifle beads trained on them. Elise squirmed, fighting to free herself, but he lodged the barrel of his own stun pistol beneath her chin.

"Stop, or you're dead. You are much more fun for me alive, but I can live with dead. Once we find my son."

The stippled patter of rain transformed into a roar, the deluge making it all but impossible for her to see anything around them. If she could not see, then neither could Jimmy or the agents. Panicked, she tried again to break free. The pistol collided with her temple, and lights flickered at the edge of her vision. Darkness tunneled threateningly; she fought to remain conscious. A continuous roar tumbled across the sky as El Lobo prodded her through curtains of rain. Her captor cursed, turning his head left and right, constantly seeking his pursuers. Behind them, Elise thought she could make out the raised voices of the federal agents. For all she knew, though, it could be the wind.

Just as suddenly as the downpour began, it ended. Steel-bottomed clouds loomed overhead, but the rain eased to a trickle.

"Help!" cried a voice off to her left. Matthew.

"Come on!" El Lobo snarled. His voice grated like tumbled gravel.

To their right, back at the rocky clearing, shouts and sharp commands split the air.

Dear Lord! she cried out silently. *Help my boy! I can't think. I don't know what to do, God. Please. Please, help him. Help me.* Incoherent thoughts tumbled like thunder as he pulled her one-handed through the woods. Her torn feet splashed in mucky puddles, skidded over slick pine needles. Tears blended into rain, both sheeting over her cheeks. Matthew shouted again, his voice closer. The Wolf, heedless of everything else, pushed forward, dragging her in his wake.

"Mama!" Matthew yelled, close.

Too close. "Matthew, *RUN!*"

He froze, his mouth gaping, a dozen yards away. His eyes shone white in the storm's gloom, terrified, as he tried to figure out what he should do. Then another voice filled the air.

"Matthew! Get down!"

Jimmy roared into the space between her and El Lobo, shielding Matthew. Her son dropped to the ground, his form barely visible behind the jumble of dead wood, shrubs, and ferns.

Her fiancé faced El Lobo. His soggy and muddied black t-shirt was plastered to his heaving chest, but his pistol remained steadily trained on the monster beside her. "I will shoot, Wolf. I don't have an agenda like the suits back there. I will, however, fight for Elise and Matthew until the end."

"How very noble of you, James Wilson. Oh, yes," he laughed. "I know all about you and your tragic resignation over the love of your life. So do not underestimate *me*. Or something dire may happen to the lovely pregnant physician and bounty hunter."

Elise, her hand still bound in El Lobo's tight grip, flinched at the threat against Cora and Ben.

Do not be afraid.

The whisper flitted across her mind like a gentle caress, but it stoked the fire within her.

Do not be afraid. I am with you.

She squared her shoulders and turned to the man she had feared since she was five years old. The one who made her life a humiliating hell, one of subjugation and slavery.

Do not be afraid. I am a strong tower.

The only good to come of the terror holding her was Matthew. Her son, her hope. The Wolf wanted to take her child away.

Do not be afraid. I am your refuge and strength.

At her side, her fist clenched. Her body was flooded with power, from her ragged, torn feet to the ends of her hair. She felt every cell's life, the blood coursing life through her veins. The fist tightened into a rock, and she faced The Wolf.

"Liza and Matthew are mine," her enemy raged at her love. "Time to say goodbye, Sheriff." The Wolf leveled his pistol at Jimmy.

Do not be afraid, Daughter. I have redeemed you. I have called you by name.

Fortitude rose within in her. "My name is Elise."

You are MINE!

Startled, El Lobo flinched, turning his surprised glare on her. She swung her arm, feeling as though a thousand giants lived within her. The blow connected with his chin, and his head whipped backward. His body followed to the forest floor. The hand gripping the pistol bounced against the ground, jolting the pistol free. She snatched the weapon, and placed her cut, jagged foot on El Lobo's throat, pinning him to the sodden earth. Elise aimed the pistol at his forehead.

"I do not belong to you anymore."

Her finger tightened on the trigger. One squeeze, and her life's terror would leave this earth. The pistol wavered. Her enemy smiled, blood trailing out of his left nostril.

"Do it," he whispered, coughing.

Vengeance is Mine.

"No."

He laughed, and spat blood onto her foot.

"I will not become a monster for the sake of one," she said quietly. The breaking of twigs behind her announced Jimmy and Matthew, but she did not remove her sight from the captive at her mercy. She narrowed her eyes, applying more pressure on his trachea. His eyes widened.

"But," she mused, flicking a button on the side of the pistol, "nothing says I can't give you a good jolt."

She lifted her foot from his neck and shot him in the shoulder. He shuddered, arching, then collapsed unconscious at her feet.

"Mama!"

Elise spun, her arms open wide. Matthew flung himself into her embrace, and the joy and relief threatened to overwhelm her. She teetered as his weight knocked into her. When had he grown so tall? Minutes passed before she finally released him. She looked up, to find Jimmy staring at her with his crooked smile. With an outstretched arm, she invited him in.

Instead, Jimmy grasped Matthew in a tight bear hug, squeezing him until he laughed. He planted a kiss on the top of the boy's head, and whispered something in his ear. Matthew rolled his eyes, and Jimmy ruffled his hand through Matthew's hair. Her son wandered off a few paces, and stood against an oak trunk three times his diameter.

Jimmy framed her face with both hands. She nestled her cheek against his rough and calloused palms, closing her eyes at the bliss of having him near once more. When she opened her eyes, they found such hunger in his that it traveled, quick and hot, to her very core.

"I was afraid I lost you, honey," he whispered, his lips nearly touching hers. His breath was warm on her rain-chilled skin. "Don't ever do that again. Okay?"

She chuckled, lowering her lashes. When she looked up once more, the love in his eyes threatened to overwhelm her. Elise placed her palm on the back of his head, and brought their lips together. The kiss deepened, as gentle rain peppered them. The fire in her core sparked to the ends of her fingertips and toes, and she tingled in too many places to count. The world around them faded into a bright, pulsing orb of light. Time dissolved in his arms.

"Ewww, gross! Mom! Cut it out!"

Until, at least, the sweet sound of her son's concerned voice jerked her into reality once more. Laughing, Jimmy scooped her up into his arms. All the aches, cuts, bruises, and scrapes flared to life, and Elise winced with a whimper. He planted a chaste, wet kiss on her dampened forehead.

"One more thing," he said, eyebrows raised.

"Hmm?"

"Teach me that right hook?"

Chapter 44

The hospital bed arched uncomfortably beneath her; but after two days of confinement, she supposed even the softest bed would chafe. The pudgy newborn in her arms scrunched up his face in a grimace, and released a blood-curdling screech. Elise juggled him gently, patting his diapered bottom and cooing sweet-nothings into his ear. He soon quieted, although he puckered his lips into a sucking shape, like an invisible pacifier was in residence.

"He's getting hungry," Elise noted, looking up at Jimmy.

Matthew grinned from the convert-a-chair across the room. "That kid is always hungry."

Elise kissed him on the head, adjusted his blankets to form a tighter swaddle, then handed him back to his looming and fidgety father. Ben's giant hands scooped the little terror from her battered and bandaged ones. Compared to the size of his dad, the baby appeared premature instead of nearly ten pounds.

"I still don't know how you birthed that monster," she laughed, smiling at Cora. "But I thank you for bringing him for a visit. It's been a long time since I held a newborn."

Cora, her wild red hair somewhat tamed into a messy bun atop her head, grinned from ear to ear. She glanced at her husband towering above her, then said, "Having a giant baby was bound to happen, I think. Thank goodness for modern medicine and creative anesthesia."

Ben laid the baby in his crib. "Now we have to name the beast."

"Beast," Cora said with a finger tapping against her lip. "Seems fitting, considering his appetite."

The robed physician pecked her son on the forehead, then ambled over to the far wall. She tapped the plate glass screen, palmed the scanner, and pulled up Elise's chart. After a few minutes' study, she nodded once, then exited the application.

"You're making good progress. I hate to tell you, though. You're going to dread the wheelchair. Trust me, I know."

Ben groaned his agreement, turning his stare to Jimmy.

"You are not going to like it much better than she does. Ouch! You would hit the father of your adorable child, Red?" He rubbed his triceps with a frown.

"Watch your mouth, father of the Beast. Come on. Elise needs rest, and I need to feed the grub. And pack. Oh, I cannot wait to sleep in my own bed and snuggle with Kitty."

With a couple of parting hugs and shoulder slaps, the door shooshed closed with a click. Cora was breaking out of the hospital, and she was stuck in it. Elise stifled a yawn. Or attempted to, and failed.

"We should go," Jimmy said, with a tilt of the head toward Matthew. "You need rest, just like Doc said."

"And I keep telling you I am fine. Sore, but fine."

The westering sun blazed above the cityscape through her window. Soon it would set, and she would begin her last day in the hospital. Two days of rehydration, immune therapy, and skin grafts on her feet had solidified her resolve to never see the inside of a hospital again, if she could help it.

For two days, she had not uttered her traitorous friend's name. But it was time.

"Is Trudy ... safe?"

Jimmy sat on the edge of her white-blanketed bed. "Yeah, she's fine. They have her debriefing in Austin. She, um, called. To check on you. Right after you arrived. I hope you don't mind, but I gave her an update."

She waved away his concern. "It's fine. I need time, to process her involvement."

Matthew interjected, "She's a traitor, and I never want to see her again."

Elise sighed. "I know how you feel, baby. But I believe her. I think we started out as a job, and ended up a family. In the end, she protected us both. That has to count toward the good."

She lay on the bed, her eyes trained on the generic ceiling tiles. "And him?" Elise did not need to say who.

"In custody. He's not going anywhere. You did it, Elise. The syndicate crumbled. Dozens of members of the hierarchy have been arrested, and nearly two hundred captives were freed."

Tears leaked across her cheek as relief overwhelmed her. Two hundred lives.

"Tandy?"

"Alive, and healing in a north Texas hospital."

Jimmy held her as she sobbed her relief. She felt Matthew's weight dip the bed, and then his arms were around her as well.

"There's one last thing, though," Jimmy alluded.

She blinked away tears, and considered his smiling amber eyes. Smiling, so no bad news, then. "What would that be?"

He fished his hand into his front jeans' pocket, then held aloft his treasure. A silver and garnet cabochon ring.

Elise gasped. "How?"

"It was found on the body of the one-eyed thug. It certainly doesn't belong to him."

"The body? Oh. And the other one?"

"He took a good knock to the head from one of the agents, but he's alive and incarcerated."

Elise stroked the red fire of the garnet with a bandaged finger. "Your grandmother's ring."

Jimmy shook his head, and her brows drew down in confusion.

"Not hers. Yours. That is," he said, sliding from the bed to kneel on the cold, hard floor. "If you'll have me."

She glanced from Jimmy to Matthew, and at her questioning look, her son rolled his eyes. "Duh. Come on, Mom. Just say yes, already." But a grin split his face, tamping down the sass.

Elise snagged her lower lip between her teeth. Then she took his hand, and guided the ring onto the fourth finger of her left hand.

"I will."

Epilogue
Six months later

Elise stood on the witness stand, her right hand raised, and her left hand resting on the Bible. She promised to tell the truth, so help her God.

She told the unadulterated facts for nearly three hours. The only person in the courtroom not in tears was the man – the monster – she faced, crouched at the defendant's table. Even his sharp-suited lawyer dabbed at tears with a cotton handkerchief.

The court recessed after her testimony. For her privacy, the court had granted a room to which she and her family could retire without media interference. Thirty minutes passed all too rapidly, and then they returned to the courtroom.

Elise's story was the last. Over the last five weeks, the court heard fifty-three men, women, and children tell their accounts of brutality at the hands of the El Lobo Syndicate. Now that all the witnesses who could legally testify in the Republic of Texas had done so, the time had come for closing statements. Katherine Miles kept her summary concise and cuttingly accurate.

To the surprise of every person in the courtroom, the defense attorney closed with one statement. "My client pleads not guilty, and I trust in the integrity of the jurors and Your Honor to proceed as you see fit."

After all, what else could the man have said?

The jury discussed the evidence for twelve minutes. The foreman passed the written judgment to the Honorable Travis Blume, who had stoically presided behind his gold wire-framed glasses for nearly two months.

"Garland Latrell Davis, also known to this court as El Lobo, or The Wolf, I hereby read the decision of your peers. You have been found guilty on all charges of all counts against these fifty-four persons."

Judge Blume read the name of each of the victims. Silence permeated the courtroom, with the exception of the judge's pleasant timbre.

"In addition, per the evidence presented, you are hereby found guilty by a jury of your peers, of eight counts of murder in the first degree."

The families of those killed muffled their sobs as the judge read each name on the list.

When the gavel rapped against the hardwood block, Elise flinched.

It was over.

Like a kicked ant hive, the people attending the trial, those families affected, and her fellow victims – most of whom she did not know – milled and congratulated one another through tearful smiles and somber handshakes. Armed federal agents surrounded the convicted murderer, a precaution against vigilante sentencing. They hustled him out of the courtroom through the judge's chamber door. Until the sentencing hearing, it was the last time she would lay eyes on the man.

She wavered, her legs suddenly liquid. Jimmy hovered at her side, his supporting palm cupping her elbow. To her right, Matthew rose as well, wrapping his arms around her waist. The two loves of her life, holding her erect when all she wanted to do was collapse in relief. A strong hand gripped the space between her shoulder and neck, and squeezed, at the same time a reassuring palm rubbed a quick circle on her back.

She turned, and found Jimmy's parents smiling; his mother through tears. "We're so proud of you, Elise, honey," Evelyn Wilson said. "You faced down the devil and won."

David, Jimmy's father, nodded and grabbed her in a bone-crushing hug. "My rifle is in the truck," he whispered. "Just say the word, darlin'."

"Oh, stop it, David. You'll get yourself arrested talkin' like that." His wife batted him with her handbag, and Elise choked out a wet giggle. "Now, no more lollygaggin'. We have somewhere else to be, if I'm not mistaken, son."

Jimmy glanced at his wrist. "Just enough time to make it across the complex, if we hurry."

They trotted across the browning grass of the expansive courtyard. Winter in Texas meant rain and sleet, sun and flip-flops, depending on the temperament of the day. The late afternoon sun cast long shadows of the statues scattered around the county's central court district.

They passed through the heavy walnut doors breathing heavily. Jimmy grinned at her, and snugged Matthew in a side hug.

"Let's do this, kid."

"Lead the way, old man."

This courtroom seemed a miniature version of the one they had vacated. Similar in style, though it was a quarter of the size. Only three rows of benches, with a walkway down the middle, led to the glossy oak tables facing the judge's bench. The Texas flag hung proudly behind the empty judge's chair. A balding man in a navy blue suit decades out of style sat at the left-hand table. He turned at the noise of their entrance and Elise smiled at her lawyer, a pleasantly round man with a constantly stuffy nose and a neverending smile. She leaned in and whispered, "Is she here?"

He swiped daintily at his nose with his hankie, and nodded at the door across the courtroom.

Trudy Blue smiled, hesitant, as she glided across the wood-paneled room. She gripped Elise in a bone-splitting hug.

"Thank you," Trudy whispered.

Beside Elise, Matthew inhaled slowly, and then nodded as if his decision was made. "Aunt Trudy. It's ... good ... to see you. But, why are you here?"

"For you, kiddo. And your mom and dad, and grandma and grandpa. If you'll have me."

Judge Waters entered the room and ascended the slightly elevated bench. She smiled, gestured for them to sit, and quickly got down to business.

"After reading your application, I see no reason why I should not grant your petition. James Wilson, please rise."

Jimmy stood, his hand gripping Matthew's narrow shoulder.

"James Wilson, I hereby grant approval for your petition of adoption of Matthew Evan Gomez. In the sight of the law, and those gathered here as witnesses, you are now the father of this young man. Do you wish to change his name, to reflect that of you and your wife, to Wilson?"

He glanced down, and Matthew nodded. Jimmy spoke to the judge. "Yes, if it pleases the court."

"It does, indeed. Well, then. All is settled here, and congratulations Wilson family."

With the clack of the judge's gavel, Jimmy had a son. Elise beamed at the sight of her husband and son wrapped in a tearful hug. Matthew's grandparents – what a remarkable gift! – surrounded them. Reflexively, she laid a hand on her belly, the barely-there bump concealed beneath the pleats of her dress. Trudy noticed, though, and her hand flew to her mouth. Elise laid a quiet finger across her lips, and Trudy nodded, grinning.

"Let him enjoy this day," Elise whispered to Trudy. "We have time."

Trudy, her soul's sister, wrapped slender arms around her, leaving a kiss on the top of Elise's head. "My tiny Blackbird. Look at you, now. I am so thankful for your forgiveness. I know I don't deserve it."

Elise laid a hand on Trudy's shoulder. "Oh, honey. None of us deserve forgiveness. But I learned from the Master. Come on, I'll tell you a story."

There was a bank of windows along one wood-paneled wall. The heavy casements framed views of the inner courtyard, winter brown. A raven perched on the sill of the window in the center of the row. It cocked its head, and tilted its beady black eye in her direction. It cawed, though the window muffled the sound.

"Yes, a story," Elise began, as she watched the bird. "It's about a man named Jesus and the love of His Father." Another silent caw, and then with an abrupt flap of its wings, it took flight, disappearing behind the tall pines of the courtyard.

She turned her back to the window, smiling at Trudy. "It is a story of hope, adoption, freedom. But more importantly, forgiveness."

They looped arms and rejoined Jimmy, Matthew, and her parents in-law. Trudy waggled her eyes, casting a significant glance at Elise's midsection. Elise grinned, rolling her eyes.

They had time.

The End

The Horror Behind the Fiction

Slavery exists today, though it goes by the modern term *human trafficking*. An estimated 21 million people are believed to be in bondage. It wears the blank stare of forced prostitution and the hopeless face of an immigrant stripped of his passport and forced to work in a sweatshop. Human trafficking is a multi-billion-dollar industry worldwide, built on the backs of captives. Traffickers threaten, coerce, promise, and manipulate the weak and downtrodden. They kidnap and sell children and teens, and enslave the desperate.

You can help.

Learn the signs of human trafficking. These are a few of the many websites dedicated to helping slaves around the world:

www.traffickingresourcecenter.org

www.polarisproject.org

www.sharedhope.org

www.slaverynomore.org

About the Author

 Jennifer was raised behind the pine curtain of East Texas, where the southern accent is as thick and heavy as MawMaw's pecan pie, and the people just as sweet. She currently lives in northern Minnesota with her husband of seventeen years, five children, four gluttonous goldfish, three Angora rabbits, two guinea pigs, two hamsters, and a sweet pup named Timber. In addition to writing, she enjoys natural light photography, graphic design, crafting and showering without an audience of minions.

www.ingramcontent.com/pod-product-compliance
Lightning Source LLC
Chambersburg PA
CBHW051333250626

47155CB00007B/2575